Andrea Semple was born in 1975 in County Durham. She has lived and worked in London and Ibiza, but is now based in York with her husband, where she writes full time. Her writing has appeared in numerous magazines and newspapers.

Visit Andrea Semple online:

www.andreasemple.com

By Andrea Semple

The Ex-Factor
The Make-Up Girl
The Man From Perfect

The Make-Up Girl
Andrea Semple

piatkus

PIATKUS

First published in Great Britain in 2004 by Piatkus Books Ltd
This edition published in Great Britain in 2014 by Piatkus

3 5 7 9 10 8 6 4 2

A CIP catalogue record for this book
is available from the British Library.

ISBN 978-0-349-40204-8

Typeset in Times by Phoenix Photosetting, Chatham, Kent
Printed and bound in Great Britain by CPI Group (UK) Ltd, Croydon CR0 4YY

Papers used by Piatkus are from well-managed forests
and other responsible sources.

MIX
Paper from
responsible sources
FSC
www.fsc.org FSC® C104740

Piatkus
An imprint of
Little, Brown Book Group
100 Victoria Embankment
London EC4Y 0DY

An Hachette UK Company
www.hachette.co.uk

www.piatkus.co.uk

Acknowledgements

I'd like to thank: Emma, Gillian, Judy, Jana, Paola and everyone at Piatkus. Paul, Camilla and the rest of The Marsh Agency. And of course, warm and fuzzy thanks to my family and friends for being supportive. Specifically, mum, dad, Dave, Katherine, Harvey, Alex, Mary, Richard, Phoebe and Clive.

Thanks to all the nice people at Harvey Nichols in Leeds who provided invaluable make-up knowledge, especially Sam at the MAC counter. And also to all the people who've contacted me on the web with kind words of support. I know it sounds obvious to say it makes it all worthwhile, but it really does.

To Matt

Beauty is truth

John Keats

Chapter One

I'm running late.

Literally.

I'm running and I'm late. This is the interview I have waited three years for – three *years* – and I should have been there five minutes ago. I mean, how did that happen?

I certainly left the flat on time. Well, the first time I left the flat it was on time.

Then I realised I had laddered my tights. So I went back.

Then I realised I looked like a vampire. So I slapped on some tan.

Then I realised I should change my tampon. Just in case.

Then I realised I had missed my bus.

Then I realised I had to get some money out for a taxi.

Then I realised the hole-in-the-wall was unable to complete my request, suggesting I should contact my card issuer.

Then I realised that I had gone over my overdraft limit to buy these shoes.

Then I realised that I had to get there on foot.

Then I realised the shoes which broke the bank seem equally capable of breaking my feet. Especially as I am currently engaged in a breathless attempt to break the land-speed record in order not to blow my chances completely.

There it is.

As I clip-clop down the pavement at hyper speed, I can see it.

The headquarters of Coleridge Communications, the biggest PR agency outside of London. There it is, six storeys of gleaming hope.

I decide to slow down to a fast walk. In fact, it's less of a decision and more of a physical necessity. I'm hyperventilating, my heart is about to burst out of my shirt, and my squished feet are now two sizes smaller than when I started running.

I come to a complete stop just beyond view of the foyer, and clutch onto some black railings.

OK, deep breaths.

Calm thoughts. I close my eyes and I'm on a beach, waves gently rolling, palm trees gently swaying . . .

'Spare some change, love?' I open my eyes and see a very skinny and ill-looking boy – no older than sixteen – holding out a polystyrene cup half-full of brown coins.

'Um, yes,' I say, as I fumble in my handbag for whatever loose coins happen to be lying about. I haven't really got time, but I need all the karma-points I can get. And he does look pretty desperate. 'Here.'

'Nice one,' he says, in appreciation of the miniscule amount I have just clunked in his cup.

I glance at the boy as he slouches off, in his faded clothes, and I try to gain some perspective. This is only a job interview, I tell myself. It's not life or death.

With that thought, I fill my chest with air and climb the stone steps towards the revolving door. On the other side of the glass I can see the foyer – within which there is a very tall and intimidating desk with an immaculate-looking woman perched behind it, talking importantly on the phone.

A sea of people are leaving the building – for lunch, I assume – and I wait timidly before attempting to jump into the flight path of the revolving doors.

This is it, I tell myself.

This is my one chance to make everything all right.

Chapter Two

Once inside the foyer, I start to heat up. And I mean, really heat up. After a two-mile run in high heels and a suit, that's just what I need. A pre-interview sauna. The immaculate-looking woman behind the desk must be a complete psycho. Either that, or she's not a human being at all and needs this kind of temperature to heat up her blood.

I arrive in front of her desk and wait for her to finish her phone call and acknowledge my presence. In the meantime, I check out her make-up. Mist foundation, sprayed on for even coverage. Perfect shading on the cheekbones. No bags or grey under the eyes. And then I start to worry. I must look a right mess. I mean, make-up is normally what I'm good at. But this morning I was all over the place. And I bet I overdid it on the tan. And the two-mile run won't have helped.

The immaculate woman finishes her phone call and looks up. She gives me a brief, but forensic assessment. I could just be paranoid, but she seems to be looking slightly amused at my appearance. Oh no. What's the matter? Have I got bird poo on my shoulder or something?

'Um, I've got an interview.'

'Sorry?' she asks, as amusement turns to confusion.

'I've got an interview,' I say again, only this time trying not to let my nerves make me incoherent.

'Which company?'

What does she mean which company? Don't they own the whole building? 'Er, Coleridge Communications. It's with Sam Johnson.'

'You mean John Sampson?'

Shit. What an idiot.

'Yes, sorry. It's Faith Wishart.' Well, at least I got that bit right.

Immaculate woman picks up the phone and presses one number. Two seconds later she says: 'John, Faith Wishart.'

My God, I think. This is how important John Sampson is. He doesn't even have time for proper sentences.

'He'll be two minutes,' the immaculate woman says, before raising her perfectly plucked eyebrows and smiling smugly to herself.

OK, now I'm really paranoid.

I sit down next to a head-high pot plant which, on closer inspection, turns out to be a fake. There are some magazines on the table in front of me. I resist the latest issue of *Gloss* and pick up a copy of *PR Week*, pretending to look interested.

Shit, my hands are shaking. And my palms are damp with sweat.

Come on, Faith. Concentrate.

I try and remember everything I wrote on the application form. All the true bits, the nearly-true bits and the completely false bits. But I can't even think straight.

Why am I a good team player?

Did I say I had a 2:1 or a First?

5

What relevant experience did I have again?

It's no good. The steady drum of my heart has now accelerated into a mad bongo rhythm. My legs are numb and my tongue is sticking to the roof of my mouth.

The lift pings and slides open to reveal a tall, smartly dressed man staring straight at me.

'Faith?' he asks in a voice so deep his vocal chords must be located in his testicles. He holds out an enormous hand. 'John Sampson.'

Oh blinking bollocks, he's gorgeous.

And look at that suit. It must be Gucci or something. Purple shirt, no tie, open at the neck, dark curly hair, confident smile, and one of those faces that actually suit being old. And when I say old I don't mean Hugh Hefner old I just mean George Clooney old.

OK, so the purple shirt does nothing for him. I mean, this is a man clearly in touch with his inner-prune. But other than that he's just like the men you read about in all those novels.

Tall, check.

Dark, check.

Handsome, double check.

If this was the nineteenth century I'd be swooning right now. I'd be swooning for England and he'd pick me up and ride me away on his black steed (whatever a black steed is) and he'd take me to his castle and ravish me and write me a love sonnet and we'd go off and poison ourselves or drown in a lake or start a revolution or something . . .

Shit, I'm delirious.

I really shouldn't have missed breakfast this morning.

Anyway, it's not the nineteenth century, and I've got a job to get.

I somehow manage to stand.

6

'Pleased to meet you,' I tremble.

He is looking at me straight on, and then I remember: eye contact. If you want to make the right impression, you have to fix the interviewer's gaze.

'After you,' he says, nodding towards the open lift door.

I hesitate.

There is a strange-looking woman standing in the lift, staring right at me. The woman is bright orange and looks absolutely petrified.

Oh shit.

It's a mirror.

Petrified orange woman is me.

Bollocks, how much of the flaming stuff did I slap on? The bottle had promised a deep, natural, radiant tan. Radioactive, more like. Mind you, what kind of tan is going to look natural in April? In bloody Leeds?

And what's more, it's started to streak, near my ear. All because mum says I look anaemic.

No wonder immaculate receptionist lady was smirking. I walk into the lift, and try and remember what exactly I put on the form. And then I get a feeling. A premonitiony feeling. As if something is about to go horribly wrong.

Chapter Three

By the time the lift door closes, the mad bongo player caged inside my chest is pounding away like it's the first day of the Rio carnival. On top of interview nerves I've now got handsome man nerves as well.

If I wasn't bright orange I'd be bright red. In fact, now I look again I realise I'm actually a combination.

A blood orange.

With added streaks.

Come on, I tell myself. It's probably not that bad. After all, I have got a bit of a critical eye for that sort of thing.

Handsome-interviewer-potential-boss-man-whose-name-I've-forgotten smiles at me. It's a nice smile, designed to put me at ease, but it doesn't.

It doesn't even come close.

'It's a nice day,' I say, although as soon as I say it I realise that I am lying. It isn't a nice day. Before I started running it was freezing. 'For April, I mean.'

He nods, not in agreement, but in another attempt to make me relax. Oh God, this is terrible. The way he combines sexy and powerful in one look, is making me feel so weak. It's like sharing a lift with Colin Farrell and Bill Gates at the same time.

'OK,' he says. 'Here we are.'

'What?' But then the lift pings open and I realise he means here we are on the right floor. 'Oh,' I say. 'Yes.'

I follow him out onto the floor and for a second I think I'm dreaming. The reason why is because this *is* my dream. I mean, when I close my eyes and imagine my perfect working environment this is pretty much it.

Open plan. Colourful seating areas. Trendy glass partitions. iMacs on every desk. The gentle hum of creativity. People wearing what they want and chatting at their desks. All generating that confident, moneyfied glow which only seems to belong to career people, not job people.

For a second, I am so impressed with the scene that I almost forget to be nervous.

'OK, this way,' says John (that *is* his name isn't it?), walking me through the room to his office.

He asks an occasional, incomprehensible query to members of his staff and he gets answered in tones which confirm that he is the boss. This is a man, I feel, who is not only respected but genuinely liked by his staff.

As I walk I can sense that I am being silently assessed. Everybody is trying to work out if I am a Coleridge Communications kind of person. Oh God, I hope no one recognises me. I hope no one . . .

Oh no.

That girl at the photocopier. The skinny one with the heavy fringe and Diesel T-shirt. With the small pointy nose and bright crimson lips. She is staring at me more obviously than most. I try and counter her gaze with a polite micro-smile, but it doesn't work.

She just keeps on staring.

9

Honestly, it's almost a relief when I arrive in John's office and he shuts the door. I say *almost*. I mean, this is an interview after all.

The interview.

'Take a seat,' he says, in the same testicular tone.

I take a seat.

John Sampson sits opposite, on the other side of his desk. A Guccified vision of power and fuckability.

'Faith ... Wishart,' he muses, as he scans my application form.

'Yes,' I say, confident that at least my name is correct.

He scans the form further, and as he does so he smiles. It's a different smile to the one he exhibited in the lift. A slightly smug smile, involving a simultaneous raising of his right eyebrow.

'I must say, right at the outset, that I was very impressed with your application. Your qualifications and your experience and your references are all absolutely superb.'

These are good words. These are the words you dream of hearing as you walk into an interview. So why are they making me feel nervous?

'Oh,' I say transferring my weight between buttocks. 'Thanks.'

'Yes,' he continues. 'On paper at least, you certainly seem made for this job.'

He places the form back down on the desk, leans back in his chair, hands cradling the back of his head, elbows wide. Then something starts to happen with his eyes.

They narrow, and sharpen. If this wasn't an interview situation, the look would qualify as sexy. But this is an interview situation. And the look is qualifying as scary.

Chapter Four

A quick confession.

It's about my job. My actual job, not the one I am being interviewed for. I am a make-up girl. I work part-time on a cosmetics counter at Blake's department store on a wage roughly equivalent to three peanuts an hour.

It might be enough to pay the rent for the cheapest flat in north Leeds, but it's a shit job.

So shit, in fact, that as far as my mum is concerned, it's not my job at all.

My mum thinks I work for a top PR company which is based, like Blake's, in the centre of Leeds. The job is full-time, pays enough peanuts to keep the entire monkey population stocked up for over a year, and is bulging with exciting career prospects. She thinks I have worked as an account executive for the last three years. To be perfectly honest, I hadn't meant this to be a lie. When I was at uni I worked for a PR company in Leeds for my work placement and they'd offered me a job for when I finished. Only thing was, when they found out I got a third the offer was cancelled. Trouble is, I never told my mum this – in fact, I never even told her about the third.

So, every phone call I have to invent some new story about what happened in the office or what some made-up colleague said to me by the made-up water cooler.

And every time it gets harder to tell the truth. Gets harder to say that I am a make-up girl. That I work part-time on a cosmetics counter at a department store.

Because my mum wanted me to be successful, to have a career, to be proud of me like she could be proud of my brother, Mark. Because we are all she's got, all she thinks about, since dad died and my sister went to Australia.

And three years ago I was prepared to do or say anything to make her happy. Hell, who am I kidding? I'd do the same thing now. Even though she can now sit down for five minutes without crying about dad.

So if she wants me to have a career and a 2:1 and everything else, then that is what I'll tell her I've got. Why should I let the facts get in the way of her happiness?

And if I can never come clean, then I'll just have to turn the lies into the truth.

Chapter Five

'I'd like to ask you something . . .' says John Sampson.

Well, of course he would. I mean, this is an interview and the whole thing about interviews is that they generally involve asking things, so I'm ready. In fact, he could ask me anything right now and I'd do it.

Hop on one foot.

Sing a lullaby.

Give him a lap-dance.

'Why us? Why CC?'

Oh good, an easy one. 'Well, you're the best agency. From what I've, um, seen. And heard. And you're the biggest outside of London . . .'

He stays leaning back in his chair, wanting more.

'. . . and I really like the stuff you do. The campaign you did for Keats Cosmetics was really brilliant, you know, with the cages and everything . . .'

I'm on shaky ground here.

I mean, I *work* for Keats Cosmetics. Well, at the lowest rung. I'm one of their make-up girls but I hadn't tried out their new tan till this morning.

And I am good at my job. Of course I am. I mean, think about it. What is make-up all about? It's about manipulating the real you. It's about covering up. Concealing. Glossing over.

But the thing is, I didn't mention my job on the application form. Because working part-time on a make-up counter for a department store is not exactly what qualifies as relevant experience for a career in PR.

But I had to say something and the Keats campaign was obviously the first that came to mind. And anyway, it *was* a brilliant campaign. You can probably remember it. You know, it was when Keats came out with the slogan 'Human Tested,' and they were going on about how none of their products were tested on animals. Well anyway, Coleridge did all the PR for it and arranged a big photo-shoot where they got a load of models to pose naked in cages in the middle of Leicester Square, while lots of pretend scientists tested on them. Apparently the pictures made all the papers and it was included right at the end of the Ten O'Clock News after all the serious bits about wars. You know, when they try and finish on a funny bit so we don't all have nightmares about the end of the world and stuff.

John Sampson doesn't say anything. He just keeps on looking at me, assessing me, as if every flicker of my mouth holds the key to my true personality. And in my head all the time there is this voice going: 'You are in an interview, ooh, isn't it scary, you are in an interview and your whole future existence depends on how you act and what you say. The rest of your life hinges on the next ten minutes . . .'

I hate the voice in my head.

It's never on my side.

Chapter Six

But while it *is* scary, I am sort of enjoying this. I mean, no one this rich and sexy and handsome and powerful and, well, *male* has ever paid such close attention to me in my life.

Hold on, this really is becoming a long silence.

'OK,' he says eventually. 'Tell me a bit more about your relevant experience.'

'Well. I studied business and marketing at the University of West Yorkshire and, um, that was when I was first, um, introduced to the whole discipline of public relations ...' *The whole discipline of public relations*, what kind of language is that? 'and then, after I graduated, I went to Australia for my year out ...'

'Oh really, which part?'

'Um, Sydney.'

'I was over there for six years.'

Shit. 'Oh. Wow.'

'Where were you based?'

Oh God. 'I stayed in ... M-anley.' Manley, yes, that was it. That was where Hope stayed. Hope's my sister. I'll tell you about her later. It's a long story. Right now I'm a bit busy being interviewed.

'Oh, Manley. How did you find it?'

'Um, I got a taxi.'

He does that heavy staring thing again, only this time it's not that enjoyable. This time I feel like I'm being interrogated, and I'm finding it harder and harder to hold his gaze. And what has my made-up year out got to do with anything?

'I mean,' he says, passing his silver pen thoughtfully between his chin and lower lip. 'What did you think of it?'

My internal bongo player has returned to the stage. 'Um, it was very, er, hot ...' John Sampson raises an eyebrow, and nods his head. '... and the people were very ... friendly ... and it was really ... nice ... and—'

He raises the palm of his hand. 'OK. Now tell me a bit about your experience.'

Oh God. I'm about to pass out. OK, now what is it you're meant to do? Think of the interviewer in their underwear, that's it.

OK, I'd hazard a guess at a neat-fitting pair of jockey briefs. Black. Calvin Klein.

'My experience ...' I say, as I picture him almost naked. Oh no, this isn't helping. He's even more gorgeous and intimidating with no clothes on. And have you seen that bulge? It's so distracting. I can't even think. 'My experience ...'

'Let me help you out,' he says, in a voice which instantly reclothes him. He starts to read direct from my application form, his eyebrows dancing as he does so. 'Two years at Glory PR in London. Account executive. Duties included writing press releases, liasing with clients, arranging photo calls, creating media packs ...' He reads on, and I nod my head at each listed duty as if it was something I actually remember doing.

By now my fake tan is the last of my worries.

It's my whole fake life which is proving of more immediate concern.

Chapter Seven

John Sampson, having finished reading my list of duties, crosses his legs and places the form back on his desk. Behind him, out of the broad office window is the rest of Leeds – the sky-rise office blocks and new hotels, cranes and construction workers, a whole city on the up. And I could be part of it. Part of something shiny and important. God, I need this job.

'It's quite a list,' he says, with an unreadable face.

'Yes,' I say. 'It was quite a job.'

His eyes twinkle with something which looks worryingly like mischief and he runs a hand through his black curls. I catch a flash of his watch, dazzling with silver expense. 'Now just remind me, if you would, who is it who heads up their operation?'

'Sorry?'

'At Glory. Who was your boss?'

His eyes are penetrating me so deep that now I'm the one who is sitting here in my underwear. In fact. I'm starting to wonder about that smile in the lift. Perhaps it wasn't meant to be reassuring. Perhaps it was the smile of a hungry lion, welcoming a tasty looking gazelle into its cage.

'My boss?'

He nods, the stare still lingering. 'Your boss.'

There is a knock at the door.

'Yes,' John calls, closing his eyes in frustration.

I turn as the door opens. It's the heavy fringe girl, popping her head through.

'Carla, what is it? I'm in the middle of an interview.'

'I know, John,' says Heavy-Fringe, chewing gum. 'Sorry. But it's quite important.'

'I'll be one minute,' he tells me, and I turn to watch his Calvin Kleined power-arse disappear out of the door.

One minute. That's just about enough time to jump out of the window. Six storeys. Yep, that should finish me off.

Oh shit, the girl. Heavy-Fringe. Now I know where I've seen her before. In the shop. I did her make-up about two Fridays ago. Violet eye shadow, pale matt foundation, translucent powder, lip liner, the works. I even told her how to place the cream blusher just below her cheekbone in order to make her face look more defined.

Well, that's fucking gratitude, isn't it?

But hold on. Easy now. It might not be that. It might be another 'quite important'. It might be nothing to do with me at all. Even so, I've still got to—

The door opens so fast it sends a breeze, fanning the front page of my application form up in the air.

'Right,' John says, in a let's-get-back-to-business, lion-gets-back-to-his-lunch kind of a way. 'Where were we? Oh yes, that's right. You were about to tell me your boss's name at Glory.'

'Yes,' I say, still stalling for time. 'My . . . boss's . . . name . . . was . . .' And then I remember, from when I was at

19

university and did my dissertation on Public Relations in the Beauty Industry. I quoted the founder and chief executive of Glory PR about fifty times and his name was '... Peter ... Richmond.'

'Ah, yes, of course,' John Sampson says, almost triumphantly. 'Good old Peter.'

Shit, he knows him. I nod my head, nostalgically. Good old Peter. 'Er, yes. Um, I thought I'd perhaps tell you about why I think I'd be good for this company. I wanted to say that I'm very much a people person and people tell me that I'm a good team player and—'

He does the raising of the hand thing again. 'We'll get to that in a minute. Firstly, I just want to know what you thought of old Peter. Quite a character, eh?'

'Oh yes, he was,' I say, without missing a beat. 'He was. But I didn't really see him all that often because he was out of the office a lot. He liked to work remotely.'

'Very remotely, I should imagine,' he says, stifling a smirk.

'But, you know, occasionally he'd come in the office and see how we were all doing.'

'And did you do any work directly for him?' he asks, the smirk now unstifled.

'Um, yes. He used to like the way I put things so he'd often ask me to write a press release or some promotional material or—'

'His obituary?'

The room closes in around me. 'Sorry?'

'Well, he's dead, isn't he? He died of a stress-related heart attack in 1998. Which, according to your application form, is three years before you started working for him.'

Oh no. 'I, um, yes. I can explain. The dates ... on the thing ... I must have ...'

'You see,' he interrupts. 'That's the thing with PR. It's a very stressful industry. It's not like – oh, I don't know, let's see, let me just take something completely at random here – completely out of the air – it's not like *working in a shop*.'

I am naked. I am five centimetres tall. I am on the brink of climbing over the desk and jumping straight through that window. 'I can explain,' I say. But my words are deflected with the palm of his hand.

He doesn't want me to explain.

He's enjoying this far too much.

Chapter Eight

All of a sudden, I want to be right back behind my make-up counter, talking to customers about finding the right foundation for combination skin. Anywhere, but right here.

'Also, it says here that you got a 2 : 1 in Business and Marketing from the University of West Yorkshire.'

'Yes,' I say, in a butter-wouldn't-melt kind of way.

'Well, having made a telephone enquiry to the head of the business department at the University it turns out that this is incorrect.'

'Um, is it?' I ask, in a butter-turning-soft-and-liquid kind of way.

'Yes,' he says, leaning back in his swivel chair and positioning his silver pen in the horizontal dip between his bottom lip and his chin.

I look behind me, contemplating my exit. Around the door the wall is bubble glass, distorting the view of the work area beyond into a few indistinguishable objects and figures. It looks suddenly like a melting dream.

'Now,' says the hungry lion. 'Can you tell me if anything on this entire form is correct?'

'I'm sorry,' I say. 'I just wanted—'

'Everything, from your A level grades to your references, is completely made up, isn't it? A complete fabrication. I bet even your interests are made up, aren't they? Here we are: horse riding, amateur dramatics, sailing and,' he looks up at me, assesses my physique before announcing my final mock-interest: '*rock climbing.*'

'I, um, once went abseiling. In sixth form. It was an outward bound thing . . .' My voice trails off.

'In all my years of interviewing I can honestly say I've never come up against a case like this.'

'I know, I just—'

'Lie after blatant lie.' He laughs incredulously, shaking his head.

'The thing is I—' His hand again halts me in my tracks.

'So Faith, assuming that is your name, let me get this straight. You're one of those make-up girls, one of those girls who work behind the cosmetics counter, and you have absolutely no experience in PR at all and you walk into one of the largest agencies in the country knowing that your application form is a complete piece of fiction.'

The window would be easy to open. And I could get there before he would have time. Six storeys.

'Well, I did really study Business and Marketing,' I tell him, because I did.

'But you didn't get a 2 : 1, did you?'

'No,' I say. 'I didn't. I got a third. But that was because of going back to live with mum in the final year, after losing dad. And anyway, at the end of the second year I was at sixty-five per cent which is precisely mid-range 2 : 1 so I know I *could* have got a 2 : 1 if things had happened differently. Or had not happened at all.'

'And you really live in a flat in Hyde Park, I take it you wouldn't make that up?'

I picture my flat. The barred kitchen window. The swirly orange carpet. 'No,' I say. 'I wouldn't.'

'And your references?'

Two weeks ago my best friend Alice picked up her phone, put on a croaky posh voice, and told Coleridge's human resource manager that I was one of the hardest-working and most enthusiastic marketing communication students she had ever taught during her twenty years at the University of West Yorkshire. Alice is twenty-five years old. The closest she's ever got to the uni is when she threw up her vodka-infested guts outside the union building, just before she stopped wanting to go out. And the only thing of value she has ever taught me is that you burn more calories hoovering than you do having sex.

'Oh, my references are true,' I assure him.

He raises a quizzical eyebrow.

'No, I promise you,' I say, even at this stage unable to come completely clean. 'I wouldn't go *that* far.'

I offer him a nervous smile, but he's not going to give me anything for it. Just a short, patronising nose-gust.

I am beginning to hate John Sampson. OK, so I lied on my form. I made most of it up, tucked a few certain details under the carpet, made myself look better than I was, but if he knew all along why did he bother interviewing me in the first place? He's enjoying this. He's enjoying watching me suffer.

I mean that's just sick.

But still, I mustn't kid myself, if he offered me the job I'd take it like that.

'Now listen,' says a voice. A confident, assured, but strangely familiar voice. And then I realise – the voice is

24

mine. I must have gone mad. What am I doing? I've just been found guilty of – well, let's face it – of *fraud*, and here I am getting all bossy. Oh no, here it comes again: 'I may have lied on the form, but it hardly makes me a serial killer.'

'No,' he admits. 'It makes you a liar.'

'Yes, I know,' I say, feeling the blood rush to my fake tanned cheeks. 'I lied, but only because I knew the truth wouldn't be enough. I knew that it wouldn't do me justice, because you see, the thing is I would make a really good account executive, I really would. Ever since I studied PR at uni I knew I'd be really good at it and I would have gone into a proper PR job when I graduated if I hadn't had to go home and look after my mum when dad died . . .'

This time he raises both hands. 'I really haven't got time to listen to your autobiography.'

'But I know I'd be good at this job,' I say, in a kamikaze, second-day-of-my-period-nothing-left-to-lose kind of way. 'I mean, I spend my whole life making things sound better than they actually are, or making people look better than they actually are, so I would be able to do the same for companies.'

'And get us sued for fraud?'

'Well, I know I went a bit far on the form but that was because I needed to, I wouldn't lie if I got the job. I promise. I'd just, well, present things . . . the way they should be presented . . . in order to make them more attractive. You see, it's not really that different from make-up, when you think about it.' I search his face for some sign of hope.

There is nothing.

Then I picture my mum's face, and all the lies I've been telling her for the last three years. All the things I have said about this company. About how I get on really well with the boss. With *him*, John Sampson.

25

'Please,' I say, my voice now desperate, my buttocks perched pleadingly on the edge of the chair. 'Please, I really need this job. I'm sorry I lied but please, Mr Sampson, I'm begging you, please, honestly, I'll do anything, please—'

'Well, actually, there is something you could do.'

This is it. I don't know how but I've turned it around. I've done it. It's just like a book. Or a movie. I've done my whole big talk like Rene Zellwegger in *Jerry MacGuire* and now he's going to come round. I'm going to get the job. He might knock the salary down a bit, or give me less responsibility, but he can see I'm a girl who needs saving. A distressed damsel. And he's going to save me. He's going to make everything OK. As if it really was the nineteenth century. I can see it in his face.

'Anything, I'll do anything. Anything at all.'

'Good,' he says. 'You can shut the door on your way out.'

Chapter Nine

So that was it. My almost-career in PR lasted approximately ten minutes. My fictional career in PR, on the other hand, is going from strength to strength. Just ask my mum. She'll tell you all about it. How pleased they all are with me, how I managed to bag the employee of the month award not once, not twice, but on *three* separate occasions. Guys, I tell you, that's quite some fictional achievement. It takes a lot of fictional hard work to get such fictional recognition.

'So, how was your day?' my mum asks me, on the phone.

'Great,' I say, suicidally, as I gulp back a glass of Bulgarian cat's piss.

'Are you having a drink?'

'Yes,' I say. 'Fruit juice.'

'Good,' she says. 'You need all the vitamins you can get in this weather. Lots of vitamins.' I can tell from her voice that she is in the middle of some hyperactive house-work as she talks. And I can picture her, on her knees, dusting the skirting board, with that slightly manic look in her eyes. A look she has worn, on and off, ever since we lost dad.

'Yes, lots of vitamins.'

'And how was work?' she asks, her voice in a forced chirp.

'Great,' I say again, checking the label for the alcohol content. Twelve point five per cent. I should have got the vodka.

'Did anything happen?'

OK, possible answers:

(1) I went for an interview for a job you think I've already got.
(2) I met the biggest wanker in the world.
(3) I decided that the way to impress him was to experiment with Keats' new fake tan.
(4) I discovered that Keats' new fake tan complements your natural skin tone. If you happen to be an orang-utan.
(5) I got found guilty of lying on my application form.

Actual answer:

'I got the employee of the month thing again.'

But of course, even my lies aren't enough for my mum. She wants more. She wants better.

'Employee of the month? That's nice, so will you be getting more money?'

You see, no matter what I tell her, it's never enough.

If the lies aren't sufficient what hope will I ever have with the truth?

'No,' I say, a little too crossly. 'It doesn't mean more money.'

'Oh, well never mind. I'm sure soon you'll have enough money to—'

Even pissed, I know what's coming. 'Mum, I'm happy here. I know that the flat isn't much but it's a nice area. It's very . . . characterful.'

And this I suppose is the truth. Hyde Park, the area of Leeds where I live, *is* very characterful. There are heroin addict characters who collapse characterfully, in the middle of the street. There are characterful kids who will gob on your back when you nip out to get a paper. There are characterful car alarms and police helicopters which will keep you awake until five in the morning. There are characterful thugs who will shout racist insults at any ethnic minority who happens to be in their line of vision. There are characterful winos who will offer a chirpy, if semi-coherent 'fuck-off' as you walk along the street, breathing in the characterful aromas of car exhaust, urine and disgarded kebabs as you do so.

Oh, there is no mistaking it, this area is nothing if not characterful.

And then there's my flat itself. Even if you take away the fact that my landlord has been noisily converting the basement flat (the one below mine) for the last six months, it is not exactly a hot property. In truth, for most of the year, it's a bloody freezing property. Bloody freezing and bloody ugly. Of course, ugly is in the eye of the beholder, but I'd like to see the beholder who could find any other term for the aesthetic catastrophe which is my flat. OK, so there are one or two quaint original Victorian features. A high ceiling. A bay window. The ghost of an old woman in a white nightie. Actually, I don't know if there really is a ghost as the only time I thought I saw her was after I'd watched *The Others* on TV, and then I had to go and stay the night at Alice's house. (Alice is my best friend, my only true friend in Leeds in fact, but more about her later).

29

But anyway, apart from the ceiling and the window the rest looks like crap. Crap orange carpet. Crap pub wallpaper. So crap that the crap kitchen flooring curls up in disgust, rather than touch the wall.

I've tried to make it look a bit better. I've painted the bathroom and I bought a nice table and some chairs. But they are small and weak weapons against the flat's overwhelming power of crapness.

Anyway, that's the problem. My mum reckons I've got this great job and then she comes to stay and she's like 'oh'. I mean, it's hardly the kind of wooden-floored swank palace you read about all these media girls having.

But it's not just the career in media that's slipped me up.

In fact, I lie about everything.

Seriously, you name it, I'll lie about it.

If the Pinocchio nose-growth theory was a scientific fact, I wouldn't be able to turn my head sideways without smashing a window.

You see, without the lies my life would look like, well, *my life*. And that's not what I want it to look like. Not to my mum, anyway. No, what I want it to look like is one of those books. You know the ones. The ones where there's a dramatic opening and a girl with a high-flying job, living in London, or New York, or some other big city, who does nothing all day except dream of the perfect man. And then she finds that perfect man in the final chapter, who happens to be someone who was right under her nose all along.

I want my life to be full of drama, to be exciting, to have a twist-in-the-tale.

I want it to be a page turner.

I want it to have a fancy cover.

But the truth is, my whole existence is about as riveting

as one of those manuals you get from IKEA telling you how to put a bookshelf together.

So to cover up the grim reality, I make things up.

I hear what you're saying. Why do I do this? Am I some kind of weirdo or something? I don't know. Perhaps I am. But the thing is I want my mum to be happy with me. I want to *impress* her. I want her to tell me that my dad would have been proud. I know these things are silly. But they mean a lot to me.

They mean the whole world.

Chapter Ten

Trouble is, there's only one person who's been able to impress my mum – at least since dad died – and that's Mark. My brother. My older, wiser, richer, and anything else with -er on the end of it, brother.

Take right now.

The phone call to my mum has got to the familiar stage where all she is doing is recounting every single word my brother told her in their last telephone conversation. Mark this, Mark that, Mark the other . . . on and on and on. Once she gets on the subject of my brother she's on for hours. It's starting to give me a headache. Mind you, that could just be the Bulgarian cat's piss.

'. . . so it looks like he's going to be too busy to come and stay that weekend. Honestly, Faith, he works so hard.'

'Yes, mum, I know.'

'Oh, and he was telling me all about his new place. It sounds wonderful. Mind you, the amount of hours he's working at the moment I suppose he hardly ever gets to see it.'

'No,' I say, sighing wearily under the weight of my sisterly sulk. 'I suppose not.'

I never really know why I get so wound up when she goes on about how hard my brother works. I mean, he does work bloody hard. He's up at about five in the morning and often works through till eight or nine at night. He works in the City, trading futures. Neither myself nor my mother knows exactly what this means, but then neither myself nor my mother understood one single element of his Oxford Maths degree which led him to the job in the first place. For my mother, it was enough that his acceptance by Oxford made the front page of the local paper (I'm from the North East, where that sort of freak occurrence is headline news.)

But anyway, that is what he does. Trades futures. I sometimes wish he was able to trade *my* future, but I'm sure he wouldn't be able to get much for it.

He is a lovely person. You would like him, I'm sure you would. He's not your typical hard-nosed investment banker type. He's quiet and gentle and never has a bad word to say about anybody.

Even Hope, my sister.

Even after leaving us all and going off to Australia instead of looking after mum.

'She was too young to handle it all,' he says. And OK, she was eighteen when dad had his heart attack, but now she's twenty-one and she still won't come home and face the music.

But anyway, my point is that my brother is a good person.

Yet now, when I listen to my mum go on about how rich and successful he is, my brother becomes someone else. He becomes someone who plans to retire in six years' time, on his thirty-fifth birthday.

He becomes someone who is always too busy to visit, or even make a phone call.

33

He becomes someone who drives a car so flash I haven't even heard of it.

The common ground has crumbled beneath our feet, and it is left to my mother to rub it in. And boy, does she know how to.

'Honestly, Faith,' she is saying. 'Aren't you proud of him?'

'Mum, I am sure that if I knew what it was exactly that he did I would be very proud.'

'Well, we don't have to understand it to realise he is successful. Just look at the suits he wears.'

'Mum, *I* have to wear a suit to work,' I lie. 'There's nothing special about having to wear a suit.'

'Come on, Faith pet, don't be jealous. It doesn't suit you.'

'I'm not jealous, I'm—'

Well, let's face it, *jealous*.

'Anyway,' my mum continues, 'the reason why I phoned is because I want to come down and see you the weekend after next.'

Oh shit. 'Um, you can't,' I say, trying to ignore the alarm bells ringing in my head.

'Charming,' my mum says, through her tense chuckle.

'No, I mean I'm working, on the Saturday, and Adam's visiting his ... parents that weekend.'

'It seems funny that they keep on making you work all these Saturdays.'

'I know,' I say. 'But there's nothing I can do about it.'

'Well, I'm going to have to meet him some time, what about the weekend after that? Or even this weekend? I can always come down and see you both sometime in the week if that's any easier ... I'm just so looking forward to meeting him.'

'Um, I—'

34

'You're not embarrassed of me, are you? I promise I won't show you up. I'll be on my best behaviour.'

'No, of course I'm not embarrassed, it's just I'd better check with Adam first if that's OK?'

'Well, OK, just so long as you do. I'm just so looking forward to meeting him.'

'I know. You said.'

'I'm so happy for you.'

'OK.' I bite my lip and fight the strange emotion rising through me.

'Oh, I see. He's there, isn't he? You're still playing it cool.'

'Yes,' I say, staring at my empty sofa. 'He's here. He's watching TV.'

Then she says something else, but I'm not concentrating.

'Faith? Are you still listening to me?'

'Yes, mum,' I slur. 'Sorry.'

'So we must arrange a time.'

'A time. Yes. We must. I promise . . .'

'I can't wait to meet him.'

'I know, you keep saying. Listen mum—' I pause, momentarily as I notice that the curtains are wide open. And so is my pyjama top. Or at least open enough to reveal my left breast to the entire Monday evening population of Sheldon Terrace.

Then I hear something.

A car boot.

I squint out the window and through the semi-darkness I focus on a strange square object heading closer. As it nears, I realise the strange square object has legs. The strange square object with legs now makes sense. It's the new tenant in the basement flat carrying a pin board. He must be moving in today. He saw my nipple. How will I ever be able to say hello to a man who has seen my nipple before he has asked my name?

'I won't embarrass you, I promise,' my mum says, breaking my trance.

'Listen, mum, I've got to go. I've got to get ready for tomorrow.'

'Oh?'

'Yes, I've got loads of stuff to do,' I say, trying to ignore the clanking and banging from downstairs. 'I'm in earlier tomorrow, got loads of admin stuff to sort out.'

'Right,' she says in the baffled better-not-ask tone she always adopts when I use words like 'admin'.

'OK then, I'll speak to you later.'

'Yes. Don't work too hard.'

'No. I won't.'

'Bye. Love you.'

'Yes, mum,' I say. 'Love you too.' If nothing else, the last three words are always true.

Chapter Eleven

Now, OK, I'd better quickly fill you in about Adam.

In many ways, I suppose he's the perfect boyfriend.

First things first, he's a lawyer, so my mum's happy.

And he never looks at other women.

He never says I could lose a bit of weight.

He never farts in bed or leaves the toilet seat up.

He never rolls over and falls asleep after sex.

He never can be found at two in the morning jerking the duvet up and down while I'm trying to get some sleep.

He never suggests a night in front of the football or anything weird involving uniforms or handcuffs or Mars Bars.

In fact he never does anything.

You see, despite his obvious credentials as the perfect boyfriend Adam has one undeniable flaw.

He doesn't actually exist.

I made him up.

Yes, I know. As relationship problems go, it's quite a biggie.

I mean, I can't exactly talk it over with a relationship counsellor. 'Well, Miss Counsellor, the problem Adam has is that he stubbornly refuses to materialise into an actual human being.'

'Don't worry, Faith,' the counsellor would reply. 'This is actually quite a common situation. Owing to the ongoing crisis of masculinity, many men nowadays have existence issues. They simply aren't *there* when you need them.'

And what would she prescribe? A course on non-existence management?

To be perfectly honest, I have only ever had imaginary boyfriends. Oh sure, they have looked real enough. They've all had real eyes, real noses, real mouths, real willies. Most have even had real hair and real teeth.

But they've never been the men I have imagined them to be. Now is that my fault or theirs? I don't know. I probably never will.

All I do know is that whenever I have met someone, someone I have felt could be The One, my imagination has always overtaken the reality.

There was Paul, my schoolyard sweetheart, who I imagined wouldn't tell his friends.

There was James, my holiday romance, who I imagined would keep in contact.

There was Cecil, the man I met in the queue at the post office, who I imagined was joking when he said that was his real name.

The point is that when you fall in love you paint this picture in your head. A picture of the person you are with. And the picture is a fantasy, maybe not a total fantasy, but a fantasy all the same.

You take a few of their best bits and magnify them to such an extent that they become a complete person. But this complete person is different from the real person you are with, who you only uncover when all those dizzy falling in love feelings have started to fade.

I read a thing about it in *Gloss* magazine once. That agony aunt they've got. Martha someone-or-other. She called it the halo effect. How you can misjudge someone only seconds after meeting them, and that is how you see them forever more.

So what I am basically trying to say is that even if I had a boyfriend I would be imagining he was someone else. Someone better.

Someone I could love.

Someone who could love me back.

But anyway, there it is.

I am a bad person who lies to her own mother. You've probably had enough of me already. You probably want to put me down right now.

But before you do, I just want to make one thing clear.

I lie for an honest reason.

To help my mum.

You see, ever since I left uni she had been on at me for not having a boyfriend. She kept on telling me that if I was 'not interested in boys' (mother code for 'lesbian'), then I should just let her know. And no matter how many times I told her that I *was* interested in boys, but I was just happy being single, she never believed me.

That's the thing with my mum. When I tell her the truth she thinks I'm lying and when I'm lying she thinks I'm telling her the truth.

Anyway, the reason I pretended I'd met a boy called Adam was because she was crying. I mean, really crying. Howling and sniffing and wailing and generally falling apart. It was a sound which sent me back to the first week after dad had gone. When all you could hear was that same snot-ridden soundtrack of grief.

It was a few months ago when she was going through a rough patch and watching all the old home videos, and spring cleaning like a maniac. I knew that the only way to lift her was to tell her some good news but I didn't have any good news to tell and I was drunk and not thinking straight and so I just came out with it.

I've got a boyfriend.

A lawyer.

Called Adam.

And it worked.

The crying stopped.

So the next time it re-started I'd just say something else like that he'd invited me for a meal at a posh restaurant or something until before I knew it I was in a full-blown relationship with someone I had made up out of my head.

But I like to see myself as an optimist. I'm a glass-is-half-full kind of a girl. I believe there is still hope for me and Adam, despite this slight technical glitch. I feel that Adam's non-existence is something which will just have to be worked out in order for our relationship to work. I'm not denying it isn't an issue, it's just that lots of couples have issues and they get past them, they move on. If alcoholics can stop drinking and nymphomaniacs can stop shagging then Adam can bloody well stop non-existing.

Chapter Twelve

Phone call over, I glug the dregs of the wine and turn up the TV in an attempt to drown out the loud music which has just started to rise up from the flat below. This strategy succeeds only in giving me a headache.

I should probably go and complain.

But what if he's an axe-murderer?

An axe-murderer who has seen my nipple.

I mean, it's not likely, but I wouldn't rule anything out after the day I've had. He's been here, for what, ten minutes and he's already acting like the neighbour from hell.

Before I have time to psyche myself up the phone rings.

'So how was it?' A voice asks, as I press the green button. Alice.

The only person in the whole world I never need to lie to. The only one who takes me as I am.

'Shit,' I say. 'It was shit.'

'Even with the reference?' she asks, genuinely bewildered.

'Afraid so,' I say. 'The interviewer knew I was lying.'

'Oh Faith, I'm sorry.' And she is, I can feel it.

'Don't worry,' I say, realising that Alice is someone whose worry quota is fuller than most.

'It will all work out, you know,' she says. 'I know it will.'

The words are like warm milk, and soothe me instantly. 'Anyway,' I say. 'Enough about me, how was *your* day?'

'Oh, good,' she says. 'We went outside.' By 'we' I know she is referring to her eight month old bump. 'To the park. And I didn't, you know, go all funny.'

'You see,' I say, offering warm milk in return. 'That's progress.'

It comes to something when walking two hundred metres to the park without having a panic attack can qualify as progress, but there you go. That's Alice. But if she can be optimistic, so can I.

'What's that noise?' she asks.

'Oh. Someone's moved into the basement flat.'

'Marilyn Manson by the sounds of it.'

'Yeah, I know,' I say, wondering if the off licence is still open.

'Anyway, I'm going to go and finish painting.'

'Painting?'

'The room. For the baby.'

'Oh yes,' I say. 'OK, I'd better leave you to it.'

'See you.'

'Yeah, I'll come around tomorrow, after work.'

'See you.'

'Yeah, see you.'

I switch the TV off, and try and block out the noise from downstairs by reading this book I started about a week ago.

It's called *Daisy Goes Shopping* and it's about this PR girl in London, who has this amazing glamorous life with this millionaire boyfriend but she feels unfulfilled. Something is missing from her life.

Poor Daisy.

Poor Daisy, with a millionaire boyfriend. Life must be so hard.

But you know what, I reckon she'll be all right in the end. Come the final chapter, it will all be great for Daisy. She will have discovered true love and happiness in the arms of a non-millionaire.

Yes, that's my prediction.

I'm currently on chapter seven but I can't get past the first sentence because of the music from downstairs. I even try and read it aloud in order for it to make sense.

' "Daisy had spent the whole day shopping and was now extremely bored . . ." '

Oh, bollocks. It's no good. I can't think past that noise. That's it. I'm going to have to complain whether he saw my nipple or not.

On my journey downstairs to the basement flat I must have been transported into a different dimension of time. For there, right in front of me is a living, breathing Neanderthal Man. I can hardly see his face, buried as it is under an overgrowth of hair. This is clearly someone for whom the words 'shave' and 'haircut' mean absolutely nothing. Judging by the smell of his encrusted T-shirt, the word 'wash' wouldn't probably have any significance either.

'Uh?' enquires the Neanderthal.

'Er, yes,' I say the combination of nerves and chill air rendering me hopelessly sober. 'Hello. I'm um sorry to um bother you but I just wondered if you could possibly, if you didn't mind, perhaps maybe, turn your music down just a little bit?' I crane my neck and venture to make eye contact for a millisecond, then look away. 'Possibly?'

The Neanderthal just stands leaning against the door-frame, staring back at me, saying nothing. What is this? National Awkward Silence Day or something?

I notice he's holding a bottle of cheap vodka in one of his hairy, unwashed hands, an indication that off licences are one aspect of modern civilisation with which he is acquainted. Owing to the surplus of hair it's impossible to work out exactly how old the man is, but he is probably younger than the beard suggests. Not much over thirty, if that.

As the silence builds up, I am starting to feel just a little bit intimidated. Here I am, face to face with one of the tallest, hairiest, smelliest men I have ever had the misfortune to come across, and I am telling him what to do. I half-expect him to whack me over the head with the bottle of vodka, drag me into his basement-cum-cave by the hair and then have his wicked Neanderthal way with me.

I decide to break the silence. 'Look, I'm sorry. Really, I shouldn't have disturbed you. It's just that I've had a very stressful day and I'm trying to relax and concentrate on my book and all I can hear is this ... *noise* – I'm sorry, this music – and it was giving me a headache, and so I just thought I'd come to ask you if you could turn it down just a little bit ...' My voice is sounding close to tears. What *is* the matter with me lately? Why is everything getting to me? I notice something else as well. The Neanderthal is staring straight at my T-shirt. No. *Straight at my breasts.*

'Um,' I say, stepping back. 'What ... what are you doing?'

'I am staring straight at your breasts,' he slurps matter-of-factly, before taking a swig of vodka. I am no longer intimidated. In fact, I am bloody furious. After the day I've had I don't have to stand here and take this perversity from this big hairy stinking sexist stig-of-the-dump.

I am about to tell him words to that effect, when I catch his eyes again. 'Um . . . look . . .' I say, wondering why I am so taken aback. They were after all relatively normal eyes. Sea-green circles surrounded by bleary, vodka-induced pink. But somehow they have a strange effect, a haunted vacancy which sends a frosty shudder down my spine. 'I just wondered if you could turn it down,' my voice is now feeble, almost lost amid the distant sound of traffic.

The man says nothing. Just hiccups, shuts the door gently, and disappears from view, his fusty scent lingering in the evening air.

'Weird,' I say, to an imaginary audience, before heading back up the stone steps to my flat and *Daisy Goes Shopping*.

And then, as I enter the living room, I notice something. The music has stopped.

He hasn't just turned it down, he's turned it off completely, 'Weird, weird, weird,' I mumble, before crashing on the sofa.

Chapter Thirteen

I didn't tell work about my interview. I mean, how could I? It was for a job which has no relation whatsoever to the careful application of eyeliner or lip gloss.

And anyway, I want to keep in with Lorraine. She's my boss. Well, sort of. She wasn't the one who employed me but she's the one who's been in charge of the Keats Cosmetics counter for the last one hundred years or whatever. She's the one I have to see if I want to change my hours or if I want to take a holiday.

She's also the one I have to explain myself to if I have overslept and turn up late. Like right now.

'Faith, we're the only people who work on this counter,' she says, in her strict schoolmistress tone. 'So, it would be good if you could turn up on time.'

'Yes, I know,' I say, sweating under my foundation. 'I'm sorry I'm a bit late. It's just that . . .' *It's just that what? That I was dreaming I was being fed chocolates by Colin Farrell and I didn't want it to end.* '. . . it's just that I bumped into that old lady, you know, Josie, who always comes in on a Saturday to have her face done. Anyway, she was asking me how to reduce the appearance of age spots. And you know what it's like once she gets talking. It's impossible to get away.' This is actually true although it's obviously not the full explanation.

For a moment I think Lorraine is looking right through me. But then I remember. She always looks like that. Well, ever since she started botoxing every square inch of her face.

'All right,' she clips. 'Just make sure it doesn't happen again.'

'No. It won't.'

Tuesdays are always quiet on the Keats counter, and this morning is no exception. In fact, as I look around the whole of the ground floor all I can see are staff. The white-coated Clinique girls, looking like they are about to perform surgery. The glowing, golden Clarins girls, all smiles and curls. The women who work for Lancôme, who spend all day swapping divorce stories. And then there's the funky girls who work for MAC, all with their Toni&Guy eighties-retro haircuts and incessant babble.

It's weird.

Although we all work within the same store, there is practically no interaction between the different beauty departments. It's like we're quarantined or something. You see, make-up girls are really loyal to their brands.

You won't catch a Clarins girl slapping on the St Tropez, or someone from Clinique covering up her hangover with a layer of Beauty Flash Balm, you really won't. And I'm exactly the same with Keats. I never use anything different. Everyday, it's the same layer of

Keats' foundation. Lorraine, who has not managed to stay true to two husbands, has also remained committed to the brand.

So it's really strange when there are next to no customers. All the girls just stand around or sit on their stools and eye each other suspiciously from behind their cosmetic trenches or play about with their make-up.

That's what I'm doing now.

When Lorraine left for an early lunch I set about playing around with different lipstick-eye shadow combinations. At the moment I'm going for a mauvey sort of effect. I think it suits me actually, this one. The lips might be a bit too much though.

I feel something weird against my leg. Then I remember. I put my phone on vibrate. Strictly speaking, it should be switched off, but as there are only about three people in the world who know my number it's not normally a problem. As Lorraine's not here, and there are no customers around I decide to answer it.

'Hello?'

From the sound of heavy breathing, it appears that Darth Vader has decided to give me a call. But then there's a voice. Faint, frightened.

'Faith.' And then the heavy breathing starts again.

'Alice, is that you? Are you OK?' A couple of the Clinique girls eye me suspiciously.

'Please . . . come.' Her voice is desperate.

'What's the matter? What's happening?'

'I need you to come . . . I . . . I'm sorry . . . I can't . . .'

'Al, I'm at work.'

'I'm sorry . . . I'm sorry . . .'

I look at my watch. This is only a job, I tell myself. It is not as important as my best friend. And anyway, I'll probably make it back by the time Lorraine finishes lunch, I tell myself. 'Where are you?'

'Spring Street,' she pants. 'I'm in the . . . phone box.'

'OK,' I sigh. 'Wait there.'

Chapter Fourteen

Alice first started having panic attacks after her mum died.

She can remember the first time as if it was yesterday. She was in Tesco, looking for a jar of pasta sauce, when suddenly everything closed in around her. Her heart raced, her skin itched with fear and she thought she was going to die.

She described to me how all the labels from the jars on the aisle in front of her flashed through her mind at hyper speed. Each word suddenly had a terrifying significance. CARBONARA and ARRABIATA were sinister messages which only she could understand. Lloyd Grossman and Paul Newman were smiling antichrists. She said that she didn't feel as though she was in her own body, as though she was somewhere else entirely, operating a remote control. All the supermarket noises becoming distant, distorted. Like a seashell, is how she put it.

When she stopped thinking she was going to die, she started to believe she was going mad. She imagined herself in a straitjacket, bouncing off the walls, as a team of doctors tried to restrain her. She had a vision of her future and it was painted white. White walls. White coats. Her own scared, white face staring back, wide-eyed, from the mirror.

But eventually the bubbling panic simmered into a manageable state of anxiety and she was able to make her way out of the supermarket (although she had to leave her basket and the pasta sauce behind). But it wasn't to be the last time. In the four years since her mother died she has had panic attacks on a weekly, sometimes even daily basis.

One of the worst attacks she had happened a year ago.

Again she was in a supermarket.

Only this time, help was at hand.

More specifically, help was *a* hand, strong and warm and masculine. A concerned hand, and it rested on hers.

'Are you all right?' the hand's owner, a tall man with a suit and a soft smile, asked her.

Alice looked up at the man and as she looked the panic left her. The pasta sauces no longer held any terrifying secrets, the supermarket aisle was no longer closing in.

The man's name was Peter. Or at least, that is what he told Alice. I never met him, but Alice told me he owned his own company. What doing, I don't know. Alice was always hazy. He was forty-one years old. (Alice always had a thing about older men.) Divorced. He told her this over orange juice and a blueberry muffin in the supermarket café.

He told Alice that she was beautiful. That a girl like her should never have a reason to be insecure. She had incredible eyes. He spoke beautiful words. He spoke them as if he really believed them, as if she really was Something Special.

And when he wasn't with her, she would want to hear them again, the beautiful words, and so she called him on the mobile number he had given her and took up his offer of a drink. When she had got to the bar he was already at the table, and when she went over he held out his hand and stood up halfway. Alice loved that. The standing halfway thing. To her that really meant something. The air was empty of any first-date nerves, and the conversation flowed as smoothly as the house red. When she was with him she realised, as the wine took hold, she felt comfortable. Relaxed. And that doesn't happen often to Alice.

And she wanted to stay feeling the way she was feeling all night, so invited him back to her place. It worked. For once, she managed to have a sleepless night which was due to something other than insomnia.

She enjoyed this new feeling. This protected, flattered feeling. Here she was, being pampered and protected by this gorgeous older man. Apparently everything about Peter was safe. If Marks and Spencer ran a male escort agency, Alice said that Peter would be the kind of guy you would expect to pick up. He had safe hands. A safe smile. A safe suit. A safe taste in music.

Alice misjudged. You see, the thing that wasn't safe about Peter was the one thing that should have been. Namely, his sex. His penis was apparently a latex-free zone. And Alice being Alice, she didn't like to broach the condom subject. Anyway, nothing could happen while she was in his arms. Nothing bad.

They saw each other again. And again. Often enough for Alice to make believe they were at the start of a relationship which could grow into something meaningful.

But she was wrong.

The only thing growing was already inside her, marking his presence with a missed period. At first, Alice pretended this meant nothing. That it was just a quirk of her biology.

But she was wrong.

The test, when she eventually took it, told her that.

52

It went the wrong colour. For fifteen minutes she had pleaded for white, but white wasn't listening. White was having a day off. Blue, it transpired, was Alice's fate.

Beautiful, horrific baby blue.

Peter would understand, she told herself. He would be pleased. Delighted. It must be what he wanted.

But she was wrong.

When she finally told him, during a meal she had spent two hours preparing, he said: 'You're *what*?' Like the test, he too was starting to go the wrong colour. It was as though the force of panic he had managed to calm in Alice was now transferred to him.

'Pregnant,' Alice said, and I didn't have to be there to hear her voice. A fragile, expectant almost whisper. The sound of hope, violated.

It was then that she noticed, for the first time, the pale band of well-preserved skin at the base of his ring finger. It transpired that the only thing Peter had divorced himself from was the truth. He was married. He had kids. He worked away from home a lot. Whatever Alice had previously thought she meant to him, she now understood the reality. She was Peter's after work secret. She was his overtime.

'I've got to go,' he said, closing the door forever. 'I've got to go.'

Time over.

Of course, I know what Alice should have done. She should have made him face up to his responsibilities. She should have asked Marks and Spencer for a refund. Most of all, she should have got angry.

But anger is an emotion of those who have something left to fight for. Right then, right at that moment, Alice felt the battle was over. She had nothing. No hope. An abortion was

53

even more impossible for her than the prospect of single motherhood.

'I'm not a home-wrecker,' she told me.

I reminded her about Peter's responsibilities. Financial, if nothing else.

'I don't want to think about him. I don't want anything. I never want to speak to him again.'

I didn't push it. Perhaps I should have, but I didn't. Ever since I first met her, five years ago, when we were both waitressing amid the clank and steam of Luigi's, I have understood that Alice is someone who has limits. Step over them, and she crumbles to dust.

Both her parents are dead – not just her mum. Her dad died earlier, to bowel cancer, when she was eleven. Her mum died in a road accident a decade later. It made the local news.

The loss of her parents may have meant that she was left with enough money to buy a one-bedroom flat in Leeds, but it also meant she had to say goodbye to the old Alice. The one who had been confident and secure. The new Alice was one for whom even going out of the house could prompt total panic and desolation. And ever since, she had recurring panic attacks.

Her whole life, on paper at least, has been one long drawn-out disaster. I am all she's got to rely on, and I cannot let her down. Alice is my closest friend, the only person outside my family who was really there for me when dad died.

She hasn't ever asked me to live with her.

But I know the real reason. She thinks that if she lived with me I would grow to hate her, that I would see how much of a burden she really is, and that I would leave her like everyone else has left her. She stays away from me in

54

order to keep me close. It sounds strange, but this is the level of insecurity we are dealing with here.

So instead, she continues to live on her own and pretends Peter never happened, even though the evidence to the contrary is now the size of a prize-winning watermelon.

Chapter Fifteen

I can see her already, even from here, her ghostly expression glancing out from behind the glass. I am out of breath but I keep running, weaving through the crowd of shoppers.

'I'm sorry,' I say, colliding with a fat man in a suit.

'What on earth,' I hear him grumble as I speed on.

She has seen me. Relief crumples her face and she turns to place the receiver down, to mark the end of the imaginary phone call she must have been having in order not to attract too much attention to herself.

I open the door, my lungs gasping for oxygen. She falls onto me and holds me tight. I can feel her hard bump, and above it her heart, beating frantically, like the wings of a frightened bird. People are looking but I try not to mind.

'I couldn't ... I'm sorry ... I don't ... it's just ... I was shopping ... and then I felt ... weird ... and ... the people ...'

'It's all right,' I tell her, keeping my eyes peeled for Lorraine. 'It's all right. Nothing's going to happen to you. You've had this before. You'll be fine.'

'My baby ...'

'Your baby's fine.'

She stands back, pulls the strand of tear-matted hair away from her cheek, behind her ear. 'Are you . . . are you sure?'

'Alice, I'm sure. You and your baby are absolutely fine.'

'Oh,' she says, her eyes flickering left to right, absorbing the bustle of people walking passed. 'Thank you.'

I place an arm around her shoulder and lead her out of the booth. 'Come on. Let's take you home.'

Chapter Sixteen

By the time I've sorted Alice out and made my way back to work, Lorraine has finished her lunch.

Oh blinking bollocks.

How am I going to explain this one?

She looks cross with me as I walk towards the Keats counter. Her lips are in a pout. But in fairness, her lips have been in a pout ever since she had half a cow's arse injected into them – as a consolation for her latest divorce – so it's not really much of a good indicator.

The folded arms and the smoke fuming out of her cosmetically enhanced nostrils are more of a giveaway.

'I'm sorry,' I say.

'Sorry? *Sorry*? Faith, could you tell me exactly what we are paying you for?'

This annoys me. So OK, I should have been here for the last ten minutes, but I hardly had a choice. And anyway, Lorraine has more breaks than I don't know what and spends half her life in the stock room when she should be on the shop floor.

Out of the corner of my eye I can see three of the Clinique girls, watching intently like shining white angels of death.

I am stuck for lies. I search my brain desperately, but I must have run out. And then just as I am on the verge of losing my job I hear a voice.

A man's voice. From behind.

'Excuse me.'

Lorraine nods, to indicate a customer, then disappears to check stock.

'Yes,' I say, turning rapidly to help.

The man is a cute, clean-cut blond neatly packaged into a baby blue shirt and navy tie. The office wear would suggest he was about thirty, while the nervous look in his eyes would look more appropriate on a three-year-old.

'I'm, um, looking for my girlfriend.'

'You've lost your girlfriend?'

'No,' his cheeks flush, Prince William-style. 'No. I mean, my girlfriend wants me to buy her some of, um, that.'

He points towards the new Keats' cover-up stick as if he was in a newsagents asking for a copy of *Afro Whores* or *Horny Housewives* or something. God, now that must be love. That's the sort of man I want. Someone who is able to buy your make-up *on his own*.

His girlfriend is one lucky person.

'OK,' I say. 'What sort of skin shade is she?'

'She's, um, I don't know. Sort of normal. Like mine.'

I look at his cheeks, and wonder if Keats do a plum tomato shade of cover-up.

'So, for fair skin then,' I say assuming that is his non-embarrassed tone.

'Yes,' he says, hopfooting left to right. 'Fair skin.'

I get him a number two shade and he hands me his credit card. Then I notice his name. Adam Stonefield.

Adam Stonefield.

Adam.

He's an Adam.

'Is there, um, a problem with my card?' he asks. *Adam* asks. Clearly wanting to leave the make-up department as soon as possible.

'No,' I say, snapping out of my trance. But as I swipe the card through I cannot help thinking.

This is him.

This is my boyfriend.

Exactly how I imagined him to be.

Perfect height.

Perfect age.

Perfect suit.

Perfect eyes.

Perfect body.

But most importantly of all, perfect name.

So OK, Adam's hardly the most unusual name on the planet. It's not like Zariah or Hendrix or Zappa Moonbeam Lovechild the Third or something. I mean, then it really would be a coincidence. It would be like, 'wow, when I made you up I didn't even know that name *existed*.' And Zappa Moonbeam Lovechild the Third would stare longingly into my eyes and say, 'that must mean we were meant to be.'

But anyway, I believe in fate.

And besides, in the context of this make-up department Adam *is* an unusual name. I mean, very few men actually get this close. Normally they hover a few feet behind their wives and girlfriends gazing over at the Mach 3 display, trying to make sure they are not sapped of too much testosterone.

So that makes it something.

And it's not just the fact that he's called Adam.

He looks right.

60

I mean, obviously I haven't gone into too much physical detail whenever my mum asks about him, but when I picture my made-up boyfriend this is pretty much what I see.

My mum would love him. She really would.

'I'm sorry,' I tell him, looking at a screen which has already authorised his card. 'It sometimes takes a while to go through.'

'That's OK,' he says, flashing a glance at my neck. Assuming he's not a vampire, this glance suggests he might fancy me.

But of course he might fancy me.

He's *Adam*.

I smile flirtatiously. His eyes respond, but his mouth stays put.

And then I remember. He's got a girlfriend. That's why he's here in the first place.

He signs the slip with a spidery crawl.

'OK,' I say, bundling the cover-up stick and the receipt into the bag. 'There you go.'

He's still here. Standing.

My non-existent boyfriend.

My existent non-boyfriend.

Whatever.

He's going to say something. Or he's expecting me to say something. He can feel there's a connection between us, I know he can.

All of a sudden, my life really is starting to feel like a book, just like I've always wanted. This is the turning point.

His girlfriend means nothing.

We were meant to be.

He's about to ask me out, I can feel it. He's going to ask me for a drink.

In fact, he has already spoken. He just said something, just then, and I was too wrapped up in fantasy land to hear properly.

'Sorry?' I say, tentatively, as I await his amorous proposal.

'My card,' he says.

'I don't understand.' I catch a glimpse of the Clinique girls, watching as my dream collapses.

'My credit card,' he says. 'You gave me the receipt but you've still got my card.'

I look down at the counter, and see the offending piece of plastic.

'I'm sorry,' I say, as I hand it back to him. 'I'm not really with it today.'

'Don't worry,' he says, having transferred all feelings of embarrassment over to my side of the counter. 'I know how you feel.'

'Sure,' I mumble, as I watch Adam walk out of the store.

Back into non-existence.

Chapter Seventeen

Before we go any further, I should tell you about my dad.

I don't know what I can really tell you but I know I must.

I loved him, I can tell you that. I hated him too, sometimes. I hated him most when he would shout at mum or us for no reason and then go out and wash the car and chat and smile to the neighbours as if he was the most easy going man on earth. The way he would explode if you accidentally broke a door handle or trod a piece of dirt into the carpet.

Or the way he would look at me or Hope before we went out and then to my mother, who was obliged to say, 'it's the fashion'. Or how he would smile at Mark in a way which he never smiled at his daughters. A proud, almost glorious smile.

But these things are nothing now. Irrelevant details which were always open to interpretation in any case. The father I choose to remember is the one I loved. The man who always wanted to do the right thing. The man who was there with us ten minutes before he reached for his heart. The one who would elbow me in the ribs when he got the giggles in front of the TV.

'Stop making me laugh,' he'd tell me, in stitches.

'I'm not doing anything.'

'Doreen,' he'd say to his wife. My mother. 'She's making me laugh.'

At which point my mother would enter and say: 'You're a couple of kids, the pair of you.'

And I'd insist: 'I'm not doing anything. It's the TV.'

Then he'd look at me, laughter stinging his eyes. 'You're a funny girl.'

Anyway, that was my dad. Gentle and tough. Kind and angry. Intolerant and welcoming. A walking, slouching, laughing, snoring mass of contradictions. In short, a human being.

A human being I can still see now, looking up at me as he attended the flowerbed, smiling broadly, or in his green-house listening to the football on the radio as he sprayed his tomatoes.

At least that is what I want to see. All too often it becomes replaced by the man lying in pain on the floor, still wearing his orange paper crown, trying his hardest to stay with us. Trying to make sure that the worry in my mother's eyes wouldn't turn into something even worse. Knowing that the attack on his own heart could end up bringing my mother's down with it.

And of course it did, at least for a while.

When dad died, Mark submerged himself in work more than ever before. Whatever grief he was feeling he somehow kept it inside, never letting a tear find its way onto his face. Even at the hospital, even when dad's whole existence was traded for a continuous bleep, he never broke down in front of us. He just stood there by the bedside, holding onto all the women, as gravity gained extra force.

'It's OK,' he said, quietly, underneath our wails. 'It will be OK.'

The loudest wail, I suppose, came from Hope. Even when it was happening, even when my dad's hand was clasped to his chest, she was visibly falling apart. While Mark phoned for an ambulance and while mum and I tried to make dad stay still, Hope was crouching on the floor next to the tree and the presents, wailing with panic and premature grief.

I can hear it now, the whole scene. Mark's ultra-composed voice on the phone, Christmas TV blaring obliviously in the background, my mum, talking fast, saying God knows what, and Hope's desperate howl above it all.

Eventually though, the howling stopped and Hope started to cope in her own way. She bought a one-way ticket to Australia and left on her eighteenth birthday. Mark had thought she would stay and look after mum, as she was the only one of us still living full-time at home.

But she didn't.

She couldn't.

So it was left to me and Mark to alternate weekends, and it was left to my mother to freefall from Monday to Friday without any one of her three children to cling to.

I had wanted to drop out of uni but my mum said she would never forgive herself. So in a way, if I can speak self-ishly for a moment, it was the worst of both worlds. The burden of guilt on top of the burden of grief.

Every other Monday morning I'd be at Darlington station, my mum sobbing onto my shoulder, her hand clutching tight to my arm.

'Mum. I'll stay.'

'No. You have to go. You have to study hard. You have to make your father proud.'

65

And so I went, but I never left her behind. In every seminar and every lecture she was always there, with dad, in some secret plot to break me down. To embarrass me in front of everybody as I struggled out of my seat, clambering awkwardly past an army of resistant knees, before letting it all out in some anonymous, graffiti-decorated cubicle.

'She's getting a lot better,' my brother would say, over the phone. 'Isn't she?'

'I suppose.'

'She's definitely back on her feet.'

And there was no denying that. In fact, she was never *off* her feet. Hoovering, dusting, cleaning the windows, sorting out the cupboards, making the beds . . .

'So much to do,' she'd say. 'So much to do.'

My dad, a man who since his early retirement from the police force managed to turn sitting down into a near full-time occupation, had now ironically converted the sofa into a no-go area for the woman he had left behind.

For my mum, sitting down meant slowing down and that was now impossible. Impossible because it would mean she would have to think and she knew too well where that would lead.

It would lead to pain. It would lead to a mountain of regret. The unsaid truths they never had time for.

It would lead to the end of the world.

Chapter Eighteen

I am breakfasting on Jaffa Cakes and Pringles in front of the TV when suddenly I start to feel like I am going mad.

Ten seconds ago everything was fine.

I was just watching this daytime show waiting for the makeover section to come on when suddenly I saw her.

Hope.

My sister.

My sister who hasn't phoned or written or emailed or texted or smoke-signalled or anything for two years, despite my mum's stream of letters. My sister who disappeared from our lives when dad died. Who packed her bags and went to the other side of the world.

And now here she is, prettier than ever, being beamed into my living room, shining like a hallucination. A very sporty hallucination, dressed head-to-toe in designer gym gear, flirting with the TV presenter.

'According to a new survey,' the presenter is saying, 'the British are now the least sexually satisfied nation in Europe. It appears that eighty per cent of men in this country get more pleasure from watching football, while nine out of ten

British women rank shopping and chocolate above sexual activity. Well, after ten years of living with my wife I don't need a survey to tell me that, I can assure you. Only joking, dear.' The presenter smiles at the camera and flutters his eyelashes while my sister – my *sister* feigns amusement behind him.

'Anyway, fear not,' he continues, reading from the autocue, 'as it looks like help is at hand. Forget about Viagra, the new way to improve our sex lives involves . . .' he pauses for dramatic effect, '. . . *yoga.*'

Yoga! What on earth does my sister know about yoga? My jaw, weighted with shock and Jaffa Cakes, is touching the carpet.

'Here to tell us all about it is yoga instructor Hope Wishart, who has just arrived back from Australia where her revolutionary Yogasmic Workout has already been a huge success. And now I understand there's going to be a book and DVD of the workout available, is that correct?'

This is too much information to handle.

Yoga.

Instructor.

Yogasmic Workout.

My sister.

TV.

Book.

DVD.

Back from Australia.

My brain is about to malfunction.

'Yes, that's right,' my sister says. 'Out in the shops today.'

'OK,' says the presenter, shuffling his cue cards. 'So how can sitting down with our legs crossed help spice up our sex lives?'

'You'd be surprised,' my sister says, flirting shamelessly. 'And there's a lot more to yoga than sitting with our legs crossed. In fact, most of the exercises and postures I use in the Yogasmic Workout are standing exercises. But really both yoga and sex are about the mind as well as the body.'

'But isn't it about relaxation, wouldn't it just send us all to sleep?'

'No. Really, yoga is very energising. Especially the tantric postures I perform.'

The presenter's eyebrows go into innuendo overdrive as he faces the camera.

'OK then,' he says. 'Perhaps you'd like to show us a quick routine.'

My sister moves forwards and faces me, along with the rest of the viewing public, head on. Then she stretches her arms high above her head and bends back.

While she does this she carries on talking to the presenter but I am no longer listening.

In fact, I can hardly move.

She is now swivelling her hips, breathing like a maniac and sticking her tongue out.

This is beyond surreal, it really is.

I am about to phone my mum to tell her but then I remember: she thinks I'm at work. But what if she's watching it? It would be too much for her.

I mean, this is Hope.

This is the girl who left for Australia when dad died.

She couldn't cope, that was her excuse. As if coping was somehow any more of an option for the rest of us.

And now, three years later, she turns up back in the country. On TV. A smiling, flirting, *coping* yoga celebrity who has found that the easiest way to deal with her family is to disown them.

When the programme ends and Hope disappears I go and visit Alice to tell her all about it.

Alice, who seems to be over her phone box nightmare, is in the middle of stuffing envelopes. It's the new home working scheme she found out about on the Internet. Sounds a bit dodgy to me but I suppose that when you can hardly walk out of your front door without having a panic attack your career options are rather limited.

'Oh my God,' she says, when I tell her. 'When did she get back?'

'I don't know.'

'Where is she living?' she asks, before licking an envelope.

'Don't know that either. London, I suppose.'

'What will your mum say?'

'She'll be devastated. I mean, she hasn't seen her for three years and now she's just come back without saying a word. It's just not on.'

'Does your brother know?'

'No. Well, I don't think so. He hasn't said anything.'

Alice looks a bit distant, and strokes her bump.

'She reckons she's going to start the yoga-sex revolution,' I tell her. 'I mean, have you ever heard anything so stupid in all your life?'

I don't like this new voice of mine. It sounds nasty. Jealous. Bitter. But I can't help it. I can't.

Not that Alice is even listening any more. She's still lost in some antenatal dreamworld all of her own. But the voice keeps going, nasty and jealous and bitter, as if it is trying to make up for three lost years.

It's a voice which pretends to be speaking on behalf of my mother. For all her tears, for those long lonely weekdays when Hope should have been there.

70

When we all should have been there.

But really, deep down, I worry that I am not speaking for mum. I worry I am only speaking for myself. I worry that secretly I wish I'd done the same thing as Hope.

Got out.

Escaped.

Gone to the other side of the world and shagged my way around Australia.

But I didn't.

I stayed here. Because it was always easier for me to make up a life than to go out and get one.

'There,' Alice says, with a sad smile, as she finishes the last envelope. 'All done.'

Chapter Nineteen

I am downstairs in HMV looking at the fitness DVDs and sure enough, there it is.

The Yogasmic Workout.

My sister, the DVD.

God, she looks good. I mean, they've probably air-brushed her a bit for the cover but still, she looks like a different person to the one who left for the other side of the world three years ago.

I smile what I hope is a proud smile but inside I know I am only lying to myself. The truth is, I am jealous as hell.

Why hadn't I done this? Why hadn't I run away to Australia and started a tantric yoga revolution?

I turn the DVD over and look at the list of contents on the back cover.

Intro: yogic breathing techniques
Warm-up
Tantric twists
Tantric toning
Pelvic rotations

Floor work
Cool down
Sexy stretches

DVD Extras:
Photo Gallery
Behind the Scenes
Hope Wishart interview

Extras! My sister's got extras!
I want a DVD!
I want extras!
Never mind yogic breathing techniques. Just being able to breathe normally would suffice right now. I mean, look at me. My hands are shaking, my palms are sweating, my legs are going weak. I must be turning into Alice.
But why do I get like this? In such a state? Why can't I just be happy for her?
She's my *sister*, after all.
In an effort to be the bigger person I decide to buy a copy of the DVD and take it home.
I am the bigger person, I tell myself.
But even though I am the bigger person – and judging by her skinny frame on the cover I really *am* the bigger person – it still takes me about six hours before I decide to play the DVD. I hoover the house, I eat dinner, I watch 'Newsnight', but I know I can't put it off any longer. So here I go.
And there she is.
My God.
How much weight has she lost? Seriously, there are stick insects with larger thighs than her.
'Welcome to the Yogasmic Workout,' my sister says, from a red, candlelit set, which is somewhere between an

73

eighties rock video and a deluxe brothel. 'I'm Hope Wishart, and over the next hour I will help you take the first steps on your journey to a better body and a better sex-life. This workout will not only help to tone up your body and lose fat, it will also help you to gain more sexual pleasure ...' My God. 'First of all we are going to start by doing a few warm-up exercises designed to help you con-nect with your tantric self and to recharge some of that latent sexual energy ...'

Now that's just the sort of thing you want your little sister to help you on, isn't it. Recharging your latent sexual energy. Connecting with your tantric self.

I grab the remote and forward to the next section.

'OK,' my sister tells me, her left leg poised delicately behind her head. 'You should be really feeling it now.'

Oh, I'm feeling it all right. I'm feeling it. Only not in my legs, which are in their customary Sprawled Out On Sofa position, but in that part of my brain which contains all those nasty feelings. Jealousy. Anger. Despair. The complete futility of human existence.

'And we're going to hold that stretch for a count of eight – one, two ...'

Suddenly I hear a terrible noise. It takes a few seconds for me to realise that this noise is not an aural manifestation of all my nasty, anti-yogic feelings. It is music. Loud, angry guitar music, and it does not seem to be going away.

Great.

My new neighbour is playing death metal at five minutes after midnight.

I turn up the volume on the TV remote but I still can't drown out the noise.

'As you lower that leg I want you to slowly exhale and release all that negative energy ...'

74

Yeah, right. But I do lower my leg, off the sofa, and stamp three times in the vain hope that the new tenant will get the message.

If anything the music gets louder.

I try and ignore it for ten minutes, but eventually realise I will have to confront him. As I put on my denim jacket, I glance again at the TV.

My sister, now in the process of fine-tuning her pelvic floor muscles, is tantrically oblivious to the deafening noise below.

'OK, now push your buttocks up to the sky and keep your tummy tucked in,' are her last words as I walk out to confront my neighbour.

I pause on the doorstep, then I knock, and as I do so I realise his door is slightly open. I strain my ears, but there is nothing but the same offending distorted guitars and angry vocals.

I knock again, only this time much louder.

When no one comes I go to the window but the curtains are shut.

I tap my knuckles against the glass, but soon realise I am out of luck. Then, as I am on the verge of admitting defeat and treading back up the stone steps to my flat, something stops me.

It's a feeling that not everything is right here.

There's no logic behind it, but it's as though I can sense something is wrong. There's something in the air.

They say you can smell trouble, and right now I think they are right.

I go back to his door and push it further open.

Unlike my flat, there is no hallway. The door opens straight onto the living room. No light is on but it is easy to see the place is a complete mess. And now the smell of

75

trouble is fused with the more immediately recognisable odours of stale tobacco and dirty washing.

I look down and see that my foot is on the carpet, next to a crumpled can of super-strength lager and a very ambiguous looking stain.

What am I doing?

This is trespassing.

This is against the law.

It's also very much against common sense.

I mean, the alcoholic Neanderthal who lives here didn't exactly strike me as the kind of individual who takes kindly to people breaking into his apartment.

And what if he's a serial killer? I mean, he's certainly got the right taste in music. And the facial hair was very much like the kind you see on all those identifit police pictures.

Yeah, that's it. I am standing in the middle of a psychopath's apartment with music blaring so loud that no one will be able to hear me scream. I should leave now.

Come on, Faith, turn around and walk back out of the door. I mean, who do I think I am. Jodie Foster? It's past midnight. It's extremely scary.

But I can't shake it.

The feeling that something bad has happened.

Chapter Twenty

'Hello?'

No answer.

'Hello?'

Still nothing.

I look around in the half light from a lamp on the floor, and see boxes. Hundreds of boxes, stacked on top of each other. Some high-rise, some low, the whole room a cardboard metropolis.

A couple of the boxes have been identified by marker pen. R'S THINGS, written in big, shaky letters along their sides.

My God. He's been here for days and he hasn't even unpacked. He must be even more disorganised than me.

Or an alcoholic. I scan the chaotic arrangement of empty beer cans and vodka bottles decorating the carpet. I follow their scattered trail towards the doorway and I see a . . . oh my God.

I freeze. Literally, the shock makes movement impossible.

Chapter Twenty-One

A foot.

A massive bare foot, peeping around the doorway.

It takes a few seconds to fully make sense of the sight, to realise that the foot is likely to be attached to a body, and that (judging by the foot's position) the body is lying on the floor, face up, not moving.

I then realise that this is the sort of scene where you can't stay frozen for long.

I rush forward, into the bedroom, and hear myself whimper in horror.

It's him. The Neanderthal. Lying completely naked on the floor.

Not moving.

There is vomit on his face, rising upwards from his wide open mouth, across his beard, towards his cheek.

An empty bottle is beside his head.

And then everything becomes unreal, fiction, the way it always does in an emergency situation.

Suddenly, I am watching myself move at crisis-speed,

crouching down, looking for signs of life. I press my fingers into his neck, waiting, trying to catch a rhythm.

Nothing.

After clearing his airway, I pick up his hand. The hand which has fallen over his groin, the hand which weighs more than I ever thought a hand could possibly weigh. It is warm.

I turn it over and again check for a pulse.

Nothing.

'Please,' I say, shaking his shoulder with my free hand. 'Please wake up.'

His eyes are open, staring blankly at the ceiling. Not seeing. Or seeing too far.

It suddenly occurs to me: he is dead. I am *touching* a dead body.

But he is still body temperature. The sick on his face is shiny and wet. His skin is pale, but not morgue-pale.

I am on the phone, my mobile, by this point.

I have heard myself ask for an ambulance, I have heard myself give the address, but these things are happening far away. In slow motion. In the third person.

It's as though I am observing the whole scene from above. Because this is no longer me. It isn't, it can't be. The girl dropping her phone to the floor and placing her hands together over the man's chest, the girl who is now pressing down, trying to bring the dead back to life. That girl is someone else. Not me. These things don't happen to me. My typical day does not involve coming across naked dead bodies in basement flats.

Fifteen attempts on the chest, then two on the mouth, nose pinched. Just like I learned at that course I went on. A St John's ambulance thing. After dad died. Equipping myself with knowledge I'd needed a year earlier. I have a vague memory of the practical demonstration, with plastic dummies, of someone telling me not to be scared of pressing down hard, because sometimes it involves breaking the rib cage.

As I press down hard, for the ninth time, a clear thought swims its way through the living nightmare. The thought is this: what if I am wrongly accused? I mean, if he has only just died, and I have only just entered the flat it doesn't look good. I can see it now: WOMAN KILLS NOISY NEIGHBOUR (THEN STEALS HIS CLOTHES).

'Ten,' I say, keeping count as I press down again on his chest, using all my upper body weight. Come on, please, *come on*. Wake up. '. . . eleven.'

I glance at his mouth, at the vomit around it, clinging to his beard. The idea of placing my lips to his is an impossible one, yet only four chest presses away.

'Twelve.'

The person on the phone had said to keep doing this until the ambulance arrives, that it would be there 'very soon.' But very soon is starting to feel like forever.

'Thirteen.'

How long can you go without a pulse? A minute?

No, it's more than that. Three minutes? Has it been three minutes? I have no idea. My mind flashes fast, like an MTV montage.

An old eighties film with Kiefer Sutherland. Julia Roberts was in it as well, I think. *Flatliners*, that was it. A group of medical students seeing how long they could survive after flat-lining. One of them made something like fourteen minutes. That's the length of time that a human being can go without oxygen. I can remember going to Sea World as a child, when we went to Florida, they had these South American pearl divers who wore no equipment. I remember watching the tiny bubbles as they made their way to the water's surface. It was the most beautiful thing I had ever seen. The pretty little bubbles, like escaping pearls, moving faster as they rose. I remember asking my dad if he could hold his breath for that long. For fourteen whole minutes. He said he couldn't but I didn't believe him.

'Fourteen.'

Every millisecond is now stretched into an eternity, and a strange, distant calm falls over me – or rather, falls over my other self, the me looking down from above. For the first time since I found him here, I notice the incredible strangeness of the Neanderthal's body. The contrast between the whiteness of his skin and the blackness of his hair. The body's weird shape. Both too fat and too skinny, an unhealthy shape, but not a wasted away shape, or a death shape, not the shape that's made for coffins.

My eyes, still not fully accustomed to the darkness of the situation, are drawn towards his penis. Lying flat, upwards, towards his belly button, it looks defeated, lifeless – as if imitating the body it belongs to.

It is a big penis. Massive, in fact, considering the lack of blood flow. Even in defeat it emerges proud and wide from its pubic mane. But can this be possible? Can I really be the sort of person who, in the middle of trying to save someone's life, is at the same time contemplating the size of their penis? Apparently, I can. Rude and ridiculous thoughts can gatecrash my mind on any occasion. Even this one.

'Fifteen.'

There is still no ambulance. No distant siren. Not that I could hear it over the noise of screaming guitars.

It is just me and the body and the unpacked boxes. The kiss-of-life is about to happen.

81

His nose is shining with alcohol sweat and is clogged with blackheads. I pinch it, then pinch my own, to try and cancel out the stench of vomit.

I gag at the realisation that there is still some on his lips, but there is no time to wipe it away. That could be the second. That could be the fatal moment when he is lost forever.

No.

I can't do it.

I now realise who I am. I am a person who can think of penis size in a life-or-death situation. I am a person who has to wipe away sick – albeit quickly, with the side of my wrist – before I can give the kiss-of-life.

But I cannot wipe it all. I can taste it, but I do not acknowledge the taste. Instead, I concentrate on the feel of his beard as it bristles against my chin. I breathe deep, pushing the air deep inside him. A man whose name I don't even know.

I lift away, tilt my head, and watch as his chest deflates. From this angle, his whole body is just hair. From this angle, he is a Yeti.

When his chest reaches the lowest point, I place my lips back on his and again exhale a slow, strong tunnel of air. As I release the breath I wonder what has happened. I wonder why he has no clothes on. Why he has done this to himself, and whether he has deliberately gone this far.

Still no flashing blue light.

I start back on his chest, using as much life-giving energy as I can muster. 'Come on . . . please don't die . . . please.'

Chapter Twenty-Two

The whole flat is with me now. It's on my side. I can feel it, the force of all the secrets contained in those unopened boxes, an almost supernatural power. He cannot die. This man, this human being, whatever he has done to himself, I must undo; whatever has happened, isn't fully over.

As I continue to press down I angle my head so I get a complete view out of the front window. The rain, beating relentlessly against the panes, is making it hard to see, although I can tell the ambulance is still not here. But of course it isn't. I only phoned . . . when? A minute ago? Less than a minute? Could it still be less than a minute? Could it be more? I have no idea. Time is playing tricks.

The music stops. A brief hiss of tape, then nothing. Just the sound of rain, a distant grumble of thunder and my own breathless exertion.

Again, I try to bargain with him between pressing down on his chest. 'Wake up . . . I'm sorry . . . I never meant to complain . . . whoever you are . . . please, just wake up . . . please . . . if you can hear . . . I love your music . . . you can play it . . . as loud as you want . . . I'm so sorry . . .'

The man, his body, his smell, his beard, his nudity, his body hair – none of this is repulsive now. He is beautiful in his helplessness and I must keep on, despite the fact that my arms are ready to surrender, despite the fact that there is still no ambulance, despite the fact that he must now surely be . . .

Something happened.

Just then.

I felt it, deep below the palms of my weary hands.

'Hello? Can you hear me? Hello?'

I lift my hands away from his chest.

A strange sound, a gasp in reverse, then his whole body is agitated by a convulsive motion. He chokes, his head lifts up, as though from a nightmare, and he struggles for air. The convulsions stop, and more watery sick pours from his mouth.

His head falls back, but a spark of life is now in his eyes.

I ask him again: 'Can you hear me?'

His mouth drops open, to release some inarticulate sound. I check his wrist. A pulse. Faint and slow, but a pulse all the same. His eyes close again.

'Keep awake,' I tell him. 'Please keep awake. You're going to be OK, but please keep awake.'

A man's voice: 'Hello?' The ambulance must have arrived.

'Hello,' I respond. 'Over here.'

A man and a woman, wearing their green uniforms, step into the living room. I have never been so pleased to see anybody in my life as I am now pleased to see these two green archangels.

The man asks: 'What's his name?'

'I don't know.'

The woman asks: 'Has he got a pulse?'

'I think so ... yes ... he has.'

The man asks: 'Have you resuscitated him?'

The words arrive faster: 'Yes ... he woke up ... his body sort of moved like a fit and then his eyes closed and I don't know what's happening now his head just fell back and his eyes closed and I don't know what to do ... I didn't know ... it just ... I ... is he I don't know ... is he going to be OK—'

The man places a hand on my shoulder. He wants me calm. He wants me to talk sense. And sense is not what I am talking.

My hands are by my mouth, shaking, more than shaking, juddering up and down. I step back, against the wall. The ambulance people crouch down and look for signs. They unfold a stretcher and heave him onto it.

There is more heaving as they lift the stretcher up.

Clothes are on the floor, caught in the door to his bedroom. Black jeans, a woolly jumper, shoes.

I pick them up and follow the stretcher.

'Are you coming with us?' the ambulance woman asks, walking backwards, and struggling under the weight.

'Yes,' I say, regaining a relative composure. 'He'll need some clothes.'

And so we head towards the ambulance, past all the boxes. Outside, into the rain.

Chapter Twenty-Three

There is nothing worse than the smell of hospitals. That antisepticy, disinfectanty, doctorly, deathly smell.

I have been sitting here, in this miserable waiting area, holding this same plastic cup, for about three hours. *Three* hours.

And what have I found out in that time?

That he's probably going to be OK.

That he went through a critical stage, but has now stabilised and is semi-conscious.

That he's called Frank.

Frank Black. I think that's what the woman behind the desk said. She was munching on a rather dodgy cheese sandwich at the time.

It sort of makes sense. If anyone was to be called Frank then it should be him. It seems to conjure his general aura of weirdness. His *beardness*.

I've learned other things too. I've learned that the woman behind the desk was clearly employed as some kind of sick joke. I mean, there are two signs on her desk. One says 'help'. The other says 'information'. And yet they must be the two words in the English language which least apply to her. So OK, she's given me his name. But that's it. Seriously, I've been up to that desk about seven hundred times asking whether he was OK, how long it was all likely to take and all the rest of it, and each time she's just greeted me with that stone-cold, nightshift, vampires-have-taken-over-my-body stare and said something like 'there are lots of other people waiting for news'.

Which was actually a lie.

There has only been one other person in this waiting area, a middle-aged man in an anorak whose wife has had an accident with the chip fat fryer. And he's been too absorbed with staring at my cleavage to go up and ask Mrs Helpful for information.

It was only when a woman with glasses and a white coat and a clipboard arrived that I was able to find anything out. And even now I still don't know if he's going to come out tonight. Or if there could be any more complications.

So why am I still here?

I've handed the clothes over, there are no more questions to be asked, it is four in the morning and where am I? I'm sitting in a chair which could have been designed by the Marquis de Sade, having my tits gawped at by a saddo in an anorak and my only other form of company is the Warden from *Prisoner Cell Block H*.

And I'm in work tomorrow.

In about five hours.

So, I am, technically insane.

But the thing is, I have to know. I can't just go home now without seeing him in the flesh. I saved his life. That's what the ambulance man said. Now, that doesn't change the fact that he's a rude Neanderthal drunkard, but it does mean

87

something. It means I need to see him for myself. Just to make sure.

I look down into my empty cup and remember the last time I did this. The night dad died. When we had been told to wait outside, and mum was the only one left with him and we were just left looking at the clock on the wall. Watching the second hand and wondering whether we wanted time to stay still or speed up.

Voices.

Footsteps.

Echoing down the corridor.

It's him. Frank. Standing there, looking half-dead.

But it's a relief to see him. After all, half-dead's a lot better than whole-dead. The doctor standing next to him smiles at me as if I'm his wife or girlfriend or something.

Frank, however, is not smiling. Even when he sees me there is nothing in his face. No recognition. He just walks straight past me.

Perhaps he's still dazed.

I get to my feet and follow him. The woman behind the desk smiles for the first time since I arrived here.

'Excuse me,' I say. 'Hello. Frank, it's me. Faith. The girl from the flat above you. I found you ...'

The automatic doors open as Frank walks ahead. It is still raining, and Frank, dressed in the clothes I brought, is still saying nothing.

I grab his arm. He stops, turns, and looks at me. In the artificial glare of the light he looks undead. His hair blacker and his skin even paler than it would be otherwise. Drops of rain decorate his beard.

'We need to get home,' I tell him. 'Have you called a taxi? Did they call you one?'

He shakes his head. 'No.'

OK, so it's not a deep and meaningful conversation, but it's a start. I pull my mobile out of my pocket and then my purse which has a battered piece of card advertising A1 Taxis.

Frank watches in glum silence as I dial and book our ride home.

'It will be five minutes,' I tell him.

He turns around and waits under a shelter by the door to the Radiography department.

I know that he nearly died of alcohol poisoning less than four hours ago. But there's no reason to be rude. Stupid beardy weirdo. I don't know why I bothered missing a night's sleep, I really don't.

We wait in silence until the taxi comes, watching puddles in the rain.

Chapter Twenty-Four

'I brought your clothes,' I say, as the taxi pulls out onto the main road. 'I went in the ambulance and I brought your clothes to the hospital.'

He doesn't answer. His face is resting against the car window, looking out. Nothing about his eyes suggests that he has heard anything I have just said.

The taxi driver – an elderly Sikh man with a sad smile – turns to confirm the destination. Frank is not answering so I nod at the taxi driver and tell him he has the right address.

As we pass the twenty-four hour Tesco, shining like a fake eternity, I catch a look at Frank's bearded face. He looks rough. In fact, rough doesn't even do it justice. He'd need a professional makeover and two weeks on a health farm just to get to rough.

'I didn't mean to enter your flat,' I say. 'I just went down to—' I hesitate, remembering exactly why I had gone down. 'The door was open,' I said, instead.

He looks at me straight. This is where it's going to happen. This is where he's going to thank me for saving his life.

'So that's what you do, is it, you go around knocking on people's doors and then when you find one open you walk straight in?' He is shaking his head. He is angry. *Angry*!

I quickly discover the anger is contagious. 'Hey you listen, Mister ... Frank or whatever you are called. If it wasn't for me opening that door. If I hadn't bothered to see if you were OK ... If I hadn't ...'

Frank closes his eyes, puts his head back against the seat and raises a dismissive hand. 'What do you want? A Nobel prize?'

My mouth opens. My mouth closes.

I am speechless.

I try again. This time there are words. 'I saved your *life*.'

The taxi driver's smile switches from sad to surprised as he looks in the rear view mirror.

Frank turns and looks at me.

'I saved your life,' I say again, only this time quieter, so the taxi driver doesn't hear.

Frank's eyes – green islands in a sea of pink – make me feel instantly guilty. For what, I'm not exactly sure.

The taxi pulls up.

While I fumble around my purse for the right money, Frank gets out.

'OK, there you go,' I say, handing the taxi driver a handful of coins.

The taxi driver counts the money, nods his head, then drives away. I turn around to ask if Frank is going to be OK.

'Are you—'

But he has already gone.

Chapter Twenty-Five

I hardly get any sleep that night.

I cannot stop thinking that there is more to Frank than meets the eye. There was something about the way he looked at me, in the taxi. It was almost like a cry for help or something.

And why hadn't he even unpacked?

I lay there, looking up at my ceiling, wondering about the story contained in all those boxes. A story which led him to poisoning himself with alcohol.

Then, before I know it, it is time to get up.

Chapter Twenty-Six

Lorraine is not wearing her happy face. Well, technically speaking, Lorraine is not wearing her face. Full stop. I mean, this is the woman who makes Michael Jackson look like the model of natural beauty.

But anyway, she's pissed off. For one thing, she's pissed off about the fact that there's just been a recall on Keats' new toner and make-up remover. It brings out everyone who uses it in a horrible rash which lasts for weeks. Apparently, we should only be selling the hypoallergenic toner from now on. Oh, and she's pissed off with me as well.

'Faith, why didn't you give that woman her free goodie bag?'

Oops. 'Oh. Um, I forgot.'

'You forgot?'

'Yes. Sorry.'

She attempts to raise her eyebrows. They move by about half a millimetre. 'Sorry?'

God. Anyone would think I've jeopardised national security rather than forgotten to hand out a flaming free goodie bag. 'Yes. It won't happen again.'

'And sort out your face. You look dreadful,' the pot says to the kettle. But I catch my own reflection and reluctantly realise she has a point. Look at those bags.

'I'm sorry. I'll put some cover-up on. It's just that I hardly slept last night.'

She fiddles pointlessly with the self-tan display. 'Faith, I'm not interested in your sex life. I just want you to get on with your job.'

My sex life? OK, so a night in a hospital waiting room being titgawped by an anorak-wearing saddo might do it for some girls, but I'm not one of them.

'I wasn't—'

But I give up. What's the point? I haven't even been able to justify to myself why I missed a night's sleep for the rudest man alive so I'm hardly going to be able to make Lorraine understand.

So I stay quiet, cover up the puffy dark circles under my eyes, and get on with my job. And, just when I think the day couldn't possibly get any worse, in walks someone I recognise.

The girl with the heavy fringe.

Little Miss Fashion Victim.

From Coleridge Communications.

The one who wanted a word with John Sampson in the middle of my interview. The one who completely blew my chances.

'Don't I know you from somewhere?' she asks, knowing that she does.

'I don't think so,' I say. 'Is there anything I can help you with?'

She folds her arms and smiles. 'You're the one who tried to get the job. Aren't you?'

Lorraine is within earshot. If she finds out I've been trying to get other jobs by lying on my CV I am as good as dead.

94

'We've got a special three for two offer on our face care range,' I say, completely ignoring her question.

Heavy Fringe glances at Lorraine, then back at me, pushing her tongue against her cheek. On a good day, I could probably handle this. I could probably think of a way to get rid of her. But today is to good days what the Pope is to a brothel.

Heavy Fringe soaks up the moment for a while, just long enough to make sure I realise she still has something over me.

'Just some lip gloss,' she says, coldly. 'And some face toner.'

As she's saying this Lorraine moves past me and says, 'I'm taking a break. Back in ten minutes.'

'Oh, OK.'

'In your own time,' Heavy Fringe says, looking at her watch, as I get her the lip gloss.

And once I've got the lip gloss I reach for the hypoallergenic toner but I realise that some of the other toner is still out. The stuff which gives you a horrible rash. I check that Lorraine has disappeared and then pop a box of it in Heavy Fringe's bag.

'With the toner,' I say, in my best make-up voice, 'you should use quite a lot at a time as it's quite mild.'

Heavy Fringe sneers, then pays, taking her lip gloss and her industrial strength toner. She leaves without comment.

'Have a nice day.'

Chapter Twenty-Seven

Alice is on a bit of a downer, possibly because she has been stuffing envelopes all day and her bump is the size of a beach ball.

'I look like a tank,' she tells me, after showing me the room she's decorated for the baby.

'No you don't,' I say. 'You look lovely. Radiant.'

'Radiant my bum. I'm the size of a mountain.'

'Don't be silly.'

'I'm fat.'

'No, you're not. You're pregnant. This is how you are meant to look.'

'Like Jabba the Hut?'

'No. Like . . . like . . . like Demi Moore. You know, when she did that magazine cover years ago. When she was pregnant and naked.'

'Oh Faith please. Your lies might work on your mother but they're not going to work with me. Demi Moore!'

I decide to change the subject and tell her about last night. The whole Frank business. She cannot believe what she is hearing.

'You actually touched his mouth?' she asks.

'Uh-huh. I had to. Apparently it's quite a key part of the whole resuscitation process.'

I then tell her about the hospital. About Frank's incredible rudeness after I had just saved his life. About the taxi home. About the way he just disappeared without hardly saying anything.

'God,' she says, before delivering the verdict. 'What a total wanker.'

I nod. It's true. There's no way he's just your everyday wanker. He's a total one.

'I would stay out of his way, the ungrateful weirdo,' she says.

'Yes,' I say. 'I think I will.'

Chapter Twenty-Eight

I arrive at work and within ten minutes I am in a state of rigid, speechless shock.

Five metres away from the Keats counter there is a promotional cardboard cut-out of a woman smiling white teeth, and sitting in the lotus position.

The cardboard woman, I now realise, is my sister. The reason I am one hundred per cent sure of this fact is that there is a sign right next to her, saying:

Yoga expert HOPE WISHART, star of Good
Morning Britain, will be in-store today to promote
and sign copies of The Yogasmic Workout DVD and
book.

And then, in smaller print, there is a time:

2.30pm.

I look at my watch. 2.12pm.

Blinking bollocks, this is not happening. This *can't* be

happening. It just can't. Why the hell is she coming here? It must be some nationwide promotional tour or something.

She can't see me. She just can't know I work here. Not because I'm embarrassed. But because mum will have told her I work in PR, in one of those letters she always used to send her. And if Hope speaks to mum, which she surely will at some point, all my lies will come crashing down on me.

I look beside the cardboard cut-out and the sign. There is a mat and a small microphone. My God, she's going to be right there, a mere five yogic lunges away from me.

I've got to think of something. And quick.

'Excuse me,' a customer's voice breaks my train of thought, 'I wondered if you had a facial cleanser suited to sensitive skin?'

I turn around and see the voice belongs to a female student, wearing a rainbow-coloured scarf and a friendly smile. I want to fob her off, but Lorraine's probably not too far away so I'd better just get the spiel over with as soon as possible.

'Yes,' I say, gabbing at hyper speed. 'It's the Keats Gentle Cleanse and Polish which is a pump action cleanser—' I feel my voice get even faster,'—containing-special-quantities-of-botanical-ingredients-such-as-chamomile-and-rosemary' and faster still 'and-it-lasts-for-months-and-comes-with-its-own-muslin-cloth-which-acts-as-a-natural-exfoliant-which-you-use-in-the-morning-and-the-evening-with-the-cleanser-taking-special-care-around-the-eye-area-while-lightly-buffing-skin-to-remove-dead-skin-cells-and-decongesting-the-face-removing-make-up-residues-but-without-stripping-your-skin-of-moisture-it's-a-very-popular-product-actually-and-won-the-best-budget-buy-award-in-the-last-issue-of-*Gloss*-magazine.'

Phew, I'm exhausted. And so is Rainbow Scarf by the

looks of things. But still, she makes the purchase and leaves in what must be something of a record time.

That still hasn't solved the problem of how I am going to make myself invisible in the course of the next few minutes. I suppose I could do a runner, but I know Lorraine would have me fired if I pissed her off one more time. And it's not worth losing my sole source of income just to avoid bumping into my sister.

But then again, this isn't just about bumping into Hope. It's about bumping into all my lies. And that could be really painful. If Faith finds out I work here she is bound to tell mum, however much I plead with her to keep it quiet. And if mum found out I was a make-up girl rather than a top PR person she would be in a right state. And then she'd start going on about what else I've been lying to her about and how ashamed dad would be if he could see me now and why did I lie to her and ...

Well, you get the picture. It would be pretty messy.

So I've got to think fast.

And then it comes to me with such clarity that if I was a cartoon there would be a thought-bubble and a light bulb above my head right now.

The stock room. Right at this moment the ground floor stock room is chock full of the latest batch of Keats make-up. Only because there's been some sort of mix up with the distributor the quantities have all got interchanged with each other and jumbled up. Lorraine's been on about sorting it out for the last two days but as far as I know she hasn't actually got around to doing it yet.

I look across at my cardboard sister smiling back at me, and then down at my watch. 2.20pm.

It's now or never, I tell myself, as my heart starts to go mental.

I locate Lorraine and tell her I'd be willing to sort out the stock for her.

'Are you feeling all right?' she asks, placing an excessively manicured hand on my forehead.

'I'm fine,' I tell her. 'It's just I've been a bit slack recently and I want to do more to help so I thought I'd save you a job and start with the stock room.'

She gives me a look which might qualify as quizzical if she hadn't botoxed her forehead into a state of muscular paralysis. 'All right,' she says, eventually. 'I suppose we're not too busy on the floor, are we, so here's the keys.'

I love Lorraine right now.

I love her so much that I could plant a smacker on that big old trout pout of hers.

Call me over the top, but this woman has just saved my life.

I think better about the kiss and settle for a submissive head-nod as I take the keys and start walking.

Fast.

Chapter Twenty-Nine

Shit.

Double shit.

Double choca-mocha-latte-frappé shit with whipped cream and sprinkly bits on top.

I've left it too late.

It's *her*. My sister. At twenty paces.

Walking through the automatic doors with another woman. Older, shorter. Her agent or something.

She hasn't noticed me.

All I've got to do is keep my head down and carry on walking.

Head down.

Keep walking.

Head down.

Keep walking.

Head.

'Faith?'

I freeze, my head staying focused towards the floor. The door to the stock room is three metres away, max. I could still make it, just about, and lock the door behind me.

102

Maybe she'll think she's got it wrong. I mean, there was a question mark when she called my name, wasn't there? Three years is a long time, after all. And *she* certainly looks a lot different so I probably do too.

But my legs have turned to concrete.

Seriously, I can't move.

Realising I am probably not going to make it in time I grab for my name badge and unpin it with fumbling fingers. I quickly shove it in my trouser pocket and turn around.

She is there, looking almost as perfect as her cardboard cut-out, mouth agape and shaking her head from side-to-side in the oh-my-God-what-an-incredible-coincidence style.

My mouth may be agape but my head remains immobile in the oh-my-God-how-the-blinking-bollocks-am-I-going-to-get-out-of-this-one style.

'It *is* you,' she says, before explaining to the shorter, older women, 'my *sister*.'

'How incredible,' says the woman, who I notice could do with a good chin pluck. She is looking around the store for whoever is sorting out the promotion. I bet it's Paolo. He oversees all the health and beauty events on this floor. He is from Barcelona. Gay as you like. And if he sees me my cover will be blown.

'Oh my God,' I say, miraculously regaining the power of speech. 'Wow. It's you. God. What on earth are you doing here?'

Of course, I know what on earth she is doing here but I had to say something. After she's finished telling me she gives me a funny look. 'Do you *work* here?'

For some inexplicable reason I act like this is the most hilarious thing I have ever heard in my life. 'Work here? Oh that's a good one. That's funny. Work *here*? Oh that's a good one. That's funny. Work *here*.'

What the hell am I doing? The first time my sister has seen me and I'm acting like a raving lunatic.

But what can I tell her?

The truth.

No.

Yes.

No.

Yes, that's what I've got to do. I've got to come clean. Set the record straight. I am trapped in a wide-open space under the glare of shop lighting within sight of at least ten people who know I work here and am currently being reunited with a minor celebrity who happens to be my sister and a woman with a beard. I'm about as inconspicuous as a gorilla in a tutu. Ice-skating. At the Olympics. It's not exactly the best time or place in the world to lie about my occupation.

'No, I work at Coleridge Communications. A PR firm. Mum's probably told you about it in one of her letters. I finish early on Wednesdays so I thought I'd just do a little spot of shopping.'

I feel a prick. No, I mean a *real* prick, at the top of my leg. And then I remember. My name-badge. The pin must be open.

I bite my lip and grimace through the pain.

She eyes me doubtfully for a second and looks up and down at my uniform. In actuality, it's not a uniform uniform. It's not one of those white coats you see the Clinique girls in. It's just a black T-shirt and black trousers which, minus the name-badge, do not in themselves give me away.

But I can tell she knows that something is not quite right here. Her body may have been yogasmically transformed but her razor-sharp stare remains perfectly intact.

The thing is, it shouldn't be like this.

I have spent the past three years wondering what would happen if and when I see my sister again, and imagining how I would confront her about deserting us all. She would break down and cry or feel awkward or apologise and then I would be the bigger person and give her a hug and everything would be all right forever more.

But here I am, panicking my socks off, petrified that she'll find out I'm lying while simultaneously trying to ignore the fact that there's a flaming great pin sticking into my leg.

In the periphery of my vision, is the skeletal figure of Lorraine, walking this way.

Shit.

I have to do something.

Anything.

Anything at all.

Chapter Thirty

I fall to the right, so I am out of view, behind one of the large pillars.

'Are you *all right*?' Hope asks me, the corners of her mouth curling downwards in curious amusement.

I pull heavy on her arm, taking her with me, beyond Lorraine's all-seeing glare. 'Yes ... yes ... sorry. It's just my knee. It just gives sometimes ... just goes completely. Badminton injury. Should see a doctor really.'

My sister looks at me like I am a novelty act. A comedy dwarf, sent here to entertain her. But I don't really care, not right this minute. All I'm worried about right now is my cover being blown.

Lorraine frogmarches past, oblivious, en route to the escalator. I phew inside, then offer a deflective smile to Hope. 'Anyway,' I say, signalling the books and DVDs set out for the star signing. 'I suppose I'd better leave you to it.'

'Oh no,' she says. '*Stay*. I'd love it if you could stay.'

'I can't. I can't stay ... because ... because ... I have to go and ... feed the ... dog.' Oh great. Not only have I managed to invent a job, and an interest in badminton, I've now added a canine to the list.

'Dog?'

'Yes,' I say. 'Actually it's my best friend's dog. I'm looking after it while she's away on holiday for a month.'

'She left her dog for a month?'

Jeez, what is she, the RSPCA?

'Um, yes. And the thing is if I don't get back and, you know, feed him he might . . . die.'

'Die?'

'Yes, *die*, the dog's hyperglycaemic. If he doesn't eat some form of carbohydrate every like six hours, that's it . . . he'll just pass out, doof. Dead. So I'd really better—'

'Fay-eef.' The sound of Paolo's voice stops my heart completely. Seriously, it goes about five whole seconds without beating at all.

'*Paolo*,' I say, turning to greet my long lost Spanish friend. He looks at the space where my work-badge should be and, before he can put his espadrilled foot in it, I wink at him and say: 'I haven't seen you for ages. What on earth are you doing here?'

He looks at me, confused, before saying in a what-are-you-playing-at sort of way: 'I wuk here.'

Hope is looking at me gone out. Then I realise why. I am still winking.

'Oh damn these stupid contact lenses,' I say, jamming my fingers into my eye. 'Honestly, I should never have given up my glasses.'

'Eneehway,' says Paolo. 'Eet eez time.'

To my relief, I realise from his servile tone he is talking to Hope, letting her know that she should make her way over to the table and start signing books. Indeed, a queue of perfectly postured Yogasmic groupies is already starting to form.

'OK,' says Hope. 'One minute.'

Paolo nods and moves away, eyeing me suspiciously.

One minute!

I haven't got one minute!

I need to get out of here before I spontaneously combust.

'I'm getting a late train back to London so why don't we meet up later? Go for a drink or something? It would be like old times.'

Old times? What old times? I honestly don't think I've gone out for an alcoholic drink with my sister in my entire life. But anyway, I've hardly got the time to quibble.

'OK,' I say. 'There's a bar just around the corner. Tiger Tiger. I reckon I could be back in town by five. Will you have finished by then?'

'Yes,' she says, with the same look of curious amusement. 'I should imagine so.'

'OK, see you later.'

'Yes, see you later.'

I walk off, past Hope's adoring public and whisper in Paolo's ear as I walk by: 'I don't work here.'

'Whatever you say Fay-eef you creezy lady.'

And then I escape. Into the stock room, fighting my imaginary badminton injury and pretending to rush back to feed my imaginary friend's hyperglycaemic dog.

Chapter Thirty-One

I'm an idiot.

A big fat imaginary dog-feeding idiot.

I mean, Tiger Tiger. It's all of two seconds away from work. What was I thinking? The last thing I need is Lorraine or someone from work blowing my cover.

I've decided to play it safe and have chosen a table in a dark corner as far away from the main window as possible. When my sister arrives I stand and wave my arms while keeping my eyes firmly focused on the outside pavement.

This time, away from the intimidatory glare of the shop lighting we hug. A proper, sisterly, it's-been-three-years type hug. And it feels good, it really does, as if bringing our bodies close like this somehow sends us back to a nicer time, before everything happened. To the days when we would sit on the bed doing each other's make-up. When our biggest source of argument was the debate over which member of New Kids we fancied the most.

'I still can't believe it,' I tell her. 'What are the chances?'

'I know. It's incredible. I should have really told you when I was coming to Leeds but I've got such a busy schedule at the moment. Seriously, I'm all over the place. Well, you know how it is?'

I smile and nod. Sure, I know how it is. My life's just one long promotional tour. Christina. Justin. Beyoncé. They've got nothing on me, I tell you.

But as I look at my sister I find it hard to resent her. So OK, when my mum needed her most she was twenty thousand miles away. And now, just as we are starting to get back on our feet, she returns home. Saluting to the sun on morning TV, embarking on a career centred around the word *yogasmic*, writing books, making videos, managing to make size eight look outsize, earning an annual income which probably equates to the gross domestic product of Guatemala, and without a single wrinkle to be seen on her symmetrical honey-toned face. Even around her *eyes*.

But despite the fact that I know all this, and that deep down I know she is a selfish person (hell, it's not even deep down – it's right there on the gleaming surface), she is my sister. We have a lot of chromosomes in common. And memories too. That must count for something, mustn't it?

Well, mustn't it?

As I watch her walk to the bar and get herself a drink I realise that I feel differently towards her than when I watched her pixelated image on TV. She is a human being. Flesh and blood. And she loved dad just as much as any of us did. She just handled it differently, that's all. Perhaps my brother was right. She was the youngest. Too young to handle death, and so she moved as far away from it as physically possible. Well, short of joining NASA and going on a mission to Mars.

So although it was easy to demonise my self-centred sister when she was on the other side of the planet, now I'm face to face (or, at this precise moment, face to perfectly pert arse, as she leans over the bar to get served) I feel a trace of that old sibling affection. In fact, I hate myself for having hated her. What sort of person does that make me?

No. I'm going to try hard.

I'm going to make an effort with her.

Put things right.

She glides back to the table, the whole male population of the bar eye-stalking her arse as she does so. She smiles and crinkles her nose and says, 'You haven't changed a bit.'

Now of course, this statement could be taken in one of two ways, but I decide to give her the benefit of the doubt. I want to say, 'Neither have you', but it would sound completely ridiculous. You might as well say it to Michael Jackson. She's transformed herself almost beyond recognition.

She's thinner, sharper dressed, and has that kind of celebrity glow to her. There's no trace of the spotty forehead or heavy eye make-up or New Look clothes I remember from her teenage years. She looks like a walking magazine cover.

'You look fantastic,' I say.

Her chest rises proudly as she inhales the compliment. 'It's my workout,' she says.

'I know,' I say. 'I've bought a copy. It's very good. You're doing so well.'

Listen, did you hear that? It was the sound of a hatchet being buried. I'm being nice to her. But not only that, I'm actually finding it very easy being nice to her.

'Oh Faith, you didn't have to do that. I could have given you one for free. I would have signed one for you.'

I look at her face for any sign that she is sending herself up. There is nothing. 'Oh, I know you would have. It's just I didn't know how to get hold of you. I hadn't realised you

111

were back in the country until I switched on the TV and saw you.'

'Oh,' she says, in a tone I would like to believe is sincere. 'I'm sorry. But you could always have got in touch with me through my agent.'

'Um, yes,' I say, suppressing at least about five negative statements I could legitimately say at this point in the conversation. 'I suppose I could.'

She smiles and crinkles her nose again. Only this time the nose crinkle is accompanied by a slight shoulder shrug. If I was not so determined to keep thinking positive thoughts right now, I would probably interpret this gesture as a patronising one. But like I said, I'm being positive.

'I suppose you must find it funny,' she says.

'Funny?'

'Your younger sister turning into a celebrity.'

Happy thoughts. 'Yes, I suppose it is.'

'Because if anything you were always the one who everyone thought was going to do bet—' She rethinks her sentence. 'You know, you must find it funny.'

I nod, resisting eye contact, and then suck on my straw.

'But do you want to know something?'

Do I want to know something? Well no, obviously. But I can't say that so I say, 'What?'

'There's one thing I've learned, you know, since *everything*. You know, after dad ... You know ... since I went away. To Sydney.'

'And, um, what's that?'

'Well the thing about Australia is that it's full of very confident people. There's this attitude that if you want something you should just go out and grab it, you know ...'

She stops, noting the two male office workers eyeing her up. She looks across at their table, and two bottles of

112

Budweiser raise eagerly. She looks back at me and rolls her eyes. It's a gesture which is meant to say, *I get this all the time and I hate it but it's the price you have to pay for being attractive and glamorous and famous.*

I try and ignore it and start to swirl ice cubes around in my glass. I swirl a bit too fast and one of the cubes goes flying across the table.

'Oops,' I say, with a slight giggle.

'... anyway ...' she says, without a giggle '... what I was saying was that Australia did me good. It made me believe I could go out and do whatever I wanted.'

'Oh, that's good.'

She looks at me quizzically, as if I am missing her point. 'You know, whatever you want to do in life you can just do it.'

Yes, course you can. If you are prepared to leave everyone else behind to clear the mess up. I do my best to smile and try to let the negative feelings pass. I stick my straw in my mouth and nod my head.

'By the way,' she says, mock-bashful. 'I've got some news.'

Oh no. This is going wrong. Suddenly I have a strange sinking feeling. 'News?'

She beams, then holds her left hand forward, her fingers flickering as if at some invisible piano.

And then I see it.

The ring.

'You're getting married.'

Chapter Thirty-Two

The ring is rising, towards my face. I get trapped in its sparkle. The diamond may be quite small, but looking into it is like looking into a tiny crystal ball. A crystal ball which tells me, in no uncertain terms, that my entire future is shit. That I will be single forever. That I will always be in the size six shadow of my younger sister. That my life will have to stay one big fat lie forever more.

'Next month. Twenty-fifth of May. In Sussex. We've found a lovely little church in Sussex.'

The ring mercifully descends and oxygen re-enters the room.

'You are sitting opposite the future Mrs Hope Richards,' she tells me. Richards ... Richards ... doesn't ring any ... 'Jamie Richards,' she says.

Now bells are ringing. 'What, *the* Jamie Richards?'

'The very same.'

Oh my God. It doesn't get any better than this, does it? It's not simply enough for my sister to become a celebrity. She's got to bloody be getting married to one as well.

114

So OK, Jamie Richards is hardly A-list. But I've heard of him. He's the originator of the Butt Blast Workout as well as Butt Blast Workout Two. I bought the second one last January after a heavy Christmas. He's the super sexy 'fitness trainer to the stars' and has his own gym in Covent Garden.

So he's a celebrity and probably a millionaire. With a six-pack. And nice hair. And an arse you could use to perch a tray of canapés on.

I know what I should say right now.

I should say 'wow'.

Or 'congratulations'.

Or 'I can't believe it – that's amazing fantastic wonderful'.

Or 'you lucky thing'.

But the words struggle to rise to my throat. The green-eyed monster inside me simply won't let them pass through.

Not tonight. You're not on the list.

So instead I say, 'since when?'

'Since two weeks,' she gushes. 'We've been together for over a year. I met him while he was filming the Butt Blast Beach Body Workout on Bondi Beach,' she giggles at the excessive alliteration. 'He was auditioning people for the video. You know, to do all the exercises behind him. And he was holding the auditions in this massive sports centre in Sydney. Seriously, there were hundreds of girls there, all from the local sports clubs and I'd heard about it through some of the people at this yoga class I was going to at the time. But anyway, where was I?'

'The sports centre,' I tell her, morbidly.

'Oh yes. We were all there and we all had to go through sequences of different exercises while he went along the different rows to analyse our technique.'

115

'Right,' I say.

'So I think we started with a warm up. And then we did glute raises, and leg curls, and crunches, and hip rotations and anyway, you get the point.'

'Yes,' I say.

'Well, he got to my row just as we were all told to start the butt-presses. You know it's the one where you lie on your back and lift your bum up in the air clenching—'

'Yes,' I tell her. 'I know the one you mean.'

'Anyway, so me and about twenty other girls were in this row on our backs pushing our arses up to heaven as if our lives depended on it. And he's walking up and down the line as if it was an identity parade or something and then he stops, right between my feet, and he just stands there smiling at me and says "I could watch you do butt-presses all day." Can you believe it? That was his very first line to me. "I could watch you do butt-presses all day." '

'Romantic,' I say.

'Oh, but when he took me out that night he was amazing. He took me to this gorgeous sea-food restaurant, he said it was his favourite because of the views of the harbour and because there were hardly any carbohydrates on the menu.' Her eyes twinkle nostalgically at the memory. 'And he told me that he was setting up his own media company to produce fitness videos and said I'd be perfect to front some of them. And I was like so totally wow that I sucked him off under the table . . .'

There must be something wrong with my ears. What I just thought she said was, *I sucked him off under the table*. 'Sorry.'

'We were sitting quite a way from everyone else and the tablecloths went practically to the floor so I thought hell, why not? Anyway, it seemed to work. He said afterwards that I blew him away. I was in the studio recording The Yogasmic Workout a month after that.'

Oh . . . my . . . God.

My brain doesn't know where to start. There's just too much information here to take in.

Jamie Richards liked her butt-presses.

He liked them so much he asked her on a date.

And made her famous.

And asked her to marry him.

But I can't digest any of that because all I have is an image of my sister under a table, moving her head up and down the way she used to every Halloween when bobbing for apples. It's not a healthy image.

And why is she telling me all this?

I mean, OK, technically speaking she's my sister but we haven't seen or said a word to each other for three years. She's been engaged for nearly two weeks and she hasn't felt the obligation to let my mum know. And how can she be so open and honest about things like blow jobs and how she got ahead by giving head, and she hasn't managed to mention one word about anything which matters.

Like dad.

Like why she left.

Like why she never made contact. With me. With Mark.

'Mum's missed you,' I say, derailing our previous conversation.

My words have a strange effect. She handles them the way a road-crossing rabbit handles an oncoming pair of headlights. 'Has she?' she asks, eventually. Her voice is different now. Soft, vulnerable.

'Yes,' I tell her. I want to add that 'we all have', but something stops me.

'Oh.'

117

'You should call her.'

She tilts her head towards the ceiling. 'I don't know,' she says.

'You were going to tell her about the wedding?'

'Yes,' she says. 'Of course. You'll all be invited. It's just ... difficult, you know, plucking up courage. After everything.'

That *everything* is a big word. It contains a lot, and I know she realises it. I feel sorry for her. Right now, she looks far from yogasmic. She knows she was wrong, to leave mum alone with her grief. I can sense it. I want to reach out to her, but there is nothing I can do or say which will change anything.

So all I can tell her is the truth. 'You owe it to her.'

'OK,' she says. 'But I don't want her to know that you put me up to this. It will probably look better if mum doesn't know I met you today.'

'OK,' I say, already wondering about the consequences of this agreement. 'I promise.'

Chapter Thirty-Three

The truth worked.

She phoned her. She phoned Mark as well.

She told them everything. Well, not *everything*. I am assuming she edited out the bit about her under-the-table antics on their first date.

Mark was the first to get back.

'You'll never guess who just called me,' he said.

Never in a million years. 'Who?'

'Our long lost relative.' His voice, as always, was flippant. Mark, for whom work can be the only truly serious and important aspect of life has always tended to trivialise family politics. While Hope may have had to voyage to the southern hemisphere in order to create distance, Mark had that distance automatically built-in. It comes as standard. In that respect, he seems to have that typically male advantage. Even when he's in the same room as you, you never feel he's that close to the action.

'What? Hope?' I said, feigning surprise. And trying to ignore the fact that Mark was automatically assuming our sister would have phoned him first.

'Yes,' he said. 'And guess what?'

And so it went. Non-surprise after non-surprise, for approximately thirty minutes. Wow! Really! Did she? By the end of it I was wondering why I had agreed to cover my sister's Kyliefied arse in the first place. If I hadn't made her feel so guilty there would have been no surprise phone calls. No apologies. And possibly even no wedding invitations.

But then, when mum phoned, I realised why I had agreed to keep quiet about bumping into Hope in the first place.

She was overjoyed.

The heartache of three years had been erased in the space of a twenty minute phone call. The absence had been re-filled.

'Isn't it all just the most exciting news?' my mum asked me, in a tone which suggested that she wasn't observing dust levels or examining the door panes for finger prints or seeing whether the carpet needed hoovering.

And at that moment I woke up to a fact I had never even considered.

All this time I had been thinking that the reason my mum was upset was because Hope deserted her. I thought that she would never be able to come to terms with why that actually happened. I thought she would never be able to forgive, even if Hope had returned to Heathrow on her hands and knees and a big apologetic bouquet of flowers.

But all this time I had got it wrong.

Mum hadn't been upset because Hope said goodbye with a note the day before the funeral. She had been upset because Hope said goodbye full-stop.

And now she was saying hello. Again.

Which made everything OK.

For all Hope has to do in order to be the perfect daughter is to be there. That is it. If being a daughter came with its own job description Hope's would be very simple. It would say 'Be There'.

Mine on the other hand would run on for pages. There would be pages of responsibilities and explanations I have to live up to, under the sub-heads 'Career', 'Appearance', 'Love Life', 'Diet', 'Family Duties', 'How you must behave in times of crisis', 'What time you must wake up, even on Sundays and days off'. My daughter job description includes a prologue, footnotes, appendices and a comprehensive index at the back for referencing.

But that's OK. I've accepted the fact.

All daughters are equal but some are more equal than others.

My mum is someone for whom the law of playing hard to get definitely works. And 22,000 miles plus three years without a phone call is definitely what you would call hard to get.

Whereas I have always played a different game. I have been about as hard to get as a teenage boy at the Playboy Mansion. I am the floozy of all daughters, ever eager to please. Mum says jump, I say how high.

'She's invited us all to the wedding,' mum informed me.

Wow. Hold the front page. Woman invites her widowed mother and two siblings to own wedding. What a remarkable act of human kindness.

And then mum said something which stopped my heart in its tracks.

She said: 'I told her all about Adam.'

Adam.

I hadn't even mentioned him in Tiger Tiger. So OK, she hadn't actually asked. But her curiosity must certainly have been aroused when mum brought him up.

'Hope said she can't wait to meet him.'

121

'Meet him? Meet him where?'

'At the wedding.'

'The wedding?'

'He's invited too.'

'Oh. Right.'

Oh right indeed.

I mean, how hadn't I seen that one coming? I could have prevented that happening. I mean, there was Hope. In Tiger Tiger. Asking me to lie for her.

So why hadn't I brought it up then? *Listen, Hope, mum thinks I've got this boyfriend. He's called Adam. She thinks I met him at work. She may have mentioned him. But I don't work where she thinks I work. I work where you saw me earlier. So if you are going to invite us to your wedding, just make sure you don't invite him as well.*

But no.

That was never going to happen.

Hope announces she is getting married to a man who is not only rich and famous and tautly-buttocked, but who also doubles as a personal trainer and careers advisor. And then I tell her that my own boyfriend is a figment of my imagination.

Me no think so señor.

So I am now back where I started. Only more so. The wedding is a month away. And I'm talking lunar. Twenty-eight days. So there's no time to dilly dally. No sir.

I need a man.

And I need one in double-time.

Chapter Thirty-Four

I am taking positive action.

If I stay in my apartment all my life the only men I will ever come across are the gas man and the postman and, last time I checked, neither of these two lard-arsed, wheezing specimens of Yorkshire manhood were in the top 100 eligible bachelor list.

Then there's work. Working on a make-up counter is not exactly the best way to come across suitable men. Or even unsuitable men for that matter.

So no. There can be no time wasting, no crossing my fingers and hoping for the best. I need to think strategically. Hell, I'm working to a deadline here.

I need a man and I need him now.

So, I'm going to do the unthinkable.

I'm going to join a gym.

No seriously, I am. Although I've always had some-thing of an allergic reaction to exercise (it's always tended to make me hot, sweaty and short of breath) I've realised that it's probably my best, maybe even my only, hope.

According to *Gloss* magazine, the gym is the best place to meet potential partners. In fact, sixty per cent of people who join a gym cite this as their main incentive. It comes in above bars, nightclubs and your place of work as the number one pulling palace.

Of course, I don't actually plan to do any intense physical activity. After all, if I'm going to pull my dream man I'm not going to do it disguised as a hyperventilating plum tomato. A hyperventilating plum tomato with streaky make-up and a sweat problem at that.

It would be better if I could take Alice with me. But Alice only needs to close her front door behind her to come over all hot and sweaty. And besides, carrying her bump is probably exercise enough.

OK, enough talking.

I'm going to find me a man.

Chapter Thirty-Five

In the Middle Ages, there used to be rooms filled with strange-looking metal contraptions designed to cause immense human pain and physical exertion. They were known as torture chambers. In the twenty-first century, the equivalent rooms are referred to as gyms and people actually pay for membership.

I am not normally one of those people. However, if I am to solve my current boyfriend's non-existence problem, it looks like I will have to change my sofa-dwelling ways. Immense human pain and physical torture here I come!

'The Bronze membership package for one year is eight hundred and ninety-nine pounds ninety-nine pence,' the ginger-haired Total Fitness representative says. He says this in a way which implies that eight hundred and ninety-nine pounds ninety-nine pence is a small price to pay for a full year's worth of immense human pain and physical exertion.

'Right,' I say.

Ginger Fitness proceeds to give the payment options – one lump sum, quarter payments or once a month.

'Is there a daily option?'

'No.'

'OK, then I think I'll take the monthly.'

'And how would you like to pay?'

With magic beans, preferably, 'Um . . . I . . .'

'Card, cash or cheque?'

'Do I have to pay right away?'

'You will need to pay before you use any of our facilities,' says Ginger Fitness, gingerly.

'Right,' I say. 'Right . . . It's just that I don't know if I've brought my cheque book.'

'A credit card will be fine.'

'I'm waiting for a new one,' I lie. 'My purse got stolen last week.' Nope, that's not going to work. Not a flicker of sympathy passes across his freckly face. Time to go for broke. 'Oh damn, I don't know what to do. My editor wants something by the end of today.'

'Your . . . editor?'

'Yes, I'm doing a piece for the *Yorkshire Post*. It's for a new fitness column called 'Gym and Tonic', and I'm basically going to describe my first day at the gym. *This* gym if that's OK. I haven't contacted the manager or anything because I didn't want any, you know, special treatment.'

I look at Ginger Fitness's body-built chest, and at a badge saying STEVE. 'The only thing I wanted to ask is whether it would be possible to interview one of the instructors. Would you be up for that, Steve? I mean, obviously we'd have to send a photographer around next week to take a few shots. But I can't imagine you're camera shy, are you, Steve?'

He flashes a glance in the mirror behind me.

'Um, well, no, no, that would be, um, fine.' His face is now the same colour as his hair.

'Right, but what about payment?'

126

'Oh, don't worry,' he says, in a special treatment kind of way. 'Pay when you're ready.'

'My favourite colour?' says Ginger Fitness, echoing my question. 'Red, I suppose.'

'Like your hair!' I say, journalistically. 'Right, I think that's probably a good place to end the interview.'

'So, is that it?'

'Uh-huh. We'll send a photographer around next week.'

'OK. And you don't have to take down anything?'

'No,' I say, tapping the side of my head. 'Photographic memory.'

'But—'

'OK, right, so let's get started on those machines!'

Chapter Thirty-Six

Although Ginger Fitness spent ten minutes explaining how to use the treadmill, I still have absolutely no idea. It's like staring at the control panel of the Starship Enterprise.

Fortunately though, another Total Fitness instructor – a reassuringly unhealthy looking woman called Sharon – is on hand to get me started.

'The control settings go from one to ten,' she explains. 'One is a walking pace, while ten is a fast sprint.'

'I think I'd better start on a one.'

The machine starts moving, and I start walking, as Sharon leaves me to it. Up in front, above my head, there are TV screens playing different MTV channels. Without any music it looks like the various singers are trapped behind soundproof glass, screaming for help.

Women of no certain age, and no certain size, lost in their own cardiovascular worlds. Jogging or cycling their way to some imaginary, far-off destination – a destination the MTV videos suggest is a reality, a place where sex and money and six-packs are freely available. A place none of us will ever be able to get to, no matter how many treadmill miles we travel.

The room is full, but only with women mainly. I therefore decide to keep the treadmill setting on one and wait for any suitable Adam candidates to turn up.

Not that I know what to say if any did.

Not that I have ever been able to approach a man without being two drinks away from alcohol poisoning.

Not that my soft, unsculpted body will hold any appeal to a gym-dwelling hunk.

Not that my wanting something to happen will actually make it any more likely to occur.

But just as I am starting to give up on the gym as the perfect Adam-hunting ground, something happens. The door to the Cardio Room opens to reveal two gorgeous hunks. For everyone else this seems like a perfectly normal thing to happen, and hardly worth turning away from the Christina Aguilera video playing silently above their heads. But for me, the scene plays like a slow-motion fantasy sequence, complete with dry ice and saxophone music courtesy of my imagination.

Through squinted eyes one of them could sort of pass for a young Will Smith. Through very squinted eyes the other could pass for a young Brad Pitt. Well, he's tall. He's in good shape. He's blonde.

Through unsquinted eyes I realise that I know him from somewhere. I have definitely seen him before.

As they move over to the cardio machines, my heart is racing faster than it could from any workout. In order not to look unfit, as I actually am, and to burn off some of that excess adrenalin, I flick my treadmill setting up to three, and start on a slow jog.

129

Oh my God. Sort-of-Brad and Sort-of-Will and their tightly packed shorts, are moving towards me. Well, not towards *me* exactly but towards the two exercise bikes next to my treadmill.

OK, stay calm, I tell myself, as I struggle to keep up with the moving surface beneath my feet. I am also trying to figure out how you can look sexy on a treadmill.

I opt for the shoulders-back-tits-forwards method and immediately begin to understand why sports bras are such a popular purchase, it seems to work. Sort-of-Will looks at Sort-of-Brad and angles his head towards my bouncing boobs. Sort-of-Brad smiles.

In other circumstances, my immediate thought might be: sleazebags. But this isn't other circumstances.

I smile back, on my breasts' behalf, and continue jogging in what I imagine to be a retro-style-Pamela-Anderson-in-*Baywatch* type manner.

They carry on titgawping for a while, before making token glances at my face. For once, I must be giving out all the right signals, because after five minutes of super fast peddling, Sort-of-Will, on the bike farthest away, ventures into conversation,

'First time?' he asks me.

'I'm sorry,' I pant, confused. Sort-of-Brad stifles a giggle.

'At the gym. It's just we haven't seen you in here before.'

'No. It's my first—' momentary pause for oxygen, 'first time.'

All three of us continue to exercise in silence for the full length of a Justin Timberlake video, then the Will Smith-a-like says: 'I'm Danny, by the way.'

'Hello, Danny,' I say, on the verge of a heart attack. 'I'm . . . Faith.'

'Hello, Faith.'

130

My eyes are so clogged with sweat that Danny's friend, on the exercise bike closest to me, actually *is* the young Brad Pitt. He smiles at me again and holds out his hand to introduce himself.

Now, the thing you have to remember is that my co-ordination skills aren't that hot. So the act of simultaneously running on a treadmill and shaking the young Brad Pitt's hand is quite a challenge. But somehow I manage it. Or at least, I manage it until he says, 'Hi. I'm Adam.'

Adam.

My God.

A.D.A.M.

It's him, The One.

The shock causes me to squeeze Adam's hand rather too hard. It also causes me to stop running. Unfortunately, the treadmill doesn't share my sense of surprise and carries on moving. A moment later, I am flat on my back. A moment after that, Adam is flat on my front. Incredibly, my grip must have been so strong that I have managed to pull him off the exercise bike and bring him down with me. Unless, of course, this is a voluntary arrangement on his part.

'That's quite a grip,' he says, completely unembarrassed by the fact that he is lying on top of a total stranger in a gym full of people. I can hear his friend Danny laughing somewhere in the background.

'You're Adam,' I say, half-concussed, and saying his name in the same way Lois Lane may have said 'Superman'.

'I am,' he says lust sparkling in his eyes.

As I start to become fully conscious, I begin to feel a growing sense of shame. I also begin to feel a growing sense of penis, and wonder why Adam is taking so long in lifting himself off me.

'Are you OK?' he asks, in a voice which I interpret as concern.

'Yes. I'm sorry. Are you?'

Now he is lifting himself off me in one athletic press-up action. He looks quickly to his friend, shrugs, and then, for the second time in the last minute, he holds out his hand. I take it, and pull myself to my feet.

Once I am there I let go of his hand, but am determined to hold onto the opportunity presented before me. OK, so anyone vaguely resembling Brad Pitt is going to be out of my league, but it's not as if I could exactly embarrass myself any more than I already have.

I need an Adam, preferably a good-looking Adam. And here he is.

So this, as the great song puts it, is my moment.

'This is really embarrassing,' I say, with eyes on full-flirt.

'It was my fault,' he says.

'That was *funny*,' says his friend Danny, still laughing and peddling.

But then I remember where I have seen him before. He was the one who blushed when he came to the make-up counter to buy a cover-up stick for his girlfriend.

His *girlfriend*.

My heart sinks. But after I've told him all this he says, 'It's over. I dumped her,' and then we carry on where we left off.

'Listen,' Adam says, picking up on the flirt signals in my eye. 'Let's go for a drink.'

Let's go for a drink.

Let's go for a drink.

Let's go for a drink.

Yep, no doubt about it: that's what he said. I try to speak, but there is too much going on in my head. There are the hundred exercisers still looking in our direction. There is Jennifer Lopez, trapped behind the soundproof glass. There is Ginger Fitness, walking through the room, smiling as he passes. There is the pain in my lower back, from where I landed.

In the end I manage: 'A drink?'

'Yes,' he says. 'They've got a bar here. I mean, normally I try and do it the other way around. You know, buy a girl a drink and *then* try and get on top of her . . .'

He seems so confident in what must be his natural environment, compared to the nervous creature I'd first met at the make-up counter.

I smile and realising this could be my last chance of turning my fictional Adam into a factual one, manage to nod my head and squeeze out the words: 'I'd love to.'

He smiles back and mops his brow with his wristband. As he does so, I notice the incredible feat of human engineering which is his anatomy. The sharp, triangular contours of his upper-half. The way his T-shirt clings to his chest. The subtle horseshoe shading of his triceps. He's not that big. At least, not *big* big. But there is no doubt he is perfectly formed.

'OK,' he says. 'Let's go.'

And so I walk, on trembling legs, out of the cardio room. Adam by my side.

'Hey,' shouts Danny. 'Where are you going?'

Adam turns, shrugs his shoulders, and nods towards me. 'I'm sorry, man. See you tomorrow.'

'Hey . . . hey . . .' But Adam ignores his friend as he opens the door.

'Thanks,' I say, as he holds it open for me.

'No problem,' he says, with a naughty smile. 'No problem at all.'

Chapter Thirty-Seven

Right now, right at this very moment, I am having sex with someone I met properly less than six hours ago. Someone who sort-of-looks like Brad Pitt. Someone called Adam. Someone who lives in one of those flash city centre apartments. You know the ones. Silver kitchens, white walls, wooden floors, lights which shine up rather than down and beds wider than they are long.

That's where I am now. His bed.

The wider-than-long duvet has already decided to leave us to it, having sulked off onto the floor.

And so we are left, him lying on top of me, like in the gym – only this time we are naked, this time the arrangement is a deliberate one, this time we are only being watched by ourselves.

I am too busy trying to look like I am enjoying myself to be actually enjoying myself. You see, I want him to want to do this again. I want him to need to do this again. Because this is Adam. This is *the* Adam. Flash city centre flat and all. And if he wants my sex I will be able to raise my bargaining power.

What could have been a one-night-stand, could then turn into something else. A relationship. In so doing, I could convert my lies into the truth.

Base metal into gold.

OK, so there would still be problems.

Like the issue of when we actually met. Like the issue of Adam not actually being a lawyer (this was revealed over our first fruit smoothie in the gym bar. He is, in fact, a marketing consultant. His friend Danny – he's a lawyer).

OK, so these are things which will need to be resolved at a later date.

The important stuff is all in place. He's got the name. He's got the face. He's got the body. He's got the bank balance. He's got more than enough to impress. His Brad Pitt smile will dazzle them all into belief.

But for now, I must concentrate on the, ahem, job in hand. Getting him into bed was easy. In fact, it was probably *too* easy. By our second drink, we were already there. Our eyes weren't just undressing each other, they were onto foreplay. Not that I should be complaining – hell, I'm on a tight deadline here. It's just, I don't want to come across like a complete slut. A partial slut will do fine.

We switch positions. I am now on top, in full view, and I can see he wants a show. And so, being a guest in his house, I do the courteous thing. Grab both my breasts, throw my head back in an apparent state of orgasmic euphoria, and start groaning like there's no tomorrow. Well, it's only polite.

'Oh yeah,' he says. 'Oh *yeah*.'

Then the sex-lies begin.

'You are so *big*,' I tell him, in a panted whisper.

'You like it, don't you?' he asks, but his tone is rhetorical.

'You are so *good*,' I say, despite the fact that I garner more sexual pleasure from a sneeze, than from Adam's currently misdirected power thrusts.

'You want me,' he says, endearingly, into my ear. 'You want me so much.'

You want me so much. I tell you, this guy really knows how to sweet talk.

'Oh yes,' I lie, clawing my nails into his buttocks. 'Please don't stop.'

Then, as I feel he is reaching the final straight, I move into the Little Red Riding Hood routine. You know, 'what big arms you've got', 'what big hands you've got', 'what big—' that sort of thing. Big big big. And, judging by his expression (tongue pressed between his lips, eyes scrunched) he seems to welcome this flattering aggrandisement of his physical assets. But of course, the biggest lie of all is saved till last. The orgasm. The big O. Or, in this case, the big zero. Still, he's put in quite a performance so I'm sure he expects a standing, or lying, ovation.

So I fake it. Starting slow and low and rising to a shrill falsetto, I produce an ascending musical scale of sexual pleasure. A doh-ray-me orgasm, only without Julie Andrews running over Austrian hilltops.

Then, he collapses back on the bed and stares up at the ceiling. I watch his gym-sculpted chest rise and fall as he recovers from eight minutes and thirty-five seconds of heavy thrusting (not that I was watching the time or anything).

I move my head onto his body, and he places his arm around me. Somehow, despite the fact that only one of the orgasms was genuine, this feels sort of right. This feels like it could be a relationship.

137

Chapter Thirty-Eight

It feels good.

OK, so he's a bit full of himself. But that sort of makes him more attractive. He's too full of himself and I'm too, well, empty of myself, so together we might make two normal complete human beings.

It's almost like encountering a different species. Someone who not only has no reason to lie about himself, but who actually likes himself.

I mean, think about it. With a neurotic for a mother and an agoraphobic for a best friend, that's going to be one hell of a unique selling point.

And besides, it's only the things he says which make him sound arrogant. If I was deaf I'd just be able to enjoy the view.

And what a view. Seriously, he's like one of those sculptures.

But anyway, all of this is really beside the point.

The point is he seems to like me. And when I wake up, the next morning, he still seems to like me.

In fact, he likes me right up against the bathroom wall (he interrupted me when I was in the middle of getting ready). And then when he is putting on his shirt and tie he looks at me and says: 'What are you doing tonight?'

What are you doing tonight! Not, like, 'What are you doing tomorrow?' Or, 'what are you doing a week Friday?' Or, 'thanks for the shag, see you around.'

'Um, nothing,' I say, a tad too desperate.

'Well how about I come round to your place?'

'Yes. Great. Er, I mean, that's OK. If you want to.'

He smiles, pulling the last length of his tie through the knot. 'OK, then,' he tells me. 'I'll come round about eight.'

'Eight,' I say. 'Great.'

Eight, great? Do I always sound this stupid, or is it just when I am trying to impress members of the opposite sex?

'OK,' he says, turning to view his own reflection. 'Eight it is.'

Chapter Thirty-Nine

As soon as I am out of the swanky dream world of Adam's apartment it dawns on me.

My flat.

My orange carpet.

My barred-up kitchen window.

My noisy Neanderthal neighbour.

He'll see my flat and he'll think I'm a right scruff bag. He'll think I'm a smelly pauper. A charity case.

He'll take one look at it and he'll say 'nice tits, shame about the flat'. And then he'll turn around and walk out of my life twenty-four hours after entering it.

And then I'll be back where I started. I'll be back to my sad, hopeless, Adamless state.

I need a lie but I've left it too late. I've already told him my address. So when I get home I try and tidy the place up.

In fact, I spend the whole of today hoovering, dusting, polishing, bleaching and pointlessly moving objects around. Which of course is a mistake. I mean, now the carpet is even more orange than it was in the first place.

But anyway, if Adam is going to become *the* Adam, he might as well get used to seeing the true Faith Wishart, garish orange carpet and all.

As I embark on the final round of dusting I switch the TV on and start flicking. *Neighbours*, no … Cricket, no …

And there she is. My sister. The nation's flexible friend. On the floor, legs over her head, feet on the floor in a kind of motionless backward roll.

'And once you've reached this position,' she tells her knees and five million TV viewers, 'you want to make sure you hold it for as long as possible. And if you feel comfortable and secure, place your arms behind you, flat on the floor. Like this. And then take a few deep yoga-breaths in this position.'

I angle my head to the side to try and read my sister's expression. It appears that folding her body like a deck chair is a perfectly painless activity for my bendy sister.

I wonder, for a second, if we can really be related.

I look at her small, perfectly pert boobs.

I look at her sinewy arms.

I look at her impossibly long, impossibly flexible legs.

I look at her ability to smile, regardless of the fact that she would probably be able to fit into a tin of sardines right now. Regardless of the fact that five million depressed housewives and hung over students are staring at her lycra-clad arse right at this very moment.

I then look down at my boobs. I remember at secondary school how everyone called me by my middle name, Melanie. But they called me this not because it was my name, but because it was a physical description.

As if two whopping honeydews were shoved under my jumper.

141

Not that I minded. Back in those days big melony tits were a must-have fashion accessory. Who cared if they were as soft as bean bags? Who minded if one was slightly bigger than the other? Back then, I loved the fact that boys couldn't keep their dirty little eyes off them.

But I know why I really loved it.

I loved it because my boobs were something I had which my sister didn't. That sounds terrible, doesn't it, but it's true. My sister may have been prettier, but at the age of fourteen she didn't have so much as two little molehills under her school shirt.

And there was me, only a couple of years older, with a chest Sam Fox and Linda Lusardi would have been proud to call their own.

But of course, as time went by, my attitude changed. So OK, they still got attention. But did I really want that kind of attention? Wouldn't it be nice, just for once, if I could engage in conversation with a male member of our species without him cramping his neck?

And now tits aren't even fashionable any more. Ever since J-Lo shifted the world's gaze below and behind, my jugular torso has looked so 1980s.

Not that my boobs can't make an impact any more. They can. I mean, am I really naïve enough to think that Adam was attracted to my eyes or my smile or my pleasant demeanour?

Of course he wasn't. He was dreaming of hillocks and valleys from the first moment he saw me.

Don't get me wrong. When you're fishing for an Adam, breast-bait is better than no bait at all. It's just that I don't want them to be the only thing men think of when they think of me.

I mean, it's not like I'm a lap dancer. My boobs may be marginally out of proportion with the rest of my body, but it's a thin margin. It's not like I'm one of those skinny girls with giant, silicone-packed bazookas. I'm not Jordan or Carmen Elektra or anything.

My arse is too big. Not sprightly and bootilicious. Not perky. Just big. OK, so it's not *Big Momma's House* huge, but it's about two Beyoncés short of a Kylie. In fact, I reckon Kylie's arse is equivalent to one of my buttocks.

More annoyingly, I reckon my sister's arse is equivalent to one of my buttocks.

So although I may still have bigger tits I've got bigger everything else as well. And add to 'bigger': softer, wobblier, droopier, paler and blobbier.

While gravity starts to take effect on me, it seems to be having a reverse impact on my sister. It's as though Isaac Newton landed on the apple. Everything points upwards.

Her arse.

Her boobs.

Her cheekbones.

Her career.

Her love-life.

But hey, I shouldn't be bitter. My love-life's on the up too.

I've found my made-up boyfriend. And he seems to like me – soft, flabby, downward pointing bits and all. And if he can cope with all that I'm sure he'll be able to cope with my flat.

'OK,' beams my sister, from her candlelit mock-Tibetan set. 'That's all for today. Hopefully you will feel alive and refreshed. And remember,' she says, pushing

143

her belly in and inhaling in an exaggerated fashion, '*keep breathing.*'

Good advice, sis.

Good advice.

Keep breathing.

Chapter Forty

After a relentless day of cleaning I phone Alice and tell her all my news.

First about Hope. About the ring. The wedding. The butt-presses. The oral sex under the table.

'You're joking?' she says, gob-smacked.

'Straight out of the horse's mouth.'

'*No!*'

And then it's on to Adam.

'Oh, he sounds gorgeous,' she says.

'Yes, he's not bad,' I say, as a dream-bubble of his hunky physique drifts above my head.

'So is it serious?'

'I don't know.'

'Are you going to get him to meet your mum?'

'One step at a time,' I say, but secretly I hope beyond all hope that he will be the Adam to fill my invented boyfriend's shoes, the next time my mum comes to stay.

She starts singing 'It Must Be Love' and I tell her to stop it.

She stops it.

'Oh,' she says. 'I meant to ask you something. Would you be able to get me some of Keats' anti-stretch mark cream the next time you're at work? I'll pay you.'

'Yes,' I say. 'Of course. Anyway, how's it going? Are you getting nervous?'

'Yes,' she says. And then, she pauses, wondering whether to say something. 'I keep thinking I'm going to die or that something might happen to the baby or something will go wrong . . .'

'Alice, Alice, calm down. Nothing's going to go wrong. Nothing. And I'll be there, when it happens, you know that. Just make sure you call me when your waters break and I'll be there.'

'OK,' she says, semi-reassured. 'OK. I will.'

Chapter Forty-One

There is a knock on the door.

'Alice, someone's here, I'd better go,' I say. 'Just remember you'll be all right.'

'OK.'

'OK.'

I go to answer the door.

Oh my God. It's the Neanderthal. It's Frank.

But he looks different. I mean, he's still got the beard and the scruffy clothes but there's something about his eyes. There's a healthy gleam to them which wasn't evident before.

'Hi,' he says.

I hesitate. I'm not even sure if he deserves a 'hi' after the way he was so rude after I saved his life, but eventually I succumb. 'Hi.'

'I just want to say sorry,' he says staring at the ground. 'About the other night.'

'It's OK.'

'And I just want to say thank you. For, you know, for saving my life.' He pauses, frowns. 'It's just—' He is debating whether to tell me something. 'It's just that ... I'm not really myself ... I haven't really been ... but I'm sorting it out ... I'm getting there ...'

'Right.'

'I've stopped drinking,' he says.

'That's good,' I say, wondering whether I should invite him in.

'And about playing the loud music. I'm sorry about that as well.'

He looks about twelve years old. OK, so a twelve-year-old with a rather alarming amount of facial hair, but still, there is a vulnerability to him which softens my heart. 'Do you want to come in?'

'No,' he says, for the first time looking straight at me. 'It's OK. I've got to get on with some work, anyway.'

'OK,' I say.

'OK, bye.'

Chapter Forty-Two

Adam has just arrived.

He's eighteen minutes and forty-seven seconds late but hey, who's counting?

'All right, gorgeous,' he says at the door, pushing forwards a bottle of wine.

'Oh thanks,' I say. 'You shouldn't have.'

He kisses me on the lips and then pinches my bum, before brushing passed me into the hallway. I can feel him making a silent assessment of his surroundings, and it doesn't take Lloyd Grossman to realise the assessment will be a bleak one.

But anyway, he doesn't say anything. Or at least, he doesn't say anything until he encounters the living room.

'Nice carpet,' he says.

'OK. Sorry. I should have warned you. My flat's a bit skanky.'

'Hey,' he says, arms sneaking around my waist and something in his trousers indicating he is pleased to see me. 'Who cares, babe? I'm not here for the interior design.'

'OK,' I say flushed. 'I'll, um, open the wine.'

I unhook myself and go into the kitchen, bottle in hand. When I re-emerge into the living room Adam is squatting down next to the TV, flicking through the DVDs.

When I get closer, and hand him the wine glass, I realise he is holding my sister's DVD.

'The Yogasmic Workout,' he says, eyeing me with happy suspicion.

'Oh, yes. That. It's actually my sister. She's a yoga instructor. That's her. Hope. Hope Wishart. She's on the telly now and everything.'

'What?' he says, incredulously. '*That's* your sister?'

Jeez, Adam, you sure know how to make a girl feel good. 'Yes,' I say. 'That's my sister.'

'Seriously?' His eyes are filled with genuine disbelief.

'Seriously.'

'She is . . . *fit,*' he says, almost to himself.

'Yes. She is.'

'I mean, you know, healthy-looking.' He pauses, realising he is digging an even bigger hole for himself. 'Not that you're not. You are very healthy-looking. In fact, I would say you are—'

I hold up my hand. 'All right,' I say, trying not to smile. 'I get the picture.' But Adam just wants to make sure.

'She looks very different from you, but not better. Just different, you know, with the blonde hair and the green eyes . . .'

And the size six body. And the skyward-facing breasts. And the legs which stretch behind her head.

'Yes, I know,' I say. 'We just look different.'

'My God,' he says. 'You must love it, having a famous sister.'

'Oh yes. Every minute.'

150

'I mean, her own DVD,' he says, studying the pictures on the back a little too attentively. 'That's really amazing. Do you, um, do you see her a lot?'

'No. Hardly at all, actually.'

'Oh.'

'Anyway, do you want something to eat?'

'No,' he says, placing the DVD down. 'Only you.'

'Or my sister.'

He studies me closely.

'You've got a very bad opinion of yourself, haven't you? A very *wrong* opinion.'

I don't know what to make of this. He moves closer, his hand gently touching my face.

'You're stunning,' he says. 'Absolutely stunning.'

I tingle inside and, as his lips meet mine. I have only one thought in my mind.

This really could be it.

He really could be the one.

Chapter Forty-Three

It is a crisp beautiful morning, I notice, as I wave Adam goodbye on my doorstep. Before I go back inside I spot Frank, walking up the road towards me. He waves. I wave back.

He has a book under his arm. The book is called *Universe or Multiverse? Theories of parallel time and alternate space*.

Frank sees me looking, and says, 'I've just been to the library.'

I look at my watch. 'It's eight o'clock in the morning.'

'It's open twenty-four hours now. I think the university's doing it for mad insomniac PhD students like me.'

Of course. He's a PhD student. What else would he be with that beard and shambolic dress sense living in that grotty flat. 'Oh,' I say, pointlessly. 'You're doing a PhD?'

'Yeah,' he says, then a sad look crosses his face. 'Only I've been granted a year out from it by the university, and I've only just got back into the swing of studying again.'

Although I feel like he wants to tell me the reason for the year off, I can tell this is a sensitive topic, so I decide to ask him what he's studying.

'Alternative universe theory,' he says.

'Alternative universe theory?'

He places his hand on the back of his neck and looks up. 'The alternative universe theory suggests that for every possible outcome of an event, an alternative universe is created. So there are an infinite number of alternative universes, to account for every single outcome.'

'I see,' I say, although I am not sure that I do.

'But then it starts to get a bit complex.'

'Right.'

He nods. 'Yes. You see, it involves the quantum rules which govern the subatomic level of the universe.'

'Oh.'

'This is the idea that parallel universes are created out of this one, for instance if someone travels back in time. So the original universe remains and the new universe is initiated at the point at which the time traveller has gone back to . . .'

I try and look like I am interested in whatever it is he is saying. But really I am wondering how anybody could possibly care.

Unfortunately, the signs of boredom must have made their way to my face because Frank says, 'Sorry, I'm prattling on.'

'No, it's OK. I'm just a bit tired that's all.'

'Oh yeah,' he says, a subtle acknowledgement that he saw Adam leave. 'Anyway I'd better get on.'

'OK. I'll leave you to it.'

He smiles, softly and says. 'I really am sorry, you know.

About the way I was before.' Again he looks like he wants to tell me something, but it's just too painful.

'Yes,' I say. 'I know.'

'OK,' he says. 'Bye.'

Chapter Forty-Four

I do enjoy my job.

I mean, that doesn't mean I don't want to change it. I do. But I sometimes think, if I had a bit more money, and if my mum knew about it – and more to the point, was happy about it – I would be perfectly happy doing it for the rest of my life.

Lorraine's a nightmare, but I get on with the customers and I enjoy doing makeovers. There's something incredibly rewarding about bringing out someone's best features, and making them feel better about themselves for the rest of the day.

Take that sweet old lady, Josie.

I don't know her full name. She always says, 'Just call me Josie.' So I do.

Lorraine never has time for her, owing to the fact that she could deprive every donkey on Blackpool beach of their hind legs, but I love chatting to her. Anyway, she comes in every Saturday for her makeover, regular as clockwork and this Saturday is no exception.

'Hello, dear,' she says.

'Hello, Josie.'

Lorraine looks at me and rolls her eyes, knowing I'll probably be out of action for the next half an hour.

Josie must be pushing eighty but she has wonderful skin. 'Rosewater,' she tells me, when I enquire. 'I use it twice a day, without fail.'

'Well, it does the job, anyway.'

'Flattery will get you everywhere,' she assures me. And we laugh, and I can see Lorraine in the background, rolling her eyes again.

Josie asks for a bit of blusher, and promises she'll buy some after. I start dabbing it gently on her cheeks when I notice someone behind her. A big fat bald man holding an unlit cigar.

I recognise him instantly. It's Mr Blake, the owner of the whole store. I've never met him before, although I've seen him around often enough.

He is walking over, but I pretend not to notice and carry on gently applying Josie's blusher. Lorraine, by contrast, cannot move fast enough. She literally strides ten paces in about a second and smiles as wide as her cosmetic enhancements allow.

'Hello, Mr Blake,' she says in such a servile manner that I think she's about to curtsy. She then embarks on a lengthy monologue but I can't quite pick up what she's saying above all the garbled shop sounds.

Josie is smiling at me. It's a nice, grandmotherly smile. I smile back, trying to not look too bothered about the conversation a short distance in front of me. 'Don't worry dear,' she says, as if able to read my mind. 'You'll be all right. Don't worry.' She rests her speckled hand on mine. 'Everything will turn out rosy.'

Chapter Forty-Five

After work, I deliver the Keats anti-stretch mark cream I had promised Alice and she gives me the ten pounds it cost.

I tell her my news. About work. About Josie. About Frank. But she quickly turns the conversation around to Adam.

'Anyway, are you seeing lover boy tonight?' she asks.

'Yes,' I nod, bashful. 'I'm going around to his flat. He's making me a meal.'

'Oooh,' she says. 'Sounds like it's getting serious.'

'Oh stop it.' I tell her. 'It's only a meal.'

But I cannot stop that feeling. That tingly, excited feeling in my stomach. A feeling which comes from knowing that I am no longer single. That somewhere in this city a man is getting ready to prepare a meal, for me. And that the lies in my life are slowly, one by one, going to be erased.

Chapter Forty-Six

That feeling lasts right up until the moment I get to Adam's flat and he says, 'Oh shit. Yeah, I was meant to be cooking a meal, wasn't I? I forgot to get some food in.'

My face crumples, despite my best efforts to keep it in place. 'Oh,' I say. 'Right.'

'Tell you what though, why don't I take you out for a meal.'

'A meal?' No, he can't get out of it that easily. He can't just buy me off. I should be strong, play a bit hard to get. 'Yeah, that sounds great.'

That's me. Faith Wishart.

Anyone's for a tenner.

We go to Brasserie 44, near the waterfront. It's very swanky and we are the youngest in here by about two generations. While I'm looking over the menu I debate whether to tell Adam about Frank. I don't know why, but I feel strangely guilty about it.

But for some reason I remain quiet. I don't know why, but I think he'd take it all the wrong way. Especially the bit about waiting in the hospital all night to see if Frank was going to be OK.

The waiter comes and takes our order. Adam goes for the steak while I opt for the peanut risotto. Which is the only vegetarian option on the menu.

I ask him about his work but I can tell he doesn't really want to talk about it. He wants to talk about me.

'You look so sexy,' he says.

Is he mad? 'I don't feel it,' I tell him.

'You must be the fittest girl in Leeds.' OK, so on the face of it, this is a compliment. But if he really thinks I am the fittest girl in Leeds, why his fascination with our waitress's arse?

'And you must be the biggest liar in Leeds.' But of course, he's not. I'm the biggest liar in Leeds. Hell, I'm probably in the running for the biggest liar in England, if they were ever to hold such a competition. But then I realise that now might be a good time to clarify a few things. 'Adam. Can, I, um, ask you something?'

'Fire away,' he says, swirling his wine glass.

Deep breath. 'Are we, like *official* now?'

He laughs. 'Official? Official what?'

'Official, you know. Boyfriend, girlfriend. I mean, is it at that stage?'

He frowns, and then necks back his wine. He looks cross, just for a second, but then, when he's gulped back his Shiraz he says, 'Sure. If you want. Yeah. We're official. Boyfriend, girlfriend.'

'OK, so I can like, tell my mum and stuff?'

He gives me a baffled look. 'Of course.'

I smile and stare into his eyes. He may not be the most perfect boyfriend in the world, but he must be one of the most gorgeous. *Boyfriend*. I love that word. *Boyfriend*. I could say it all day.

'Thanks,' I say. 'That means a lot.'

He smiles a cheeky, but lovable smile. 'Did I tell you you looked sexy?'

'Yes,' I say. 'I think you did.'

And then I tell him I'm going to the loo, and I do, taking my make-up bag with me.

Even the toilets are posh in here. With perfume and little engraved bars of soap and marble sinks and mahogany doors for each cubicle.

And there I am, mid-pee, when there is a knock on the door.

'Hello?'

'It's me.'

It's him. 'Adam. This is the women's toilets, what are you doing?'

'I came to see how you are.'

'But I'm—'

'Can I come in?'

'It's the *women's* toilets,' I remind him.

'*Please*,' he asks, cutely.

'OK,' I say. 'Just hold on a sec.' I wipe and flush and then open the door. And before I have time to pull up my knickers he is kissing me and, although part of me wants to resist, the kissing feels good.

'You're so sexy,' he says, as he nibbles on my ear. And then, before I know it, he is hoisting up my skirt and undoing his trousers.

I feel nervous. I mean, sex in public toilets is not something I've done before. Kissing with tongues is about as kinky as I've ever got. I'm normally as dirty as Christina Aguilera's granny and yet, here I am, submitting to his methods of persuasion.

But there's something about it.

Something about the confined space. The danger. The risk of being caught. The intense urgency of the moment.

It's bad but it's good at the same time.

There is a flush, a few cubicles down, which conveniently allows Adam to release a climatic groan as he finishes off. He pants heavily into my ear and holds me till he has recovered.

'Are you OK?' he whispers.

'Yes,' I tell him. 'I'm fine.'

Chapter Forty-Seven

So there can be no further denying it. Adam is a sex-maniac.

For him, life is just one long shag, punctuated by brief and depressing interludes of non-shagging. Not that I'm complaining. After all, it's been months. Having spent night after night alone in a double bed, I've had some catching up to do.

But now, I reckon, I'm pretty caught up.

The trouble is, Adam is not only willing to have it anytime, or anyhow, but also any*where*. The shower, the living room carpet, restaurant toilets.

And as I've told you before, this is all completely different for me. A totally new kettle of fish.

But there's a weird myth about sex.

People reckon that if you haven't had it for ages that you are gagging for it. But in my experience, it doesn't work like that.

When we first shagged, me and Adam, it was a total non-event. My first bit of nookie in over a year and not so much as a blip on the Richter scale.

Don't get me wrong, it wasn't unpleasant. It's just that it wasn't particularly anything.

But now I'm starting to see the point.

True, I would prefer it if sometimes – just *sometimes* – Adam wanted to do something other than shag. Like, I don't know, talk to me, or something wild and crazy like that. No, that's not fair. Adam does talk to me. He tells me I look stunning. And sexy. And it feels nice when he says these things. More than nice. So I shouldn't complain.

It's not as if Adams grow on trees.

And we're just starting to get to that stage. The stage where our relationship moves into the next level. And once it's there, it won't be long before I can pop the big question.

The big question being, 'Would you meet my mum?'

Then of course, there will be more big questions, of which 'Will you lie for me?' will be the first.

And he will say yes to both.

I can feel it.

Because he will see how much it means to me, even though it shouldn't. And he will do the right thing, because sex-maniac or not, I sense that he is a decent human being. I am also starting to sense that I would be attracted to him even if he wasn't an Adam. Even if he wasn't perfect parent-friendly boyfriend material.

And that's a scary thought.

It really is.

Chapter Forty-Eight

I go to work.

Lorraine is in a hyper mood. Probably because the fat, bald figure of Mr Blake is pacing around the shop floor, keeping an eye on everything. She is smiling, manically, at him. Quite amusingly, he is ignoring her. In fact, he is looking straight at me.

He walks over.

'Hello, Mr Blake,' Lorraine says.

But Mr Blake just holds out his hand and smiles gently at me. 'I don't believe we've met.' He has one of those voices fat, bald businessmen seem to have. Cigar smooth. Confident. Full of money.

'No. We haven't,' I say. 'I'm Faith Wishart.'

'OK, Faith, nice to meet you. Keep up the good work.'

'I will,' I tell him, a smile sitting wide across my face.

Lorraine, looking suitably miffed says: 'Don't worry, Mr Blake. I'll keep my eye on her.' But Mr Blake is already walking away.

'Keep up the good work,' Lorraine says, scowling. 'What

164

on earth are you playing at, Faith? What does Mr Blake know about your good work?'

'I don't know,' I tell her. 'I really don't.'

Back home and watching TV, I hear a noise. A clanking sound. And then I look out of the window and see Frank. He is taking all his disused bottles and cans to the bottle bank.

God, he really must be making a new start.

When he returns he sees me staring at him through the window. He smiles. Waves.

I wave back.

I think of Mr Blake today and the way he was so nice to me.

And then for some reason the words of Josie, the old woman I do makeovers for, echo in my brain. *Everything will turn out rosy.*

Everything will turn out rosy.

And I wonder what she had meant.

Chapter Forty-Nine

My mum phones.

At first I just go into auto-pilot, while I listen to her talk about Hope's wedding invitations and how I'm going to get there. Then about how Mark's going to get there. And I just 'hmm' and 'ah' and say 'yes' where appropriate.

But then she says, 'I'm definitely coming up to Leeds on Saturday. To meet Adam.'

Oh my God. To meet Adam.

I think about work. But I am off on Saturday. But I could still use it as an excuse, saying I've got a big PR campaign to do or something.

My mum continues, 'I can come at any time. So don't say you're working.'

'But ... I ...' don't have another excuse, I really don't. And in the time I have taken hesitating it has been arranged.

'So I'll see you then,' she says. 'Anyway, I'd better go and clean the upstairs windows.'

Chapter Fifty

Sometimes it's best just to come out with something straight away. You know, just to get it off your chest. So that evening, within ten minutes of Adam stepping through my door I say . . .

'I've got something to ask you.'

'Ask me?' He looks worried. As if I'm about to drop down on one knee.

'Yes. My mum's coming up at the weekend and I was just thinking, well, you know, if you didn't mind, if you'd like to meet her.'

'Meet her?'

'Yes. My mum.'

'Meet your mum?'

'Yes, I mean, she won't be here long, and you don't have to stay—'

'Fucking hell, babe.' His eyes are wide with surprise or disbelief. He is shaking his head.

These are not good signs.

'Fucking hell babe what?' I ask, genuinely perplexed.

'Fucking *hell*.'

167

He stands up off the sofa and walks into the kitchen. He is still shaking his head.

'What's the matter?' I ask.

No answer. He just stares out of the window.

Eventually he says something, more to himself than to me, so I don't hear.

'Sorry?'

'I *said*,' he says, with over-the-top enunciation. 'This is too intense.'

'Intense?' I say, noting the anger is now travelling in both directions. 'What do you mean intense? Because I asked you to meet my mum? She's not scary, you know. She's just a person.'

He looks at me as if I have missed the point. 'We've only just starting seeing each other,' he says, simmering down to anger mark four. 'It's not exactly meet the parents stage, is it?'

'I don't know. I didn't know there had to be a stage.'

He stares at the ceiling and releases an elaborate sigh. 'It just all seems to be getting heavy.'

'Heavy?'

'I just don't want you to start getting any false impression. I mean, I don't want you to think this is something it isn't.'

'And what do I think it is?'

He shrugs. 'I don't know. But you keep throwing up all these extras.'

'Extras? Adam, I'm not a DVD.'

He smiles. It's a smile he hasn't worn before and it really doesn't suit him. It makes him look smug. And pompous. And ugly.

'I just asked if you'd like to meet my mum, that's all.'

168

And then, calmer than before, he walks out of the room and out of the flat.

'Adam, wait!'

But it's too late. He is gone.

Chapter Fifty-One

One hour later, he is back.

'I'm sorry about earlier,' he says on my doorstep.

'It's OK.'

He produces a bottle of wine from behind his back. I smile, despite myself, and he follows me inside.

'I overreacted,' he explains, taking the seal off the top of the wine bottle.

'No,' I say in a tone as diplomatic as his. 'It's my fault. I'm rushing things. I've been reading things which aren't there. I mean, it's OK about not meeting my mum, I didn't mean to scare you off.'

'If it means that much to you,' he says, looking around for a corkscrew.

'It's in there,' I say, indicating the drawer with the falling off handle. 'And it doesn't mean that much to me.' This is a lie. Adam meeting my mum means everything to me. Of course, I know it shouldn't mean everything. I am well aware that it shouldn't really mean anything at all. My happiness should not depend on my mother's approval. It should come from within. But knowing what you should be feeling does not make you feel it. So when I tell him it doesn't mean that much to me, I feel a strange sinking sensation. Like when you wake up from a gorgeous dream and face the reality of your shit heap apartment.

'No, I'll meet her,' he says, as he pours the wine into two glasses. Glug glug glug.

'Honestly?' I say, a little too enthusiastically.

He stares at me for a long time before offering me a wine glass. 'Honestly.'

'Well in that case I've got to tell you something else.'

His eyebrows raise expectantly. 'Go for it,' he says.

I do my best to ignore the depressed tone of his voice and tell him: 'My mum thinks we've been together for over three months.'

His cheeks puff out as he nearly spits red wine out all over the floor. After a melodramatic gulp he says: 'What?'

I close my eyes and tell him the rest. 'And she thinks you're a lawyer.'

The air thickens.

I open my eyes and see Adam shaking his head from side to side, opening and closing his mouth like a demented goldfish. 'What . . . I . . . Where . . . Who . . . Why?'

Oh dear.

He is starting to sound angry.

I gulp my wine and pull my shoulders in the way which I know will make my nipples visible through my T-shirt.

He glances down at them, through his wine glass, as he takes a sip.

'It's a long story,' I say. 'But basically I got tired that my mother used to think I was an unemployed lesbian. And so I invented a man. And a job. And everything. But don't worry, she doesn't know anything about law.'

'Oh,' he says, still nipple gazing. 'Right.'

171

Emboldened by my first glass of wine I move closer to where he is standing and place my hand inside his T-shirt and circle my finger around his belly button.

'So is it OK?' I ask him. 'Will you go along with it?'

'Yeah,' he says, in a lustful grumble, before nibbling on my ear. 'No problem. Whatever. Anything you want.'

So this is why he came back! God, he really is a sex-maniac. One glance at my protruding nipples and he's off. But frankly, I'm not complaining. After all, he's agreed to meet my mum. The lies might be able to stop. I mean, how sexy is that? On a scale of one to Colin Farrell it's definitely a Farrell. In fact, I could rip his clothes off right now. And I'm not even ovulating.

As it happens, there is no need to rip his clothes off. He does that all by himself. Right here, in the kitchen. And then he waits, like a naked gunslinger at the OK Corral, waiting for me to make a move.

After a moment's deliberation I take my clothes off too and pull his perfectly formed body next to mine, tingling at the touch.

'Oh, right,' he says, in his now familiar sex-voice. 'You're so sexy . . .'

But then, as we are about to get underway, I remember something. 'Condom,' I say, coyly.

'Oh yeah,' he says, and reluctantly squats down on the floor to find his wallet amid the scatter of clothes.

And then I remember something else. 'I'd, um, better shut the curtains.'

Chapter Fifty-Two

The next morning I wake and turn over to hug my gorgeous, mum-friendly boyfriend only to discover that he has turned invisible overnight. And then I remember. He had to be in work early. Eight o'clock or something ridiculous.

I decide to hug my pillow instead, and start to slip back into that deep, contented sort of sleep I never knew when I was single. But then the phone starts to ring. And ring.

And *ring*.

The ringing is so persistent I know it can only be one person.

I ignore it and shove my head under the pillow.

But I know it will stay ringing until I get out of this lovely warm bed to answer it. Because I'm not in work until midday. Because it is 7.30 in the bloody morning. Because my mother is a sadist whose favourite method of torture is sleep disturbance.

There is a pause. A pause which I know will last only as long as it will take for her to place the handset down, pick it back up and press redial. The grim predictability of it could

173

weigh me down, if I wasn't already weighed down by three of the world's thickest duvets and a pillow over my head.

Ring, ring. Ring, ring. Ring, ring . . .

The rings are getting louder, apparently more annoyed by the fact that I could still be asleep. I don't even have to pick up the phone to understand what my mum is trying to tell me.

You, must. Get, out. Of, bed . . .

I strike a compromise. I get up but take the bed with me, or at least two of the duvets. Shit, where are my slippers? Even in here, cocooned inside my duvet-womb, I am aware that it is bloody freezing, and the thought of crossing the carpetless hallway with my bare feet is not an attractive one. Unable to find my slippers I decide to step-jump across the freezing cold hallway to land on the living room carpet.

But when I land I get my left foot caught in the duvet. The momentum of the jump pushes my body forward, and before I know it my head is on the floor next to the TV remote control.

'*Shit*,' I mumble, before spitting out carpet-dust.

Ring, ring. Ring, ring. Ring, ring . . .

Chapter Fifty-Three

By the time I actually get to pick up the phone any trace of that honey-glow Adam left me with has disappeared altogether.

'Hello, mum,' I say, because I know it's her.

'Are you up?' she asks, with grim predictability, in place of hello.

'Yes,' I yawn, propping myself up on the marble mantelpiece by the gas fire. 'I've been up for ages.' There it is. The first lie of the day.

'Are you having your breakfast?'

'No. I've just had it.' Lie number two. God, what is it with me? Why am I so scared to let my mother know that I like to lie in? I mean, is that really such a criminal offence?

'And how is Adam today?'

Then I remember. Adam said he'll meet her. And he'll go along with all my stupid lies. 'Oh, he's *wonderful*,' I tell her. 'And he can't wait to meet you on Saturday.'

I can sense my mother's shock as the phone line crackles away, waiting for her response. For once, she is genuinely lost for words.

I savour the moment. She now must surely realise that Adam is one hundred per cent flesh and bone, and not just some figment of my overactive imagination. For the past God-knows-how-many-years she has either thought I wasn't interested in men or they weren't interested in me. A lesbian or a minger. (Not there there's anything wrong with being a lesbian or even being a minger, it's just that I know I'm not the first one and I've always hoped I wasn't the latter, and I don't like my mum assuming that I'm either.)

I wait for my mum's gleeful, ecstatic response. I wait for her to apologise for doubting Adam's existence. I wait for her to gasp with delight.

But she doesn't.

She does something else instead.

'Mum? Are you . . . are you *crying*?'

'I'm sorry,' she whimpers. 'I'm sorry . . . I'm being silly . . . it's just . . . it's just that . . . happy for you . . . so happy . . . for both of you . . .'

'Mum. We're not getting married or anything.'

'Oh, I know that, Faithy. I know. Well not yet anyway. It's just that I'm so glad that you've found such a nice man.'

I sigh. All of a sudden the savourable moment is beginning to evaporate into thin air. I mean, exactly what was that 'well not yet anyway' about. Jesus, she's relentless.

'Mum, you haven't even met him yet . . .'

'I know that.'

'. . . and we've been together for over three months, I haven't just found him.'

'Oh yes,' she says, faltering – because she realises that she hasn't believed me up until this moment. 'I know but I'm actually going to meet him, Faithy. I'm going to meet Adam. That makes it all so . . . so *real*.'

I smile, despite myself.

I have made my mother happy.

It's only a small thing, her meeting Adam, but it means so much to her. It's all she really wants for me. To settle down with a nice man. And although I haven't fully worked out whether or not Adam is The One that's not really the point.

The point is he could be.

At least, as far as my mother's concerned he could be. And as for the nice man bit. Well, he's nice-looking, that's for sure. Nice blond hair. Nice body. Nice eyes. And agreeing to meet mum and go along with all my silly stories, that was a nice thing to do, wasn't it? Of course it was.

Of course.

So any nagging doubts are going to have to be put on hold. For once in my life everything is starting to work out. My mum was right. It feels real. And I like that feeling, I like it a lot.

I just hope that it's going to last.

Chapter Fifty-Four

Six hours later I am in work, having a quiet day, when Adam comes in to see me. It's his lunch break, and Lorraine is not in the immediate vicinity, so we talk. But as always, Adam only seems to have one topic of conversation. And it's a topic which follows me right into the stock room, where I have headed in order to get some more boxes of night cream.

He kisses the back of my neck.

'Adam! What are you doing?'

'You know what I'm doing.'

'We can't do it here!'

'Why not?' Adam asks me, genuinely perplexed.

'Because I'll get fired, that's why not.'

He looks around at the head-high piles of beauty products, 'Who will see us?'

'There are cameras,' I sigh, 'CCTV.'

Adam looks up at the cameraless ceiling. 'Where?'

'I should get back to work.'

'You're allowed ten minutes surely. You could be having a fag-break,' his eyes sparkle mischief. 'A shag-break.'

'What about you? Don't you have to be back? It's nearly three o'clock.'

'Late lunch. I'll be fine. I thought girls who worked all day behind cosmetics counters are *generally* on the look out for distraction.' He smiles his devil-smile and loosens his tie.

'Adam, please. You shouldn't be in here. Please, just go.'

'OK, babe,' he says, without moving an inch. 'Whatever you say.'

I haven't got time for this and so I turn around and start collecting the batch of night creams. 'Because seriously,' I tell him. 'I really would get fired.'

'Yeah, yeah.'

I stand up and turn around and see a bundle of clothes on the floor. And then, above them, is Adam. Standing totally naked, and propping his elbow against one of the shelves.

'I'm all yours,' he says.

'Adam! What are you doing?'

'You know you want me.'

'Ad—'

I stop.

There is a sound.

The last sound in the world I could possibly want to hear. The sound of a door handle.

'Hide! Put your clothes on! Disappear!'

But it's too late.

The door opens to reveal Lorraine. She is staring straight at Adam. The sight of his muscular body is such a shock that she is unable to speak for the first few seconds. Her whole body joins her botoxed face in a state of paralysis.

'Lorraine,' I say. 'I can explain. It wasn't my fault, we weren't doing anything. I didn't even ask him to follow me here!'

179

Adam squats down and grabs his boxer shorts. 'Yes,' he says. 'We weren't doing anything.'

'Faith,' Lorraine eventually says, gasping for air. 'The office. Now.'

Adam gets dressed and flees while I follow Lorraine across the shop floor and up the escalator, awaiting my fate.

Chapter Fifty-Five

'It wasn't what it looked like,' I tell her.

But Lorraine is not having it. 'You were with a naked man in the stock room.'

'Yes,' I say. 'I know. But I didn't want him to be there. I didn't tell him to take his clothes off.'

'So you didn't know this man? Shall I call the police? Shall I say we've got a sex attacker on the premises?'

I sigh. 'No. I know him. He's my boyfriend. He'd come to see me on his lunch break, that's all. And then he followed me into the stock room and got the wrong idea, that's all.'

'And so what *were* you doing in the stock room exactly?'

'I was getting some more night cream. We'd run out of it.'

She raises her eyebrows. (Well, OK, when I say 'raises' I mean by about one millimetre. And when I say eyebrows, I mean those thin black pencil lines above her eyes.) 'Oh,' she says, ambiguously. 'Had we now?'

'Yes,' I say.

'Only it seems that we've been running out of a lot of things lately, haven't we?'

'I don't know.'

'And it seems that you spend a lot of time in that stock room, whether with naked boyfriends or otherwise.'

Me? She's the one always disappearing into the stock room! 'I'm not sure I understand,' I say.

She pauses, and folds her arms. 'Stock is going missing.'

'And you think I am responsible?'

'Well, Faith. It would be entirely fitting with your recent track record.'

'I haven't done anything!'

'You are the only person, apart from myself, who has continual access to Keats' stock.'

'It's not me,' I tell her.

'And that woman cavorting in the stock room with that naked man. I suppose that wasn't you either, was it?'

'Lorraine, I'm sorry. I shouldn't have allowed him to follow me but—'

'Enough excuses,' she says.

'But—'

'I've had enough.'

'But—'

'That's it, Faith.'

'But—'

'You're *fired*.'

Chapter Fifty-Six

'You'll get another,' Adam says. 'No problem, babe.'

He is trying to be sympathetic. I think. But it's not working.

I just nod and say, 'Yeah.' But I know I won't get another job. If I tell the truth, I will come across as unemployable. If I lie, I will get found out again.

I can't even hold down a job as a make-up girl.

I'm going to have to leave town. I'm going to have to leave the continent.

I start to cry, the tears messing up my mascara. 'I'm sorry,' I say. 'I don't mean to cry.'

Adam looks scared. As if my head was starting to spin or an alien was about to pop out of my stomach. So this is who I am dating. A man who doesn't think twice about whipping his trousers down in public, but who descends into a blind panic every time he comes in contact with human emotion.

'Don't cry,' he says, but not in a caring way. More in a this-is-all-getting-heavy-can't-we-just-have-sex kind of a way.

I hate him right now. I know that it's irrational to feel like that. But he could still act just a teensy little bit sorry, couldn't he?

It's all right for him saying I'll get another job. It wasn't his stock room he got caught naked in. It's not him filling out his P45.

I move up off the sofa.

'Faith, where are you going?'

'I'm sorry,' I say, heading for my bedroom. 'I just need to be alone.'

Chapter Fifty-Seven

I wake up early. The alarm clock tells me that it is 6.15. I roll over and discover Adam has disappeared into thin air.

Surely he hasn't gone to work already. Perhaps he left last night.

My eyes close again, under the weight of sleep, but it's no good. I'm too restless now to drop back off.

I elbow myself up into a half-sitting position and re-open my eyes. It takes a few seconds to focus and to make sense of the dark unidentifiable shapes which constitute my bedroom.

I look at the blackish bundle on the floor. His clothes. And then at the two shadowy objects by the door. His shoes.

Curiouser and curiouser.

Perhaps he's gone to the bathroom. I lie and listen and wait to hear a flush or any other bathroom noises but there is nothing.

I look at the alarm clock again.

6.19.

Then I hear it.

A noise.

A slight gasp.

Coming from the living room.

My heart starts to race as paranoid night-thoughts enter my brain. Perhaps it's an intruder. An attacker. Perhaps they've gagged Adam and tied him up on the sofa and now they're coming for me.

I peel back the duvet, trying to make as little noise as physically possible. I then tiptoe slowly towards the doorway. I hesitate, after causing one of the floorboards to creak, then continue out into the hallway.

Once there, I look around for a weapon.

Remembering I am not a member of the secret service, I grab my umbrella instead. Perhaps I could prod the intruders to death.

And then I hear it again.

The slight gasp. Only this time it is accompanied by a equally slight whimper. He sounds as though he is in some kind of pain. Perhaps he's got some information on a secret terrorist plot which is being tortured out of him by government agents which don't officially exist.

I wonder if I should call the police, but realise that the phone and my mobile are both currently situated in the living room. If anyone is going to save Adam from whatever horrible fate is being inflicted on him then it looks like it is going to have to be me.

I try and control my breathing as I inch closer to the living room door, umbrella in hand. I feel a pang of guilt about yesterday. About how I made Adam feel guilty after I lost my job.

Don't worry, Adam, says the film star voice in my head. *I'm going to save you.*

I wait by the side of the door, back against the wall, holding the umbrella towards the ceiling, rifle-style. I can hear Adam again.

He sounds hopeless, desperate.

That's it.

I can't bear it any longer. I'm going in.

My hand rests flat against the door, then slowly pushes it open. I can't see anyone at first. But then I notice the TV is on, with the sound turned down.

The programme which is on seems strangely familiar. Which is weird, because I am never up at twenty past six in the morning.

And then I realise exactly what I am watching.

It's The Yogasmic Workout DVD.

It's my sister. Or in this particular position, my sister's arse. She is facing away from camera, bending her body over, down between her legs.

I push the door open wider.

There are no intruders.

There are no burglars, kidnappers or government agents.

There is only Adam, sitting on the sofa, completely oblivious to his umbrella-wielding girlfriend two metres behind him.

He is crying.

Or maybe he's not.

Actually, now I come to think about it, he doesn't sound like he's crying at all. He sounds like he's doing something else. Something implied by the jerky movements of his right shoulder.

A right shoulder which is connected to an arm.

Which is connected to a hand.

Which is connected to a . . .

'Oh,' he whimpers, softly. 'Oh yeah.'

He's *wanking*.

'Adam,' I say. 'What are you doing?'

He jumps. Then freezes. Then stands up. Then turns

187

around, trousers caught around his ankles, his erection already heading south.

He looks at me. He looks at my umbrella.

I consider using it. Right now, it could probably do some serious damage.

'I was . . . I was . . .'

'. . . masturbating in front of my sister's video.'

But then he does something I wasn't quite expecting. He smiles. And then he says, 'Yeah.' As if he's not even bothered that I've just caught him with his trousers around his ankles and his hand around his cock.

In fact, he is starting to laugh, expecting me to join in.

'You—' I am furious. I am trying to find an appropriate insult. '*Wanker.*'

'Yep,' he says, hands raised in surrender, penis dropped in defeat. 'That pretty much sums it up.'

At least he could have the dignity to lie. Or to try and cover it up. Or to look even *slightly* like this is an embarrassing situation for him. But eventually, reluctantly, he offers the lamest of lame explanations. 'I couldn't sleep.'

'You couldn't sleep?'

And then it dawns on me. This is the moment I am meant to kick him out. He's already lost me my job and now I've caught him with another woman. So OK, the other woman doesn't know about it, and is two hundred miles away. But the other woman is my sister. And can I really stay with a man who so openly lusts after her, that he doesn't just confine himself to mental images and private fantasies but actually whacks off in front of her DVD? On my sofa? At six in the bloody morning?

But already I know the answer.

Already I know I will let him back into my bed. Because the other option is to tell my mother, and my lusted-after

188

sister, the truth. And I hate myself right now. I hate my weakness. I hate myself more than I hate Adam. Because although Adam is, without doubt, a wanker, he is an honest one. At least he can face up to what he is.

So we argue, for a while, but then we go back to bed, where I stay looking blankly at the ceiling until it is time to get up. Wondering exactly how this is all going to end.

Chapter Fifty-Eight

When Adam has gone to work, my mum phones.

She is asking me about work and I am telling her it's great, because what else can I say? I can hardly tell her that I've got sacked from a job she didn't even know I had in the first place.

And then, she starts talking about Hope's wedding.

'Have you bought your outfit?'

'No, mum, I haven't really had time.'

'Isn't it all so exciting,' she says. 'I bet you can't wait to meet Jamie?'

'No,' I say. 'I can't.'

'Hope called last night. She says she's going to send you an invite to her hen party. It's going to be in Paris. Isn't that exciting?'

'Yes, mum,' I say, already wondering how I am going to get out of it.

Then, out of the blue, she says, 'Only three days.'

'Only three days what?'

'Until the weekend. Until I meet Adam.'

'Oh yes,' I say. 'I forgot.'

'Oh Faith, I'm so proud of you all. All three of my children doing so well.'

'Yes, mum, I know. I know.'

The day lasts forever. I sit, doing nothing, watching TV. Frank is playing music. Only it's not loud music this time. It's not heavy metal, and the volume's on low. In fact, it sounds quite nice. Soothing. I know the song. It's Al Greene. My dad used to have his album. A greatest hits. He used to put it on loud and try and get mum to dance with him but she'd always tell him to get off, because she had work to do.

And then I start to think about Frank.

It feels really weird to have saved someone's life. And then I think about how he seems to have changed. How there has been no further evidence of alcoholic rude behaviour.

I start to think about what Frank said when he was talking about his PhD. All that alternative universe stuff. I mean what if it's true? What if there really are as many universes as there are possibilities? What if somewhere out there I'm making all the right decisions?

Maybe my lies aren't lies at all. Maybe they're truths that are being lived by another me. The truths I myself should be living.

Yeah, that sounds good. I'm not a liar, I'm just speaking other possibilities. The reality of the alternative universes. The universes where I really did get the job with Coleridge Communications. And where my boyfriend doesn't sit masturbating in front of my sister's DVD.

There must be a better universe than this one.

And there must certainly be a more sorted Faith Wishart. One who isn't scared to live life for herself, not just for her mum.

191

Chapter Fifty-Nine

Adam arrives back at my flat in a bad mood.

'How was your day?' I ask him.

'Shit,' he says, without asking me about mine.

I suddenly consider what he might be like on Saturday, when mum comes. He may look the part, but he isn't half temperamental.

'Do you want a cup of tea?' I ask him, like a good wife.

'No. Something stronger.'

I pour him a glass of wine.

He downs it in about five seconds.

'That's better,' he says. Then, looking at me lecherously, he says: 'Give me a kiss.'

I give him a kiss, but even as I do so I can't help wondering. Does Adam want a girlfriend, or is he after a Geisha, love-slave and housewife rolled into one? There is something about him tonight. Something I don't like. Something which is charging the air with a negative energy.

His eyes are a million miles away. On planet lust. I wonder, momentarily, how well I know this man I have invited into my life. Yes, he is willing to lie for me. But I can't deny the decision was guided by his trousers as much as his brain. And ever since he's agreed to it, he seems to act like he has got some sort of power over me. As if it's perfectly OK to lose me my job or wank over my sister.

He grabs my breast. 'Adam—' Then he lowers me to the carpet, by pushing me back over his leg. And then he's on top of me.

'Adam, please. Not now. I'm not in the mood.'

He laughs. 'Not in the mood.'

Chapter Sixty

He is on top of me, just one of his hands enough to suppress two of mine. The other hand is working below, grappling with buttons, greedily tugging like some desperate animal.

'Stop, don't, no,' I say. Weak, pathetic. My voice as feeble as my body.

I kick my legs, heels banging against the floor, but I cannot shift his weight. The gym-worked body I was drawn to for its strength, is now teaching me the lesson of my misguided attraction.

He brings his head closer, his mouth seeking mine. I twist away and he reaches my cheek. Then his voice, whispering menace into my ear. 'You're such a ...' My whole body struggles against his words. '... cock tease.'

His head raises back, and as it does I spit at him. He laughs as the saliva hits his cheek. A genuine laugh, as if he really finds this funny.

I feel his legs kick above me as he sheds his jeans. My mind flashes with dead frogs and experiments with electricity, an image preserved in my memory from some long gone children's TV show.

Then skin meets skin. The hairs of his legs prickling against me. He has pushed my trousers around my ankles and now his free hand is clawing at my knickers.

My body freezes momentarily, as every muscle tightens. Then somehow I muster a scream, something resembling the word 'help'. The sound of a victim. A sound which makes everything real. Which turns the scene into horror.

And then I feel it. The teased cock. Hard against my naked leg, as he tears at the crotch of my knickers.

'Stop,' I scream. 'No.'

My body is in a fit but it is still too weak to fight him off. I have done lessons before. Self-defence classes which taught you how to punch and kick and block and weave. But my resistance is not working, I have no energy. I am not a fighter. I am soft.

I look to the side, my face against the carpet. I am still screaming as I look for something, anything. Something which could stop this from happening. I see the whole scene reflected in the black glass of the TV monitor and see the terror in my own face, as that of a stranger.

Some strange, helpless girl lying flat on her back with this blond, blue-eyed monster on top of her.

I look across to the phone and think of mum. Just two metres and seven numbers away from me. She's probably cleaning right now, hoovering or dusting, thinking about Hope's wedding, not knowing anything.

And then, as his hand's against my mouth, trying to shut me up before starting his business, I think of dad. For the first time since he died I pray there is no heaven, I hope more than anything in the world that he is not looking down, watching.

I hope he has gone forever.

It is about to happen.

It is about to happen and I have no fight left. I am exhausted.

I have said no. Please. Don't. I have been saying it for what seems like forever but what was probably sixty seconds.

Less than forty-eight hours ago I had held him close, I had wanted him, and I had wanted to feel him inside me. But that was a different me. A different Adam.

The Adam weighing down on me now is a stranger. I don't know him and he doesn't know me. He cannot, to want to do this.

'Stop, please. Stop.'

He laughs, his breath hot in my ear. And then I realise something. He is capable of anything. He could . . .

There's a noise.

A knock at the door.

He hasn't noticed. He just keeps on, now pinning down my wrists, fighting against the resistance. I scream help.

'Hey, Faith, it's OK. It's OK.' His voice is calm, with a tone which in any other context would be reassuring. And then his free hand covers my mouth and he closes his eyes. I try to bite him but I can't push my teeth far enough forwards.

I struggle again but I can tell he is almost there. Any moment . . .

Another noise.

Louder this time. The sound of a body throwing itself against the door. And then the sound of wood, breaking.

Adam freezes. Looks at me. The fear he forced into my eyes has now returned to its rightful owner. 'What the fuck was that?' His hand relaxes, forgetting its duty.

Now is my chance.

I bite hard, nearly hard enough to lose teeth, and don't stop until I can taste blood.

'You bitch,' he squeals, flinching his hand away, raising it high, and clearly ready to strike it back down. His hand, marked with blood and smudged make-up, hovers in the air eagerly awaiting the order.

I squeeze my eyes shut, anticipating the hit.

It doesn't happen.

For a second, or a whole lifetime, there is nothing but the forced blackness from my scrunched up eyes. And then I hear footsteps. Heavy, travelling fast.

I open my eyes. Adam is twisting away from me, his arm still raised as he turns towards the unseen intruder.

'Get off her,' I recognise the voice, vaguely, but I still cannot see who it is.

'Mate, piss off,' says Adam. 'It's not what you—'

He is caught in a headlock, and suddenly there is less weight on top of me. I can breathe.

But still the vice-gripped intruder is anonymous, his face shielded by a mop of black hair as he struggles to lift Adam off me. Adam, turning red and gurgling manically, is staring at me with wide, psychopathic eyes.

Then, as Adam's body is yanked up and away from me in a kind of forced limbo, the intruder looks up. It's Frank. From downstairs.

'Are you hurt?' he asks me, the question causing a momentary lapse in concentration. Adam takes advantage and wrestles himself free.

A second later Adam has punched Frank on the nose. A second after that blood is being soaked up into Frank's beard as Adam bends down to pull up his trousers. He doesn't have time. Frank lunges forward and holds him in an awkward body grip.

197

I quickly yank my jeans up and do up my shirt, fear and adrenalin making the buttonholes smaller than they were this morning.

Things smash as my living room becomes a wrestling ring.

Adam reaches for the empty bottle of wine.

'Watch out!' I warn Frank.

Frank watches out and swerves left, slamming the side of Adam's leg into the coffee table. For a surreal moment, the scene takes on an almost comic effect. With Frank upright, grappling with a bent-double Adam, it's as if a demented, de-costumed pantomime horse is throwing some kind of fit right in the middle of my living room.

Adam swerves back, crunching the TV remote underfoot, and makes another attempt at the wine bottle.

This time he succeeds and slams it against Frank's back. The bottle doesn't break, just causes a painful thud.

'Agh!'

The action is repeated.

'You fuck!'

As I watch I feel instinct take over. Before I know it I am on my feet, trying to restrain Adam's Herculean arm. As a reward for my efforts I get elbowed in the chin and sent flying back onto the carpet.

Frank observes this and decides to get nasty, yanking Adam's head down by his hair and bringing his knee up to meet Adam's nose.

It becomes clear that what Frank may lack in muscle he more than compensates for with imagination.

Everything is happening so fast. It's not like those fights in movies. You know the ones – when there's a pause between each punch and where it's really well choreographed. No. Watching a real fist-fight in your living room is quite a different experience altogether.

As they rip at each other's clothes and smash the vase my mum bought me, I elbow myself across the floor and reach for the phone.

'I'm calling the police,' I say, my hand shaking like mental.

'No you're fucking not,' Adam says, pushing Frank away and making a dive for the phone. He misses, but from where he's crash-landed he makes an easy swipe for it.

I get to my feet as Frank boots him in the stomach. I remember that if it wasn't for Frank barging though the door I would be a rape victim right now and I boot Adam in the stomach as well.

Adam is coughing and retching but I am shouting and swearing at him until I feel a hand on my arm.

Frank wipes the blood from his nose and hoists Adam up and drags him coughing and whimpering, out of the apartment. Something is said in the hallway. The door opens, and clicks shut.

Adam is gone.

Chapter Sixty-One

Frank comes back into the room.

I am back on the floor, shaking. A mess.

Frank clears away the broken glass and porcelain and straightens the furniture.

'I'll go if you want.' he says. 'He won't be coming back.'

I look up at him. I don't know what I want. To be honest, I can't really come to terms with what just happened. Or what nearly happened. It still doesn't make any sense.

I had trusted Adam. I had invited him into my life. Into my bed.

I thought he respected me. I had duped myself into thinking that he wanted more from me than my body alone could provide. I had started to convince myself that sex wasn't the only thing I had to offer.

I was a sucker.

Frank translates my silence as a signal to leave.

I hear his footsteps pad softly down the hallway as I look around the room. The TV, the DVDs, the settee, the gas-fire, the marble mantelpiece. Every object feels different now.

Treacherous, almost. Like mute observers to the scene, implicated by what they have witnessed.

I do not want to be left alone here.

I cannot be.

'No,' I call out, as I hear the front door open. 'Stay.'

Chapter Sixty-Two

The door closes, and the footsteps pad slowly back to the room. Frank offers a gentle smile as he re-enters.

Something about his presence soothes me instantly. Perhaps it is to do with his complete difference to Adam. Physically, they are almost opposites.

Frank is dark, bearded and scruffy, while Adam is blond, clean-shaven and obsessively well-groomed. Frank is the exact opposite of my Ideal Man. And so now, as my Ideal Man has proved himself the exact opposite of ideal, Frank is a welcome presence.

'I'm sorry,' I say, pushing my hair off my face.

'You have no reason to be sorry,' he says. Matter of fact. 'But you should call the police.'

His words arrive into my head as an echo. It is not that I don't know what he is saying, it is just that it sounds like he should be saying it to someone else.

You should call the police.

'I . . .' but I don't even know what I am about to say. 'No.'

I hardly even know my own name at this moment in time. The thought of starring in some gritty police drama and running through what just happened is not a tempting one.

And anyway, I don't even know what did happen.

I wasn't raped.

I wasn't beaten.

I wasn't robbed.

He wasn't a stranger.

All I know is that he frightened me. He pinned me down and he frightened me. And what would the police say then? They would ask me questions. They might be cross, angry at me for wasting police time. Or they might be sympathetic. That would be worse. I don't know why, but it would.

I expect Frank to insist but he doesn't. He just stands there in his too baggy jumper and looks at me with soft eyes. 'If you are sure,' he says. Part of me knows I should still be scared. After all, I had trusted Adam and he has proved himself capable of anything. And I don't even know anything about this bearded, scruffy, smelly and previously very rude man now standing in my living room. Yet somehow I know he will not harm me.

He disappears into the kitchen. Cupboard doors open and close. He gets something out of the fridge. The kettle starts to grumble.

He has read my mind.

'Thank you,' I say, when he re-enters with a cup of tea in his hand.

He smiles, and makes a friendly noise through his nose. 'No,' he says, 'Thank *you*.'

My head tilts in confusion. 'Thank me for what.'

His eyes switch to the area of the carpet where I struggled with Adam. He suddenly looks sad. 'For saving my life.'

'Oh,' I say. 'You've already thanked me.'

203

'No,' he says. 'I'm not just talking about that night. Well, I am. But I mean, since. The way it's changed me. The way that you did that, without even knowing who I was.'

'Anyone would have done it,' I say.

'Maybe. Maybe they would. But thank you.'

Frank sits down on the settee.

'It's OK,' I tell him.

I can tell he wants to say more. That he has something to get off his chest, and I remember the state of his flat. All those unpacked boxes.

But I am not going to force him to say anything. Secrets should be respected, I should know that. 'I should go,' he says, sitting forwards.

'You don't have to.'

He stands. 'You'll be OK now. But if you're scared I'm only downstairs.'

I get to my feet. 'Thanks,' I say. 'For . . . you know.'

'It's OK.' And then, at the door: 'If you want me to stay with you I will.'

'No,' I say, wearing my brave face. 'I'll be fine.'

But as soon as I close the door my brave face starts to wear off.

Chapter Sixty-Three

Within five minutes I am knocking on his door.

'I'm sorry,' I say, as he opens it.

'Don't be,' he says. 'Come in.'

The place has been transformed. There isn't a vodka bottle or beer can in sight. Most of the cardboard boxes have disappeared. The only ones that remain are those marked R'S THINGS.

'You've tidied up,' I say.

'Yes,' he says, about to embark on the understatement of the century. 'It was a bit of a mess.'

'Do you like Al Greene?' he asks me.

'Yes,' I say. 'Actually I do. My dad used to have his greatest hits.'

He puts on the CD he was playing earlier and turns the volume down low. 'But I thought you were into heavy metal?' I say, with reference to his former neighbour from hell antics.

'Oh,' he says. 'No. Not really. That was just a tape someone gave me.'

'Do you want to phone anyone?' he asks. 'You can phone your parents if you want?'

'No,' I say. 'It's OK.'

I think of my mum. I think of having to see her at the weekend. I think of her itching to see Adam. For some reason I am thinking aloud. I am telling Frank all about it. All about my lies. About dad. About my sacking from Blake's. About everything.

'So, let me get this straight,' he says, after listening to my half-hour monologue. 'Your mum is coming on Saturday to meet a lawyer called Adam who she thinks you have been dating for over three months. And you only really stayed with that bastard I . . . *met* . . . tonight because he was called Adam and he was willing to go along with your lies.'

'Yes,' I say. 'That makes me pretty sad, huh?'

'It makes you pretty eager to make your mum happy.'

He then tells me about his parents. About how they divorced a few years ago and how his mum lives in Edinburgh, while his dad still lives in Leeds, where Frank grew up. I ask him what his dad does and he seems pretty keen not to talk about it, just saying that 'he owns his own business'. He also says that he lived with his dad, right up until he moved here, because things got 'difficult'.

'Right,' I say. And then, looking again at the boxes, I ask him: 'Who's R?'

He sighs, and waits a while before answering.

'It stands for Robert.'

'Oh,' I say, trying not to seem overly-nosy.

'My brother.'

He is shaking his head hard.

I can tell from his face we are now on sensitive ground. There is a vulnerability to him now, and I can start to see now why he may want to stay hidden away behind all his facial growth.

I don't understand. But I don't want to push it so I say nothing. The silence extends way into the discomfort zone before he finally cracks. 'He's dead.'

'Oh,' I say, suddenly at a loss for words.

Just as he says that he looks at me, straight in the eyes and, for that split-second I feel a chill run through me. 'I'm so sorry,' I say, in that awkward and pathetic way people do when responding to someone else's loss.

I don't ask him what happened but we both know the question is hanging in the air. 'Car crash,' he says eventually, his lips tense as they hold back a flood of emotion.

Car crash.

But there's something else, I can feel it. Something else he wants to say.

He starts to lift up his jumper.

I feel awkward. I don't know why. After all, I've seen him naked before.

Once his jumper is off he turns around to show me his back, the only part of his anatomy I haven't had a proper look at. I don't notice anything at first, just smooth pale skin and gentle contours. But then I see it. A long, pink-brown scar at the base of his spine. Curved, like an upside-down smile.

The scar, I realise, is meant to tell me that he was in the car as well, alongside his brother. But the scar can only tell part of the story, so Frank decides to complete it.

'I was driving,' he says, with a ghosted expression. He puts his jumper back on. 'So there it is,' he says, with an artificial shrug. 'There's my big secret. I killed my own brother. Eleven months ago today.'

'Frank, I'm so sorry.'

207

'Don't be,' he says. 'It was my fault.'

He says the last four words with his eyes up towards the ceiling, as if waiting for a nurse to give him an injection.

He carries on.

I do not ask him, but he wants to tell me. Or tell someone. And I am here, listening, wanting to hear, and so I will do.

He tells me that it was dark. Raining heavy. That all the lights and distances were blurred. That he was sober. That his brother, four years younger, wasn't. He had been to a concert. He was in a band, lead vocalist. But it wasn't his band playing that night. He was just there, drunk. It was at Rock City. In Nottingham. Where his brother lived. Frank had gone with him because all Robert's friends were busy that night. Even though it wasn't Frank's type of music he had agreed because things hadn't been that great between them and he wanted to try and make amends. Build bridges. And he was so busy building these bridges, talking, laughing, listening to music that he wasn't paying too much attention to the road ahead.

He was overtaking.

He was overtaking on a road where all the lights and distances were blurred.

There was a slight bend in the road.

A slight bend which coincided with a slight dip. So he hadn't seen the oncoming headlights until too late. And when he saw, he swerved. They avoided the car but it was still too late. He had lost control and they were heading for the verge and a road sign.

'They called it a tragic accident,' he says, in conclusion. He shakes his head. 'A *tragic* accident.' He shakes his head again. 'But you know the thing with tragedy? There's always got to be a fatal flaw. You know, that's what they

208

teach you at school, isn't it? When you do Shakespeare. In tragedy. And I knew, even as it hit, I knew it was my fault.'
He stands still, looking out of the window. Curtains wide open. Rain pattering against the panes. He looks up, towards the streetlight, watching as it weeps golden tears down onto the pavement.

Chapter Sixty-Four

He tells me what happened after.

About how he stopped wanting to study.

About how he filled the days with vodka and how he came to fear mornings and all the clear-focused memories they brought with them.

And as he talks I cannot believe I got this man so wrong. I was blinded by the beard, by the empty vodka bottles, by the inability to say anything polite.

Well OK, anyone would have thought the same thing. A noisy Neanderthal piss-head.

But I didn't read into any of it. I didn't wonder why.

He stopped shaving because running a steel blade over his bristles suddenly seemed the most trivial task in the universe.

He uses that word. Universe. And I wonder if he really believes there is some alternative universe where his brother is still alive. Where he kept his eyes on the road. I wonder if studying the subject helps him believe. Not in an after-life, but in some sort of parallel life, where everything is still OK.

He started drinking because sobriety was no longer an option, and because cirrhosis of the liver, or any other fatal drink-induced condition for that matter, was something which now held no fear.

And as for being rude, well, it was just a way of shutting people out. Because that's the thing with grief, it has two opposite effects.

When dad died I had about twenty-four hours of privacy and then I wanted to go out and spill my heart to the world. I wanted to make everyone love my dad the way I had. I wanted them to share their memories of him, and I wanted to share mine back. I wanted to talk and to smile and to talk and to smile and to talk, because so long as I was talking and smiling I wasn't curled up under the duvet waiting for the world to end.

But Frank is obviously a different kind of griever. The male kind, I could say. The kind that wants to lock grief up and keep it for themselves.

Who can only tackle loss by drowning it out.

With booze.

With chaos.

With loud noise.

No wonder his dad couldn't live with him anymore.

As he keeps on talking I start to wonder what the old Frank looked like. The Frank who washed his clothes. The Frank who washed, full stop. The Frank who didn't need to drink in order to face the day. The Frank who may be about to return.

'But I've stopped with the drinking,' he says. 'It's not been easy, but eleven months ago I was practically teetotal so it's not as if I'm George Best.'

'Right,' I say.

A silence builds up between us.

211

A sad silence.

Frank's mouth is a smile but it is a forced one. A smile contradicted by his eyes.

He's not crying, but I sense the effort he is making to stop the tears. An effort which makes me want to move closer towards him, to help him out. There is a hug waiting to happen. If I just could go over, put my arms around his back, and let his head fall into my shoulder. I picture it, in my head, but I haven't the courage to make the moment real . . .

'I'm sorry,' Frank says, regaining his composure.

'It's OK,' I tell him, realising the hug opportunity had been and gone and I hadn't taken it. 'You must have found it so hard.'

Frank moves past me, goes over to the stereo in the corner of the room and crouches down. 'I want you to listen to something.'

'OK,' I say, not knowing what else to say. I just stand and watch as Frank fumbles around his scattered collection of old cassettes. His jumper rides up his back to reveal pale skin and the delicate indentation of his lower vertebrae, and the scar running along it. Something about this brief glimpse of flesh makes me feel the heat of embarrassment rise to my cheeks. Why am I starting to blush? After all, I've witnessed Frank's naked anatomy in its entirety.

I go to sit on the sofa and decide not to look at Frank's back anymore. I look out the window instead.

It is still raining heavy. The kind of weather which turns the outside world into a TV with bad reception.

'Found it,' Frank says. I turn back to see him flapping a black cassette in the air. He opens up the tape deck, slides it in, and presses play.

I wait for whatever it is Frank wants me to hear. The tape hisses. Frank sits back on his heels and turns around, watching my face. Waiting for something to happen.

The music starts. The familiar heavy metal guitars which have filtered their way up through the floorboards. The drums, which instantly remind me of those late-night migraines. And then the vocals. That same gravely, angsty voice.

Only this time, I can sort of make out what he is singing.

Come and join us
Come and get to know
Everyone's welcome
At the freak of nature show

More loud guitars. More drums. And then the second verse.

Look around it's good to see
Me with you and you with me
Everybody gather close
Our love's a giant pop-up toaster

I think I probably misheard that last line. The tape was a bit distorted at that point. The guitars a bit too loud. But then, as the song heads into the chorus I make the connection.

A connection which causes my mouth to drop open. It's him. Robert.

'It's your brother.'

Frank nods.

A wave of guilt passes over me. Those times I went downstairs to complain about the noise, I was telling him to switch off his dead brother.

'It's beautiful,' I tell him. Because it is, somehow. Oh sure, I hated it when it used to disturb me. When it was just noise. Noise I hadn't even asked to listen to in the first place.

But now, with knowledge, the noise becomes music. The voice, his brother's voice, hides something inside it. A sweetness not quite covered by the gravel on top. And even though the words – or at least the words I am hearing – don't make any real sense to me, the voice itself communicates clearly, even from the grave.

Frank turns it down slightly then stands up, awkward.

He is still looking at me, wanting me to feel what I am already feeling.

'I'm glad . . .' he hesitates, aware of the crack in his voice. 'I'm glad you like it.'

'I love it,' I tell him. 'He was very talented, your brother.'

There is still an awkwardness in the air, but also a closeness. It's as though in deciding to play his tape to me he's letting something go. Not his grief exactly, but the selfish hogging grief. I sense that this is the first time in the last eleven months that Frank has been able to let someone in.

To share something which had been private.

'He was . . . he was just about to get a record deal,' he tells me. 'An A and R man had been to one of their gigs in Nottingham.'

Frank looks up to the ceiling, and his breathing goes funny. There's a slight sinusy rattle, as if he is going to cry.

I stand up. I don't know why, it just seems like the appropriate thing to do.

The song comes to an end and we are left with nothing but the hiss of tape. I look again into Frank's eyes, and see they are sad, but still dry.

214

The hug possibility is back with us. The sight of this man – this towering, bearded, thirty-year-old man – suddenly made so vulnerable, does something to me. Something strange. Something I can't quite explain, even to myself.

I move closer to him. The hug happens.

His arms are strong around my back, but he is too weak and exhausted to hold back the tears any more.

'I miss him,' he says.

'I know.'

'I miss him so much.'

Chapter Sixty-Five

The next evening, when it gets dark, I get scared again. I start to think that Adam will come back. I go downstairs, but Frank is not there. And then I remember, he said something about going to the university library to work.

To take my mind off things I call Alice. Of course, this is not the obvious thing to do. I mean, ringing Alice to help me calm down is like joining an Internet chat room for intellectual stimulation or playing an Eminem CD to help you get to sleep.

I tell her the truth about what happened with Adam. I don't tell her that I thought I was going to be raped, because now I don't want to believe it myself. I want to believe he would have stopped. I want to believe he would have suddenly realised what he was doing and listened to his conscience. Because I do not want to think he could have done the unthinkable.

Not for him.

For me.

'But you're OK now?' Alice is asking, her voice packed with so much sympathy I could cry.

'Yes. I'm OK now.'

'Because if you want me to come round.' She sounds like she means it. And that's a big deal, for Alice. I mean, it's after dark, and it's quite a trek.

The trouble is, I *do* want her to come round but I can't tell her that, so I just say: 'No. It's OK. Honestly. I'll be fine. Seriously, I'll probably go to bed in a minute, after I've watched a bit of telly.'

Thankfully, she doesn't believe me.

In twenty minutes she is there, on my doorstep. 'It's me,' she calls through the letterbox, to put my mind at rest.

When I open the door the sight of her provides instant relief. So OK, as bodyguards go a nearly nine-month pregnant woman suffering from panic disorder and agoraphobia might not be the most ideal candidate, but I cannot think of anybody I would rather see more.

Chapter Sixty-Six

Alice and her bump decide to stay the night and I am grateful for their company.

We share the same bed. Alice is a good listener. And so is her bump. When Alice has gone to sleep I carry on talking to the little person inside her.

I sit there, in the dark, looking at Alice's bizarre silhouette. Her skinny frame at odds with her gigantic bump. Like a flat horizon and a setting sun.

I tell the bump everything.

About Adam.

About my lack of job.

About mum.

About dad.

About Frank.

About all the stupid lies.

About how there are alternative universes where all the stupid lies may actually be true.

And the bump understands. The bump, like Alice, does not judge.

I put my hand gently on the bump, and I can feel a pulse.

A tiny heart beat? My eyes well up with tears. I am proud for Alice, for her body's ability to do something which is so natural and so miraculous. I have never really felt it before. What it must actually mean for Alice to have another life growing inside her. A life as yet untarnished by the outside world and its relationships and jealousy and grief. And lies.

And then I understand just why we worship babies as much as we do. Why we coo and ga-ga over their tiny wrinkled faces. We look at babies and we see ourselves, only without all the baggage. We can look into a baby's face and somehow imagine that life will be different for them. That it will be better. Kinder. Free from pain.

And even though this is just a different kind of lie, it is a comforting one. It is a lie which can help you fall asleep, one hand resting on your best friend's pregnant belly.

My eyes grow heavy. I am drifting. My hand still picking up the gentle signals. The baby's heart beat.

I smile, as sleep finally arrives.

219

Chapter Sixty-Seven

After a deep, dreamless sleep I wake feeling totally refreshed.

I thank Alice again for coming round and do her make-up. She has beautiful, pale skin which requires only the lightest of powders.

'That tickles,' she says, as I start the soft brush strokes.

'Sorry.'

'No. It feels nice.'

One thing that I learned from my job, when I had it, was that people have two appearances. There is the way they look when you are standing talking to them, which is the appearance we normally use to judge if someone is pretty or handsome or ugly.

And then there is their appearance close up. The thing you soon realise when you spend most of your working life applying make-up is that a face is not a smooth flat surface. There are blood vessels to contend with. Pores, be they open or blocked. Contours. Muscles. Various crevices, lines, nooks and crannies even before the ageing process begins.

You see, that's the thing I didn't fully understand. I used to think that it was just my face which was like that. That mine was the only face in the world that *needed* to wear make-up. I thought for everyone else it was an optional extra rather than a physical necessity. Because, unless you are a make-up girl, you analyse your own face a lot more than you analyse anyone else's. And in a sense, you analyse it *too* much.

In fact, some of the top make-up artists recommend standing back from the mirror when applying foundation, powder and blusher before zooming in for close-up work with eye shadow, lipstick and concealer.

The logic behind mid-distance make-up application is simple. You are looking at yourself as the world will see you. But no matter how far you stand back you never get the true picture.

After all, you are the last person in the world who can every truly know how you look. Because when we are looking at our face we are not really looking at our face. We are looking at a map we have seen so many times that we can no longer see the landscape it represents through fresh eyes. We know every line. Every contour. Every inconsistency.

And we are drawn to the bits we don't like.

It's like getting out the ordnance survey map for the British Isles and only being able to detect Grimsby and Bognor Regis. It's part of, but not the complete picture.

You see, with me I only really see two things when I look into the mirror. I see my dimples and my lips. No, might as well be precise about it, my dimples and my bottom lip.

My dimples I hate because I have always hated them and I think they make my cheeks look fatter than they already are and because I have no control over them whatsoever. Make-up can't hide them. Cosmetic surgery wouldn't be able to extract them.

My lower lip, though, is even worse. Seriously, it's freaky. *Deformed*, is how I used to see it but I've matured a bit since then.

Now I just think of it as pig-ugly.

They say that beauty depends on symmetry. The more symmetrical a person's face the more beautiful they are. Well if that's the case I have the ugliest lower lip on the entire planet. The left side is plump while the right side is narrow.

On a good day (a *very* good day) I can justify the existence of my dimples by seeing them as characterful. Or cute. In a Shirley Temple type way.

But my lower lip warrants no such justification. It is cute in the same way ET is cute. Ugly, disfigured cute.

As I said, it's freaky.

Yet despite my knowledge that it makes my whole face circus-ugly, Alice insists that I am mad. She does not know what I am talking about. Even when I haven't tried to sort it out with lipstick she still reckons there's nothing wrong with it.

But then, she is exactly the same. She's got this mole on her cheek, which is about the size of a pea, if that. And she's convinced it is like this gross and hideous thing which makes her ugly.

I am brushing over it now and she is saying, 'make sure you cover that horrible thing up,' as if it was a giant wart or boil or something. And I'm saying the whole thing about it being a beauty spot and that having a mole didn't stop Cindy Crawford or Enriqué or Pink.

222

And then she is about to say something else with a smile on her face when suddenly she sits back and holds the bottom of her bump and winces and makes a slight pain sound.

'Are you OK?' I ask, ready to call an ambulance.

'Yeah,' she says. 'Sorry. I just get pains sometimes. The doctor says it's inevitable but it still bloody hurts. It's when the baby moves about.'

I look at the bump.

She looks at me, with worried eyes. Of course, Alice *only* has worried eyes. Quite worried eyes. Moderately worried eyes. Seriously worried eyes. And totally panicked eyes.

Right now they are in the seriously worried bracket.

'What if the baby has it?'

'Has what?' I ask, anticipating some deadly hereditary disease.

'My mole but bigger. What if he or she gets picked on at school about it, what would I do?'

'I think you'd cross that bridge when you came to it. But if it's as tiny as yours you wouldn't notice it.'

She considers this for a moment. Then nods solemnly.

'Whether it's a boy or a girl, your baby will be beautiful,' I say. 'Like its mum.'

'Now I know you're lying.'

She smiles, and I go back to my make-up reverie. I think about how when you examine your face you can see ugly bits which no one else can.

I start to think, maybe that's what life is like.

Maybe we just magnify the bad things to such an extent they eclipse what is good. So that's probably why I lie. Because lies act exactly the same way as concealer. They cover up the bits of our life we think are pig-ugly. As I

223

learned last night, sometimes trying to turn the good-looking fiction into a good-looking truth can be as painful as a nose job.

A nose job which may not even be necessary in the first place.

224

Chapter Sixty-Eight

I am back where I started.

I have no boyfriend.

Of course, this shouldn't matter. What should matter is that Adam was a terrible person who is no longer a part of my life. So I should be happy.

But it's hard to be happy while you're waiting in a queue at the Job Centre. Seriously, I have been here half an hour and there are still seven people in front of me. This is not what Fridays are meant to feel like.

And then my mobile rings.

'Hello?'

'Faithy? Is that you?' My sister. 'Are you at work? I figured it would be your lunch hour.'

'Yes,' I say grimly. 'It's my lunch hour.'

'Now, Faithy, I'm ringing to tell you that you simply *must* come to Paris for my hen weekend. It's going to be fantastic.' Hope continues: 'We'll be staying at the Hotel Costes. Which is one of *the* most glamorous hotels in Paris. It's where Sting and Robbie Williams always stay.'

225

I look around the room. At the depressed-looking nineteen-year-olds in tracksuits looking at vacancies for dish washers and cabbage packers.

'It sounds great . . . but . . .'

'Oh, and don't worry about money,' she says, reading my mind. 'You won't have to pay for anything. I'll sort out your train fare and we can share a room.'

I have run out of excuses. And anyway, if ever my life needed a glamour injection it's right now. It's hardly like I've got any plans. 'OK,' I say. 'Sure, I'd love to be there.'

'Great,' she says.

'How are things going with the wedding?' I ask her, dutifully.

'Oh,' she says. 'It's going to be wonderful. I've got the dress, and everything is arranged for the reception. We'll be leaving at six though, because of our honeymoon. We're flying out to St Lucia.'

'Wow,' I say, inching myself forward in the dole queue. 'St Lucia. Fantastic.'

'Oh,' she says. 'But I'll still have plenty of time to meet Adam.'

My heart sinks. 'Yes,' I say.

The thought of turning up at Hope's wedding without the man they have heard so much about is just too much. I should tell her now, I really should but somehow I can't. And then I think of the wedding. Of mum's and Hope's and my brother's faces. When they see me arrive completely manless.

They will think there never was an Adam even when there was.

They will think I am incapable. Of telling the truth. Of finding a man. Of being a success in any area whatsoever. And I will have to stand there, the eternal bridesmaid, watching as my sister – my *younger* sister – gets married to a man so anatomically perfect he must have been designed by a computer. A man whose celebrity smile could light up the national grid.

And when Hope throws the bouquet behind her my mum will be screaming at me like an obsessed football fan at a penalty shootout. 'Go on, Faith! Come on, girl, you can do it! Keep your eye on it, Faith! Now jump, go on! There's my girl. Reach! Focus! Concentrate!'

I tell Hope I should go back to work and she says she'll send all the Paris details in the post.

'OK. Bye.'

I move another step closer in the queue and realise there's no point even thinking about the wedding. Not yet. There are closer bridges to cross. Like in twenty-four hours. When mum turns up with an eager, expectant smile on her face saying 'so where is the mystery man then?'

And I'll have to say something like 'he's not here'.

And she'll say 'so where is he then?'

And I'll say 'out'.

And she'll say 'out *where*?'

And I'll say 'at work' or 'at the pub' or 'playing football' or 'he had a family emergency' or 'he fell down a manhole' or 'he's gone to fight for his country' or 'he's setting up a Red Cross funded orphanage for sick children in Zimbabwe' or 'he's on an undercover operation for MI6' or something. But nothing I say will be enough. There is no sequence of words which can get me out of this particular pickle.

I will have to stand and watch as my mum's face falls and crumbles. As she finally realises that my boyfriend really was too good to be true. And once she has sniffed out that particular fact she is sure to discover that I do not really work for the best PR company outside of London. And I

227

will surely be too weak to lie by this point and she will eventually realise that the only thing I am good at is make-up. And making things up.

I make things appear more attractive than they actually are. Because I understand what the truth really is.

And that it always needs hiding.

Chapter Sixty-Nine

After over an hour in the Job Centre, just as it is about to be my turn, my mobile rings again.

I press the button and hear heavy breathing. 'Alice, is that you?'

'Yes ... it's me ...' My heart sinks. She's having another panic attack.

'Listen, Alice. You're fine, nothing's happening.'

'No ... something's ... hap ... pen ... ing ...'

'No, Alice. Come on, you'll be OK. You've been here before. In ten minutes you will start to calm down. You know you will. Try and think relaxing thoughts, you know, a beach or something. You're lying down on a beach, you can hear waves, the sun is shining and there's a clear blue ...' The rest of the queue is looking at me as though I am mad.

'No ... something's *really* happening ... my waters broke ... the contractions have started ...'

It takes a full five seconds for me to understand, and then it hits me.

Oh my God.

'Oh my God. OK, stay—' She makes a loud primal noise on the other end of the line. 'Are you all right?'

'It's ... a ... contr ... aaagh ... ction.'

'Right, OK. Stay there. I'll, um—' Shit. What will I do? Taxi? Ambulance? Police helicopter? 'Is it your first contraction?'

'Yes. Yes. My first.'

'Right, shall I—'

'Phone the hospital.'

'OK, yes, right. I'll phone the hospital. And then I'll do what they say and then I'll be right there.'

'OK ...'

'OK,' I say as if saying the word will make it so.

'OK.'

'*OK.*'

The woman behind the desk looks up at me crossly, wondering why I am holding the queue up. 'I'm sorry,' I say, already heading for the door. 'I'll be right back.'

Chapter Seventy

'Aaagh . . .'

The pain is absolutely excruciating. Seriously, if she squeezes my hand any harder I think I'll collapse.

The whole room is full of people – an obstetrician, a paediatrician, midwives, and someone whose badge I haven't been able to read. They are all standing around staring either between Alice's legs or at whatever it is which is bleeping behind me.

It seems strange. I mean, this is Alice. This is the girl who feels self-conscious enough simply walking down the street. Yet here she is, knickerless, legs spread-eagled, getting ready to give the show of her life. And what's more, she doesn't seem in the slightest bit embarrassed as she tries to push this little (or, judging from the look on her face, not-so-little) human being out into the world.

The senior midwife, who looks 107 years old, smiles a smile which tells Alice: *if you think you're hurting now, wait ten minutes and then you'll really know what agony is.* She then walks over and starts to move the strange-looking

231

strap around Alice's stomach which, we were told, is used to monitor the baby's heart beat.

'Come on little one,' she says, addressing the bump. 'What are you trying to tell us?'

And then, Alice, who is clearly acting as the bump's translator, starts to make the strangest sound I have ever heard. The sound contains elements of a whimper, a howl and a full-on scream, although is somehow more disturbing than any of these in isolation.

Her whole face is a caricature of pain. You want kids to have safe sex? Take a picture of this lady right now, slap it on a poster above the strap line: PREGNANCY REALLY SCREWS YOU UP. The number of teenage mothers would be slashed overnight.

'You're doing really well,' I say. '*Really* well.'

'Aaagh,' she responds. 'You lying bitch.'

I can hardly believe it. Alice is turning into a monster before my eyes. This is the girl who wouldn't normally say hello to a goose, let alone boo. It's as though all the feelings of anger and rage she has always managed to keep bolted down, are now exploding out. It's hard to tell whether she needs a midwife or an exorcist.

She continues to hold onto my hand with a vice-like grip, as she gets ready to enter the seventh circle of hell.

'All right, dear,' croaks the senior midwife, with a seen-it-all before chuckle. 'We're going to need a really big push if we're going to help this little one on its way out of tummy-land.'

The senior midwife, I now realise, is a complete psychopath. She is loving every single minute of this. 'Dear, could you step aside from the machine,' she tells me.

I turn and see that I am standing in front of a white electric box with the words Foetal Monitor Unit on it. 'Sorry,' I say, and step aside.

232

'Don't go,' Alice says with a glint of terror in her eyes. 'Don't leave me.'

'I'm not going anywhere,' I say, as if going anywhere is even a possibility when my hand is still within her death-grip.

'*I want to die.*'

'You can do it,' I tell her. 'You really can.'

There are more people in the room now, more white coats, getting ready for the final act. There is a man between her legs. Underneath a thin top dressing of grey hair combed straight back he's wearing glasses and a warm, confident smile. He seems to know what he is doing, although he could just be bluffing. Everything about him seems to suggest that this is all perfectly normal.

I feel like a weak husband, ready to faint, but I know that I must stay strong for Alice. She needs me now more than ever before.

It is right then, right at that moment, that I realise I will never ever have a baby. If I ever start getting all clucky and maternal I'll just adopt. I really will. (By the way, if you're thinking this is one of those books where the heroine will suddenly change her tune and end up with a beautiful baby in her arms by the final chapter, I'm afraid you're wrong. It doesn't happen.)

I look back at the scene and Alice is now pushing like those Scandinavian giants you get on the World's Strongest Man contests at Christmas, heaving those enormous boul-ders. She's pushing and breathing and pushing and breathing and pushing and I'm there with her. Pushing, breathing, pushing. And everyone's looking at me as if I'm mad but I don't care because this is my best friend in the whole world and this is beautiful, it is, it's the most beautiful thing in the whole world (although obviously I still don't want to do it).

233

'Come on, Alice,' I say, 'we're nearly there.'

'*We*?' she says, her eyes flashing murder. And then it arrives, the final contraction. She pushes like no woman or weightlifter has pushed before. As I begin to doubt whether my hand will ever regain feeling, Alice makes that sound again, that whimper-howl-screaming sound, and somewhere high up on a hilltop a lone prairie wolf is probably answering her call.

The senior midwife, who is now staring intensely up Alice's legs says: 'Here comes the little one. Here comes the little head.' The double use of the word 'little' is clearly ironic, judging by the fact that Alice looks as though she is about to split in two. 'Push harder, dear. There's a good girl.'

She pushes harder, and I can feel her effort. We all can. But she is on her own now. She is in a different world, a world of intense physical pain and exertion, and we can only look on.

'Aaaaaargh. Aaaaargh. Aaaaargh . . .'

Then I see it, the baby's head. And I never realised that something so hideously ugly – with all the blood and slime and fluids – could simultaneously be so incredibly beautiful. So incredibly innocent. I mean, this is what it's all about, isn't it. This is life in its purest, most undiluted form. And suddenly, right then, I feel a complete part of this. Like a proud father.

When the baby is finally, fully out, screaming as loud as you would expect someone to scream if they had spent nine months in a nice warm womb and then arrived into the outside world only to be greeted by a pile of gunk landing on their head, the senior midwife and one of the doctors check the baby and clean him.

'It's a boy,' the senior midwife tells Alice as she gently places him in her arms.

Alice breaks down at the touch of his soft, wrinkled skin.

Soft, satisfied smiles are exchanged around the room and, for a moment, life seems capable of perfection.

She looks exhausted, the life-force drained from her, but somehow her eyes are more alive than I have ever seen.

'My baby,' she says, above the screams, and looking at his tiny crumpled pink head. 'My beautiful baby.'

Chapter Seventy-One

It is Saturday morning and the screaming is no longer coming from Alice's baby. It's in my head.

I still haven't told her.

My mum.

I tried phoning her an hour ago but she must have already left.

I can imagine her right now. Sidling into the fast lane, leaning forward at the wheel, humming 'Oh What A Beautiful Morning', smiling manically in anticipation of the one event she has been looking forward to for over a year. Meeting Adam.

I feel sick.

I haven't eaten a thing all morning but I know I'm going to vomit.

I rush to the bathroom and retch over the toilet bowl. Nothing comes. I retch again. Silvery water dangles from my mouth.

Oh, this is ridiculous.

Pull yourself together, Faith.

You've just got to tell her. You've just got to tell the truth.

The truth.

Another retch. More watery nothing.

Mum, a little something I forgot to mention . . .

I'll just tell her that we broke up. How hard can that be? I mean, really? It's the truth for God sake.

But she won't believe me. She'll think there never was an Adam even when there was.

Come on. Deep breaths.

I go into the bedroom and do my make-up. Normally this has a calming effect, but not today. I am applying foundation at hyperspeed, listening out for the sound of her car and the familiar yank of the handbrake.

I'm all over the place. Nearly taking my eye out with my mascara.

I then look in the mirror and realise I am over made-up. My mum will end up saying something like I look easy. Or that no wonder I haven't managed to keep a man. Or that I'm sending off the wrong signals.

I quickly wipe it off and opt for a slightly more subtle approach. Tinted moisturiser, pale pink lip gloss and a quick brush of mascara.

Then I hear it.

The car.

Shit, she's early. But then, of course she's early. She wouldn't have been able to wait one extra minute. She'll have jumped into her Renault mum-mobile at about five this morning. I run into the living room and my horror is confirmed. I can see her trying to parallel park into a space the size of a matchbox.

As soon as the engine's off and the handbrake yanked, she leans forward in her seat and sees me standing in the window.

She waves, grinning madly.

I wave back, and force my face into a smile.

As she locks the car door and trots across the road, I realise this is going to be harder than I'd imagined. I look frantically around my living room.

Nope, still no boyfriend.

And, unless I metamorphose into Victor Frankenstein in the next five seconds, it looks like I will be unable to create one.

There is a knock on the door. My mum's eager tappety tap-tap.

OK, I tell myself, as I head out to the hallway. This is it. Over three months of fabrication completely down the drain, I realise, as I head towards my mother, distorted by the textured glass.

'Hi, mum,' I say, opening the door.

'Hi, sweetheart,' mum says, coming forward for a hug. I hug her back, breathing in the smell of her hair, temporarily forgetting why I had dreaded this moment. I hold onto the hug for as long as possible, not as a stalling tactic, but because I need this hug. Whatever else happens when I see mum, this is always the most important part. It is the fuel that keeps us going through every weekend we have had together, especially since we lost dad. More is said in these five, silent seconds than in any of our lengthy telephone conversations.

But the thing with hugs is, they don't last.

Her arms release themselves from my back and she pulls back, her hands excitedly taking a shoulder each. 'So where is he then?' she asks. 'The great mystery man.'

Chapter Seventy-Two

'Do you want a cup of tea?' I ask my mum, deflecting her enquiry.

'That would be nice,' she says. Worryingly, she walks straight down the hallway without examining the carpet for dust and mess. This is a bad sign and reminds me yet again of the sole and exclusive purpose of her visit. Meeting a man who is not here.

'Hello,' she calls, as soon as she enters the flat. My heart sinks as I fill the kettle, turning to watch her head peep into the living room, then the kitchen, and then the bedroom. 'Is he on the loo?' she asks eventually.

'No,' I say, realising that this is it. The moment I come clean. 'You see, mum, the thing is—' I look at her face, a face which has aged more in the last three years than in the previous ten. 'The thing is—'

The thing is me and Adam have finished.

The thing is we split up.

The thing is he turned out to be a complete bastard who tried to rape me.

Come on, Faith, just tell her. How bad can it be?

But as I look into her eyes I realise this is a rhetorical question. It can be very bad. Her smile is becoming vulnerable now. It is about to crumble as she starts to realise that Adam may not be here. The mystery man may still be a mystery.

'Mum, sit down,' I say, through clenched teeth. 'I've got something to tell you.'

She sits, as the kettle starts to bubble away in the kitchen. 'Well, what is it? What do you want to tell me? Have you got a promotion?'

'It's ... well ... it's ... it's about Adam.'

'Yes?' she asks, as worry shadows her face. 'What about him?'

'Well, he's not ...'

She nods, her eyes trying to usher me along.

'We're not ...'

Her face is entering a transitional phase. By the time I manage to finish this sentence, any trace of happiness or motherly love will have evaporated from her features in place of total disappointment. None of our telephone conversations will ever be the same. She will never trust me again. Never. I know that, but it's too late to turn back now.

OK. OK. Here I go.

'Mum, Adam—'

There is a knock at the door.

At first I think I am hearing things, a side-effect of the delirium I am now feeling. But then I hear it again. Three hard, steady raps on the door.

'Aren't you going to get that?' mum asks me.

'Yes,' I say, standing up in a daze. 'Of course.'

I walk out of the room and into the hallway. Through the door pane I see the blurry figure of a man in a neat blue shirt. My heart sinks as I realise I don't recognise him. It's

240

probably a Jehovah's Witness. They're always smartly dressed, aren't they? Or a door-to-door salesman, selling vacuum cleaners or something.

Anyway I'll soon find out, I think to myself, as I open the door.

Chapter Seventy-Three

The door is open and I still do not recognise this man. He is tall, dark, clean-shaven, wearing a smart blue shirt and excessively good-looking. He is a parents' wet dream. In fact, he is a wet dream, full-stop. But what the hell is he doing on my doorstep?

'Yes?' I ask, waiting for sales patter or passages from the Old Testament.

He doesn't say anything. Instead, he smiles and his eyes widen.

Oh dear.

I think he expects me to know who he is. There is something familiar about him. Something about the eyes.

But then, my life is just so jam-packed full of smart hunky strangers turning up on my doorstep it becomes easy to forget. After a while, they all just blur into one.

'Who is it?' my mum warbles from the other room.

'Is that your mum?' the man on the doorstep asks in a voice I definitely know from somewhere. Maybe he does voiceovers on the telly or something.

'Um, yes. Why?'

'Right,' he says. 'Better go and meet her then.'

'Meet? Her?'

The man walks past me and down into the hallway. I start to panic.

He could be a hit-man or something. Or a kidnapper. Or a serial killer. I mean, they always dress smart, don't they? Like in *American Psycho*. Maybe someone's got a grudge against my mum. Maybe it's one of those rude sales assistants she always goes on about, stalking her and exacting their revenge. Someone from House of Frasers or Debenhams she's managed to push over the edge. The poor bloke she bawled at for not having her new sofa in on time.

I follow the trespasser inside. 'Hey! What are you doing?'

He continues into the living room and stands himself right in front of my mum. Any minute now, I think. Any minute now he is going to pull out a gun and shoot her, right between the eyes.

His hand raises.

He doesn't have a gun!

He's going to strangle her instead.

I lunge forward and grab his arm. 'Faith,' says the man, in that strangely familiar voice. 'What on earth are you doing, darling?'

Darling.

Oh my God. He must be a sex-attacker.

And then he winks at me.

He winks!

At me!

But wait a minute. I know this man. Those eyes.

No. It can't be.

'Frank,' I gasp. And then all the colours begin to blur, and the room tilts away from me and disappears into nothing . . .

Chapter Seventy-Four

I have fainted.

When I slip back into consciousness there is a pain in the back of my head from where I have landed. My mum and Frank – *Frank* – are above me, looking worried.

'Are you OK?' Frank asks.

'Yes,' I say as they hoist me back to my feet. 'I just went dizzy.'

'You gave me the fright of my life,' my mum informs me.

'Sorry. I didn't mean to scare you.'

'I'll get you a glass of water,' says Frank. Adding: 'darling'.

I sit down, and so does my mum. After he has given me the glass of water, Frank turns to my mum and says: 'Where were we?'

'I think you were about to introduce yourself,' she tells him.

'Yes, that's right. I'm Adam. Pleased to meet you.'

Oh my God. This is too much. Not only has Frank lost his beard, tidied his hair, found a smart dress sense, along with some manners and the ability to clean himself, he has changed his name.

And then I remember.

I told him everything. I cried and blubbered my heart out to the poor lad. He knows exactly how much this means to me. Mum meeting Adam. And so, for the second time in the space of a week, he has come to my rescue.

But who'd have thought he would scrub up so good? If you ignore the fact that his eyes have a slight pink infusion and look rather tired, he looks absolutely perfect. He looks far better than Adam ever did. I mean, the real Adam. *Adam* Adam.

Well, you know what they say. Underneath every bearded, ex-alcoholic Neanderthal there's a well-groomed, sexy homo erectus just itching to get out.

But it's not just Frank who has been transformed. Look at my mum.

Before, when I used to faint at home she would work herself up into a frenzy, interrogating me. What did you have for breakfast? Are you on heroin? Are you going to bed too late? Why don't you stop this silly vegetarian nonsense?

But now, after a couple of minutes of quiet reasoned concern, she is lost in a happy trance, hanging on Frank's – sorry *Adam's* – every word. But I know she will not really be listening. She will just be lost in proud mum-thoughts.

Hasn't she done well!

Isn't he handsome!

What a smart-looking young man!

He looks rich!

After a while though a slight frown forms on my mother's forehead. 'Excuse me for asking,' she says. 'But why did Faith act so strange, when you arrived?'

'Strange?'

'Yes. She jumped on your arm.'

245

'Oh, *that*. Yes ... well ... that must just be my animal magnetism, I suppose,' he laughs. 'She can't keep her hands off me.'

Oh dear. Animal magnetism might not be the top quality my mum looks for in a prospective son-in-law, but Frank did his best, I suppose. There is an awkward pause, but then my mum is smiling again. The danger has passed.

Well, almost.

'But why did she call you Frank?' God, who is she? Jeremy Paxman?

'Frank,' I interject. 'Did I really?'

'Yes,' Frank says. 'She always calls me Frank. It's just her pet name for me. Because I've got a thing for old swing music. You know, Frank Sinatra. Mind you, I suppose he was a bit before your time, Mrs Wishart.'

'Oh no,' my mum says, bashful at the compliment. 'I love old Frank.'

I sit slumped on my chair, watching in disbelief as the scene gets even more surreal. Hell, even Salvador Dali himself couldn't have imagined what comes next. They both start singing 'Fly Me To The Moon'. No seriously. They do. Frank serenading my mum from his seat on the carpet, as if to Juliet on her balcony.

OK, so on a scale of cringe-worthiness it is up there with Celine Dion videos and those soppy bits in *Friends* they used to have before there was a wedding, but I don't care. Since dad died, any moment when mum is happy is worth its weight in gold. And I have no idea why Frank is doing this for me, but I am so grateful that I could cry.

They carry on crooning, my mum humming where she doesn't know the words.

But I don't need flying to the moon.

I'm there already.

Chapter Seventy-Five

We pulled it off.

He pulled it off.

I don't know how, but he did it. In fairness, it was touch and go for a while. I mean, my mum seemed very keen on asking him twenty questions about his job as a lawyer.

And then mum said she'd take us for a drink down the road. So we went for a drink down the road. And she asked what Frank wanted to drink and this seemed to be the question of all questions. It was as if he was being forced to rat on his own brother to Jack Bauer or something. His eyes went into panic mode as they darted over to all the upside-down spirit bottles over the bar.

'I'll have a . . . um . . . a . . . er . . .'

I was praying, silently. *Don't say vodka. Don't say vodka. Don't say vodka.*

'I'll have a mineral water,' he managed, eventually. And then, in case my mum thought he was too boring, he added: 'sparkling.'

I smiled at him. He smiled back. Somewhere in Antarctica an iceberg melted.

247

'Thank you,' I tell him, when mum goes home. 'You saved my life.'

'No,' he says. 'If we are being accurate about this, you saved *my* life. I'm simply repaying the favour.'

'You've already done that,' I remind him. 'The other night, remember. With Adam.'

'Oh well,' he shrugs. 'Let's just say you owe me one.'

'But you shaved off your beard! You bought a new shirt!'

'Steady.' He says, hand raised. 'I may have shaved off my beard, but I already had this shirt. I don't just own jumpers and T-shirts, you know.'

'OK, but still. What you did, it was a lot.'

'Well, it takes a lot,' he says sombre-faced. 'To impress parents.'

I nod. 'There's no denying that.'

But I still don't understand, I still don't know why he did it. I mean, what should he care if I lied to my mum about having a boyfriend? That's just my own stupid fault, isn't it? It's no reason to change your whole identity and meet the mother of a girlfriend you don't really have.

Chapter Seventy-Six

'Have you had any luck?' Frank asks me. 'With work?'

'No,' I say. But it's OK. I'm going to start looking properly next week.'

He nods. 'It will be all right, you know.'

'Yes.'

He then tells me a bit more about his brother. About the hospital. About what happened when he got out.

'I wanted to get drunk. I wanted to get out of my head. Because my head wasn't exactly a great place to be,' he said.

I nod and tell him, 'I can understand that.' Because I can. When dad died the whole world changed overnight, and I felt it intensely. I used to wake up in the middle of the night and feel the quiet all around and I sometimes just wanted to scream to block out my thoughts. I thought I was going mad, getting all these horror movie images in my head. And I reckon I probably would have gone mad if it hadn't been for mum. I mean, one of us needed to keep their head together.

'So about two days after I got out of hospital I hit the pub and stayed there till I was thrown out.'

'Oh dear.'

'Yeah. But I didn't go home.' I detect a freshness in his voice. As if he has never spoken about this to anyone before. 'I knew if I went home it would still be too much. So I went to find another bar and the only place nearby was this club. But it was like this house club where everyone was off their tits on E, smiling like maniacs and in walks this pissed miserable bastard in a raincoat. So anyway, I get to the bar and pay God knows how much to keep any sober thoughts at bay and I'm just standing there and this guy comes up. Not much older than eighteen. And he says, "Why the fuck aren't you dancing?" And I didn't answer him. I just carried on drinking. And then he says, "you miserable bastard" and danced off. I didn't understand it. I mean, what sort of world do we live in if you can't just go out and be a miserable bastard if that is what you want to be?' He smiles, though his eyes are trapped in the sadness of the memory.

I smile back. 'People just get scared. They think some of your misery might rub off on them.'

'That's probably it,' he says. 'But anyway, that was just it. From that day, getting pissed just seemed to be the best option. The only option, actually, if I am being honest about it.'

He carries on talking. And talking.

And talking.

But I don't mind. In fact, I am glad that someone can talk this openly and this honestly about something which hurt them so much.

It's almost as if a switch has been flicked inside him. As if all these words have been kept locked up until now and once he has started to speak there is no stopping him. And it is right now, as I listen to him try to untangle himself from the experiences he is talking about, that I realise something. Something which excites and scares me all at once.

This is a man, I realise, who needs to be loved. And then, immediately after this thought, there is another one. Even scarier.

I could be the one to do it.

To love him.

And, looking into his soft, strong eyes, I realise this wouldn't be hard at all. It would be the easiest thing in the world.

Chapter Seventy-Seven

Alice's baby is the most beautiful creature I have ever seen in my life.

At least, he is once you get over the smell. And the goo which comes out of his mouth and dribbles all over your sleeve. And the screaming at the top of his lungs – every time I touch him. And the sight of his nappy when Alice changes him.

'Well done,' she says to him, clapping her hands. 'What a big one.'

She's calling him Oscar, so I should really refer to him by his name rather than calling him 'him' all the time, shouldn't I? It's just that he's at that really early stage where even a name seems too big for him somehow.

I have never seen Alice like this.

So focused. So happy.

I had been worried that she was going to go the other way, that it was all going to be too much for her.

'Who's a lovely boy,' she is saying, nose-rubbing Oscar as he lies entranced on the carpet. 'Who's a lovely, little boy?'

'Ga,' says Oscar.

It's been two days since the birth and it is fair to say that Alice is looking knackered. In fact, she could probably walk onto the set of *Night of the Living Dead* and get concerned looks from passing zombies. But she doesn't even seem to care. Nothing is likely to break that broad maternal smile.

Nappy changed, she hoists old dribbly face back onto her knee and gets her right breast out.

'Come on, Oscar,' Alice says. 'It's your round.'

Oscar locates the nipple with as much steadfast determination as a heat-seeking missile and, nipple located, he starts to suck. Boy, does he start to suck.

'My God,' I say. 'Looks like he's thirsty.'

Alice smiles.

Then, once it looks like Oscar is in for the long haul, she asks how things are with me.

I tell her about yesterday. About Frank and how he saved me. How he looks completely different without the beard.

'Oh, how romantic,' Alice says, while Oscar tries to create more suction power than a Dyson.

'Well, I don't know about romantic, but it was very kind of him.'

'He must have a thing for you.'

'A thing?'

'Well, how else can you explain it?'

Good point. 'He's just a . . . a . . . a nice person.'

Alice laughs. 'The lady in the post office is a nice person but I doubt she'd change her identity for me.'

'Well, I don't really think of him like that.'

'So, come on, how do you think of him? Oscar really wants to know.'

But of course, Oscar couldn't give a shit. Oscar just wants booby milk, and lots of it.

'I don't know how I think of him,' I tell her. 'I suppose I had thought of him as someone I felt sorry for, you know, with all that happened with his brother. But now I'm not sure. I mean, I still feel sorry for him, but not in a charity case sort of way. I just feel grateful to him, that's all.'

'Right,' she says, teasingly.

'Oh Alice,' I say. 'Stop it.'

'Well, he must feel something for you.'

'I suppose.'

'You don't seem that happy about that fact.'

'Well, it would make things more difficult.'

'More difficult?'

'I just . . .' I wait, while Oscar loosens, then regains, his nipple-grip. 'I just don't think I'm ready for any of that. You know, after Adam.'

Alice nods her head. 'But it must be nice. To have an admirer.'

'He's *not* an admirer,' but even as I'm saying it, I am already doubting my statement.

'OK, OK. Whatever you say.'

Chapter Seventy-Eight

An hour later and we are going for a walk. Me, Alice and Oscar.

This is a big occasion for Oscar. His first proper walk outside.

It's also a big occasion for Alice. I mean, before Oscar came along she rarely made it as far as the park without having a panic attack.

But so far, she seems to be doing OK. She keeps on nuzzling Oscar in his papoose.

'Lovely boy. Lovely, lovely boy.' She blows warm raspberry kisses onto his cheek.

On our way to the park Alice asks me about my work situation.

'I'm still unemployed,' I say. 'What about you? I mean, when you get sorted out?'

'Back to stuffing envelopes.'

'High-fliers, aren't we?'

'Richard Branson eat your heart out,' she says.

We arrive at the park and the sun decides to make an appearance. Alice still seems completely panic-free as we walk around the perimeter path, passing joggers, foreign students and other young parents. We get to one of the benches and decide to sit down.

Oscar is wide-eyed with what could be amazement, but which could in fact be trapped wind.

'Yes,' Alice is saying in her baby voice. 'It's the park, isn't it? We like the park, don't we? We like coming to the park! Yes, we're a big boy now, aren't we and we go to the park with all the other boys, don't we? Yes we do. Yes we do. Yes we do.' She bounces him gently up and down.

While Alice is lost in baby-babble, I lean back and enjoy the warm breeze. A magpie lands near our feet. Then another. His beautiful wife.

The happy-feeling yesterday left me with still hasn't gone away. In fact, it seems to be getting stronger. I just cannot get over the fact that someone went to that much effort. For *me*.

So OK, I saved his life. But still, I couldn't get Alice's words out of my brain. He must feel *something* for me. But what?

I look around at the people sitting on the other benches. On the closest bench there is a group of baggy teenage boys analysing their skateboards. On the next bench along there's an old couple, dressed in beige and munching on sandwiches. On the bench after that there's ... there's ... there's ...

No.

It can't be.

Is it?

With ...

No.

But as my eyes focus properly there is no denying it. It's John Sampson, dressed in smart jeans and smart T-shirt.

And with him, canoodling, flirting by his side is Heavy Fringe.

'Oh. My. God,' I say aloud.

Alice stops bouncing Oscar. 'What?' she asks.

'You know that PR job I really wanted. And can you remember me telling you about the interviewer and how he had found out about all the bullshit I had put down on the application form?'

'Uh-huh.'

'Well, don't look now, but he's over there, with the girl with the heavy fringe. On the third bench along.'

Of course, whenever you say 'don't look now' to someone they look straight away. So Alice looks. And as she looks her face loses colour. Her smile freezes, then falls. I have seen this face before. It is the face which indicates that she is about to have a panic attack.

'Are you all right?' I ask her.

'No,' she says. 'I don't think I am. I'd probably better go home. Only, that way.' She points to the direction away from John Sampson.

'Yes,' I say. 'I think that's probably a good idea.'

Chapter Seventy-Nine

While I'm sitting on the sofa eating my Coco Pops, I see a man leave Frank's flat. A bald, fat man in a long coat. I have a strange feeling that I recognise this man, but I cannot think where from.

I'm pretty sure he must be Frank's dad, but I know we haven't been introduced. But still, there's definitely something familiar about him.

Then the phone rings.

As I go to pick up the phone I am anticipating one of three voices. Alice's. My mother's. Or the woman from the bank who keeps on saying I'd better come in and see her about my overdraft agreement.

But it's none of these voices.

It's a man's voice. 'Hello, Faith.'

'Hello?'

'It's, um, me.' Me? Who's me? Who on earth is me? 'John. John Sampson. From Coleridge Communications. I interviewed you a short while ago, for the position of account executive.'

Oh my God.

258

I remember yesterday, in the park. Him and Heavy Fringe.

'Oh,' I say. 'Um, hello.'

'Well, the thing is another vacancy has appeared. And I was, well, wondering if you were still available?'

'Available?'

'Yes. For the position?'

'Position?'

'Hmm. It's another account executive role.' His voice sounds flat, depressed. Completely different to the tone he displayed during the interview. But his words are music to my ears.

He's offering me a job!

And not just any old job, a PR job!

A *career* job!

'Um, yes,' I say. 'That sounds . . . great. I would love to.'

'OK then,' he says. 'Pop in at two today and we can talk it over in detail.'

'OK.'

'OK, bye then.'

'Yes, bye.'

Even after I have put the phone down I cannot believe what has just happened. John Sampson. *John Sampson*. The same man who made me feel about five inches tall during the interview. Talk about a change of heart.

Perhaps he realises he made a terrible mistake.

Perhaps he realises Pinocchio would make an excellent account executive.

Or perhaps not.

Perhaps he saw me in the park yesterday. He didn't seem to, but perhaps he did. And perhaps he's having an affair with Heavy Fringe and doesn't want his wife to find out.

But how am I going to tell his wife?

And why?

I don't even know who she is. And it's not like we saw anything that incriminating. They weren't kissing. They weren't holding hands.

Or perhaps he just saw me and remembered how incredibly beautiful I was and wanted to see me again.

Yeah right.

But then I remember something else.

Alice.

The way she started to panic the moment she saw him. The way she made sure we walked the other way home.

But why would Alice know John Sampson?

Why would . . .

Oh Faith, why all the questions. Just enjoy it. You've got the job you wanted. The one your mum thinks you have already. So relax.

Faith Wishart, account executive.

It does have a certain ring to it.

Chapter Eighty

On my way around to see Alice, I bump into Frank. Still beardless. Still beautiful.

He is clutching a pile of books from the library with pictures of stars on them.

'I've just got a job,' I tell him.

'Oh, that's great,' he says, genuinely pleased for me.

I tell him all about it.

He then looks a bit nervy. 'Faith.'

'Yes.'

'I was just ... I don't know ... I was just wondering ... if you fancied coming around for dinner tonight?'

My heart lifts and I go all tingly in my stomach. 'Yes,' I say. 'That would be great.'

'Great,' he says.

'Great.'

'Great.'

'I'll come round at about half seven?'

'OK. I'll see you then.'

'Yes,' I say. 'See you.'

Chapter Eighty-One

When I get to Alice's I fill her in on the Frank and job situations.

She seems happy for me about the job, but not exactly what you would call surprised. Well, her mouth falls open and she says 'Wow, that's amazing' but I can read Alice like a book. I am able to distinguish between genuine surprise and the forced variety.

And this is definitely the forced variety.

'So when are you going in?' she asks me, patting Oscar's back as he rests over her shoulder.

'Today at two.'

'And what did he say?'

'Well, he didn't say much really. Not much at all. He just offered me the job and that was it, he put the phone down. No chit-chat, no nothing.'

'Oh.' She looks worried, as she continues to help Oscar with his current wind problem.

I just sit there, watching them both, for a while. Then I get up to leave.

Halfway home I suddenly make the connection. It

suddenly all makes sense. The phone call. Alice's reaction. Her face in the park.

I phone her as soon as I get through the door.

'It was him, wasn't it?'

She doesn't say anything. Just breathes into the receiver.

'He's the father, isn't he? John Sampson is Oscar's dad. John Sampson is Peter. He'd lied about his name, hadn't he?'

'I—' her voice quivers. A quiver which tells me my suspicions are correct.

'And you phoned him, didn't you? On Monday morning. You phoned him and told him to give me the job and he rang and gave me the job because he was scared that if he didn't give me the job you would tell his wife about the affair. And about Oscar.'

'Yes,' she says, feebly. 'I'm sorry.'

'But—' My voice is cross. Angry even. But then I realise something. I realise that this isn't just about me. It's about Alice, and Oscar. And if I should be angry with anyone then I should be angry with John Sampson. After all, he's the one who lied to Alice. About not having a wife. About loving her. About his name. His job. Everything. He's the one who ran away as soon as she was pregnant. Who wanted nothing more to do with her. And Alice's only crime was to be too weak to stand up to him. Until she saw him in the park, with yet another victim. And then when she realised that he had been the one who had humiliated me in the interview, she must have finally cracked. And got on the phone. And blackmailed him.

'No,' I tell her. 'I'm sorry. But, Alice, there's no way I'm going to work for a wanker like that, whatever the circumstances.'

And I mean it.

263

There is no way.

But that doesn't stop me from going along to see him, with Alice's bank details. She had insisted I didn't do this, but I insisted it was the least he could do, and she eventually complied.

'Five hundred quid, every month,' I tell him, in his office, outlining the arrangement. 'Direct debit.'

'Right—'

'Of course, it's entirely up to you. I certainly don't want you to think I'm blackmailing you or anything. It's just that I am sure you wouldn't want Oscar to go without.'

'No,' he says. 'Of course, I wouldn't.'

I walk out of the office with a smile and a promise I know he is going to keep. En route to the lift I pass Heavy Fringe, throwing me a bitch stare, I then notice the rash running across her jaw line and down her neck.

'Oh dear, you should see someone about that,' I tell her, as the lift pings open.

Chapter Eighty-Two

'So,' Frank asks, checking on the spinach and ricotta lasagne baking away in his oven. 'You've got a job.'

'Actually, no,' I say, before embarking on the whole story.

'Oh my God,' he says. 'And what did he say?'

'Nothing. He couldn't say anything.'

'I sure wouldn't want to get on the wrong side of you.'

'No, sir,' I say, laughing. 'You wouldn't.'

'So what are you going to do about your job?' he asks.

'Oh, I don't know. I'll think of something.'

'What about your old job? Is there any chance of getting it back?'

'I doubt it,' I say.

During the meal, Frank tells me more about the theory of alternative universes. But to be honest, I am not listening. I just keep nodding my head and thinking about how gorgeous he looks all smart and beardless. His pale skin, green eyes and black hair dancing in the light of the candle he has put on the table.

He asks me what I am doing at the weekend.

I tell him about the trip to Paris. And this leads into the subject of Hope's wedding. And how everyone thinks I've got a boyfriend.

'What if I came with you?' he says.

'Are you serious?'

'Yeah,' he says. 'Why not?'

'Because you've already lied for me.'

'Faith,' he says. 'If I don't come to the wedding I've only made it worse for you.'

'But why . . . I don't understand.'

'Because,' he says, wanting to say something else. 'Because I want to.'

Chapter Eighty-Three

The night before Hope's hen weekend I stay at my brother's flat in the City. The Eurostar is going to leave early in the morning and I wouldn't make it if I had to travel down from Leeds.

I haven't seen my brother for ages. Well, not since Christmas anyway. He's been too busy working. I've been too busy inventing boyfriends.

Anyway, it's good to see him. It's Friday night so he's only just finished work. He hugs me, kissing me on the cheek.

'It's good to see you,' he says, quite formally.

In fact, everything about him is formal now I come to think about it. His suit. His side-parting.

'You look well,' I tell him.

'Likewise,' he says.

Likewise?

I have a brother who says 'likewise'? What's happened to him?

I sit down on the sofa while Mark stands there, then paces, then stands there. I start to talk about mum, about how excited she is about the wedding, about how she can't believe that one of her children is getting married.

Then the front door opens and a man with glasses and a suit walks into the flat.

'This is my flatmate,' Mark says. 'Lee.'

'Pleased to meet you,' I say.

'Likewise,' he says.

Likewise?

He looks even more nervous than Mark. And even smarter. Seriously, I don't think I've ever seen a tidier looking man in my life.

His shirt, at the end of a working day, is positively creaseless. In fact, now I come to think about it the whole apartment is shimmering. I look at the bookcase and see that the books are arranged in height order. The pot plants on the windowsill are placed at identical distances apart. The wooden floor is shiny enough to double as a mirror.

How on earth did Mark find a flatmate with his excessively high hygiene standards? Did he post a classified ad in *Anal Retentives Weekly*? (Flatmate required. Creaseless shirt and allergy to dust essential.)

I mean, when I grew up I used to have the suspicion that my brother was some kind of a freak. I loved him and everything but I used to wonder if other boys used to arrange all their cassettes in alphabetical order. I can remember once that I put back his Swing Out Sister tape between Duran Duran and Erasure. He went mad. Almost as mad as the time I spilled Ribena on his bedroom carpet. Or the time I said the reason he didn't have a girlfriend was because his legs were too skinny. That was a nasty thing to say actually now I come to think about it, but I was thirteen so I can probably blame it on the hormones.

But anyway, they are good hosts. They make me a nice pasta meal and give me some red wine and make interesting conversation. They then give me Mark's bed while Mark sleeps on Lee's floor.

Yet when I am lying there, in my brother's bedroom, I get a strange sad feeling. I remember his bedroom as a teenager. It was just as tidy, but it had character to it. There had been posters on the wall. There had been a pin board full of photos, postcards, letters and concert tickets. On every shelf or surface there had been some reflection of his personality.

But looking around this room, even in the half-light, I can feel its anonymity. It could belong to anyone. It feels stripped of identity, like a spare room.

And then I think of the evening as a whole. Of the strange air of formality. Of all the politeness.

And of how it's funny that you can grow up with someone, scream at them on a daily basis, go through the same process of losing someone you love, and yet still feel the need to be all stiff and polite with each other just because we haven't seen each other for a while.

But perhaps it's my fault, just as much as my brother's. Perhaps it's because I cannot talk openly about one single aspect of my existence. I have to carry on telling him about a job I don't have and a love-life which is now a piece of fiction.

Or maybe it's just because we've turned into grown-ups.

But I don't feel like a grown-up.

Grown-ups don't make up boyfriends.

Grown-ups don't say they work somewhere they don't.

Because that's what being a grown-up means.

It means telling the truth.

Chapter Eighty-Four

This is a nightmare.

Right now, I am somewhere under the English Channel. I am on a train surrounded by a group of women I have never met. And my sister. Who might as well be a woman I have never met.

And they are all talking in loud, competitive voices about their favourite members' clubs. Their favourite dress designers. Their favourite sexual positions.

For the first time in my life I realise why they call these things hen parties.

All this clucking and squawking and talking about cocks.

Oh, and they're all skinny. And tall. And they've all got that VIP look about them. As if they spend each night sitting in a giant tub of Crème de la Mer.

My sister keeps smiling at me, inclusively. But surely even she realises that these models and media top bods are out of my social league.

She introduced everyone when we were in the departure lounge at Waterloo. But I've forgotten all their names already. They were all called things like Natalia and

Clarissa and Tara-Jane Von Skinnyarse, but I forget who is who.

Occasionally, when I am concentrating, I join in with the giggles and nod knowingly at the right moments and I think Hope appreciates the effort. And anyway, I really should try as Hope has paid for my hotel. And on the phone she genuinely did seem like she wanted me to come.

But I keep drifting off. I keep thinking about Frank. About all that he has done for me. And even just thinking about him is starting to make me feel vulnerable. I start to worry about him. About him turning back to his old bearded, alcoholic self.

And then I start to wonder why this would bother me quite so much.

Chapter Eighty-Five

We are eating at a place called La Cantine du Faubourg, although the word '*cantine*' doesn't quite do it justice. It's all white and pink and beautiful with cartoonish artworks on the wall. It's the kind of place you'd imagine celebrities would go to, and it's probably full of them, only they'd all be French celebrities so we wouldn't be able to recognise any of them. Unless it was that woman from *Amélie*. Or Gérard Depardieu. Or Jean-Paul Gaultier. Or the guy from Eurotrash.

We are seated at a large table by one of the screen walls, where a subtle light show is going on above our heads. It's like sitting in a giant lava lamp.

The waiters, contrary to the Parisian stereotype, are very nice when they come to take our orders. Most of the women order salads although my sister, surprisingly, opts for a large pasta meal. I have the same, because it is one of the few vegetarian options.

They also order two bottles of the most expensive champagne. Well, of course they do. I mean, they would, wouldn't they?

'I can't believe you two are sisters,' says skinny-arse number one, shaking her head in disbelief.

'Neither can I,' says skinny-arse number two. 'Although you do have very similar eyebrows.'

'So tell me,' says skinny-arse number three. 'Why on earth do you live in Leeds?'

'Where exactly *is* Leeds?' asks skinny-arse number four.

'Oh,' says skinny-arse number one, as my meal arrives. 'I'd love to be like you. I'd love to not give a toss about my weight.'

I smile and smile and smile but inside I am plotting their very painful, drawn-out deaths.

After the meal my sister heads for the toilets.

I instantly panic at the thought of being left alone with these squawking hens. They all start talking about how lucky she is, to be marrying someone as sexy and rich as Jamie Richards.

'What about you?' skinny-arse number two asks, turning to me. 'Is there a man in your life?'

'Um, yes,' I say, keeping up with the lie. 'Adam.'

'And what is he?'

'He's a, er, lawyer. In Leeds.'

'Ah,' says skinny-arse number one, scrunching her nose. 'How sweet.'

Bloody hell, even my lies are being patronised. My sister still hasn't returned and I cannot take another second so I too head for the loos.

I pick a cubicle next to the only other locked door. I assume it must be my sister but don't say anything just in case. I just sit there, not able to pee, killing time.

There is a sound. A whimpering sound. My sister is crying.

273

After she has blown her nose and controlled her tears, she flushes the chain and leaves her cubicle. I leave mine too.

She is surprised to see me. 'Hi,' she says, her skin pale.

'Hi,' I respond, not knowing what else to say. This is her hen night, after all. And I don't want to ruin it. But I can tell she wants to say something else.

'I felt a bit funny,' she says. 'I think it's probably just wedding nerves.'

'Right,' I say. 'Oh dear.'

She takes a deep breath. She wants to say something else, I can feel it. But she doesn't say anything, because tears get in the way.

'Hey,' I say, placing my arms around her. 'Hey, it's all right. It's all right.' A smart-looking Parisian eyes us suspiciously as she walks past.

'No,' Hope says. 'It's not. I'm a mess. I know you think I've probably got everything but I feel terrible. I feel fat and terrible.'

'Fat? You're a rake!'

She smiles through the tears. It's a you-mean-well-but-you-don't-know-what-you're-talking-about sort of smile. 'It's not like the real world. I'm not surrounded by real people, you know, like you. I'm surrounded by stick insects, like *them*,' she says, indicating the table of skinny-arses beyond the toilet wall. 'There's so much pressure. If I want to do another yoga video I should lose at least five pounds. And Jamie—'

'And Jamie what?'

'Jamie says I'm being silly.'

'Well, Jamie's right. You don't need to lose it,' I tell her, but realising that, as a 'real person' my words will only have so much effect.

'You won't tell anybody, will you?'

'No.'

'You won't tell mum, will you?'

'No.'

'You won't say anything tonight?'

'No. Course I won't.'

She looks at me with eyes which were never so helpless. I cannot help but wonder what has happened to her. I realise that all the things I have been jealous of – her looks, her money, her career, her love-life – haven't really helped her one bit. She's more insecure now than when she was fifteen.

And then I realise. Perhaps it affected her more than I've given her credit for. Dad dying. Perhaps she went to Australia not because she couldn't handle grief. The pain. Perhaps she's never really faced up to it, and perhaps she's still living with it now.

'Thank you,' she says. And then she hugs me.

And then we go back out into the throng and realise that all the skinny arses are standing, giraffe-like, next to the sculpted slate bar.

My sister buys me a cocktail. And I decide not to mention another word about what just happened.

'What do you think of them?' she asks.

I look over at the giraffes, sucking on straws. 'They're very nice,' I lie. 'Very friendly.'

'Pants on fire,' she says. 'They're complete bitches, the lot of them. But they can be quite a laugh sometimes, when you get to know them.'

I laugh. I haven't seen this side of my sister for a while. Make that a decade. And we talk and we carry on talking and then we move onto the topic of Jamie. She says how much she loves him. And how romantic he is. I cannot deny that – for Hope at least – it seems like the real thing. But

275

even the real thing doesn't seem enough to make her secure about herself. But yet however depressed she gets at the moment, she would probably be happier with him than without him.

As the skinny-arsed hens cluck and squawk behind us I clink her glass and wish her luck. She holds my hand and says thank you for being a true sister. And a true friend.

Chapter Eighty-Six

When I get back to Leeds I go around to see Frank.

In fact, every day before my sister's wedding I go around and see Frank. With Alice preoccupied with midwives and mother and baby groups (so preoccupied that she hasn't had a panic attack since the John Sampson incident), and with my mum focused solely on Hope's wedding, Frank is the only person I can really talk to.

And every day brings us closer. So close, in fact, that weird things are happening to me.

Frank, the man I brought back to life, is now doing the same for me.

It's true. I really do feel alive. I think that, for once in my life, my existence actually means something to someone. Someone who isn't my mother or Alice. Someone I like, and like a lot, is liking me back, and that's a nice feeling. All of a sudden I feel there is a point to being me. Not a very big point, not a Nelson Mandela point, not a Ghandi point, not even a Beyoncé Knowles point, but a point all the same.

I want to bottle this feeling. I want to store it and save it for a rainy day. But even rainy days aren't what they used to be. They just seem like the backdrop to one never-ending pop video. And it's a pop video for The Carpenters. Or Sister Sledge. 'Frankie,' that would be appropriate, I suppose.

Because the world looks different. Different enough to make me believe Frank could be more than just a good friend. Everything connects. The trees, the roads, the cars, the buildings, they are all as much a part of each other as lips and eyes are part of the same face. I can see the beauty in everything. The whole world has had a makeover.

But then, on the evening before the wedding, Frank says he has noticed it too. That whole Carpenters' video thing.

' "The way birds suddenly appear," ' he says. ' "Every time, you are near." '

I laugh, nervously, but then I stop and realise that Frank's face is rather close to mine. A short, kissing-distance away. I look into his eyes and get scared. Scared of how easy it would be to love him.

'Why are you doing all this?' I ask him.

'Because I care about you. And I think I will always care about you.'

I find it weird how someone can say that about me. Someone who knows the truth, about all my lies. 'Well, you shouldn't.'

'Well, I do.'

His lips are moving closer. But instead of heading for my mouth, they land on my forehead with a soft peck. 'Anyway,' he says. 'We should probably have an early night. Big day tomorrow.'

Chapter Eighty-Seven

On the start of our long train journey down to Sussex and the small village where my sister is getting married, Frank looks uneasy. At first, I assume it's just nerves. That he's just nervous at all the lies that lie ahead.

But as I am on the phone to mum (who arrived on Hope's doorstep at seven this morning after a night on the motorway), I know something else is bothering him.

'Frank,' I ask, once I have told my mum exactly where we are on the rail network and put my mobile away. 'Are you OK?'

'Yes,' he says.

'Is it about today? Are you nervous?'

'I just wonder where it's going to end?'

'End?'

'I mean, after today. There will be other times you have to lie to your mum about Adam. What then?'

He has a point. It's not as if I can expect Frank to be a continual stand-in replacement. 'So what are you saying? Are you saying I should tell my mum I don't have a boyfriend? I should tell her the truth? That you're just my friend?'

He says nothing. Just rests his head against the window as we pass through a station too quickly to read the sign. 'Maybe.'

'But if you think that then why are you here? What's the point of even coming if it's not to help me keep up the lie?'

Again, he says nothing. And this time he looks hurt. I think of what I have just said, and an answer to my own question forms in my mind. Perhaps he's here because . . .

'I have . . . I care a lot about you, Faith,' he says. 'That is why I'm here.'

I look at his soft, beautiful lips. The delicate cupid's bow. I remember how much I wanted to kiss him last night.

'I know,' I say. 'I'm sorry.'

'I—' He says something else, but I cannot hear because just at that moment we pass another train travelling in the opposite direction.

'Sorry?'

He pauses. 'Nothing,' he says. 'It was nothing.'

'So you think I should tell my mum that I don't have a boyfriend?'

And then he says, 'Not necessarily.'

'What do you mean?'

He stares straight at me, and leans forward over the table.

'I mean, what if I was your boyfriend?'

My heart is racing. Suddenly this makes sense. All those weird music video feelings I've got. For a moment I am not even thinking about my mum or my lies or the day ahead. I am thinking about what Frank just said.

He wants to be my boyfriend.

I lean forward, across the table, and kiss him softly on the lips. My eyes are closed. And nothing else matters. None of the other train passengers. Nothing.

Then there is a voice, from above. 'Tickets please.'

280

We pull away from each other and look for our tickets, smiling like embarrassed children. We show our tickets and I think about all that Frank has done for me. How he even bought his own train ticket, on what little he must have left of his student loan.

When the ticket inspector has gone I know exactly what to say. 'OK.'

'OK what?' Frank asks.

'About you being my boyfriend. And about telling mum.'

Frank smiles. He knows what a big thing that was for me to say. 'Faith, if you don't want to. I mean, I know I'm not a lawyer or anything.'

'No,' I say. 'I want to.' And then, thinking for a second about mum I say, 'But is it OK if we wait till after? You know, at the reception.'

'Sure,' he says, still smiling. 'Of course.'

Chapter Eighty-Eight

I cannot believe it.

I have agreed to tell the truth.

For Frank.

And it will change everything. Because that's the funny thing with telling the truth. You go around stewing in the juices of all the secrets you lock inside feeling like a terrible person, but knowing the lies make you look wonderful. And then, when you pluck up the courage to tell the truth, to actually feel good rather than look it, everyone thinks you are the terrible person you've actually said goodbye to by coming clean.

Because telling the truth is about revealing the lies. And the moment you've done that, that can be all anyone sees. The lies.

But I don't care anymore. If it all boils down to a choice between feeling good and looking good, I'll opt for the first one.

Chapter Eighty-Nine

We are all in the church.

Frank, who for now must remain Adam, is by my side. As is my mum. And behind us is Mark, who has brought his flatmate Lee as his 'plus one'.

Standing in front of the altar is Mr Fitness Guru to the Stars himself, Jamie Richards. He looks smaller than I had imagined, and seems to be wearing less fake tan than on the cover of his videos. But he seems OK. I mean, he turned and smiled at us, having guessed who we are.

The church is small but perfectly formed. It's like one of those picture postcard English churches you get in Hugh Grant films, apart from the laminated hymn sheets which let the side down a bit. I mean, this is a place of holy worship not a flaming Little Chef.

But no, hymn sheets aside this is the business. Quaint old wooden pews. Big stone arches. Stained glass windows depicting scenes from the Bible I'm not familiar with. There's that whole churchy atmosphere. Oh, what's the word for it?

Reverential, that's it. If I was religious (which I am, sometimes, when I'm in the right mood) this is definitely where I'd want to come. It's the perfect place to come and stand, quietly waiting for heaven.

I look at mum and can see that she's already there. In heaven, I mean. Her cheeks are flushed, she is biting her top lip, her eyes are starting to well up, and she's got that kind of radioactive glow proud mothers always seem to generate on these types of occasion. She looks like she could explode as a result of an overload of sentimental feeling. By the end of the service there'll probably be a queue of UN weapons inspectors wanting to see whether she is likely to detonate.

'This will be you one day,' she says, loud enough for Frank to overhear.

I turn to him and roll my eyes. 'I'm sorry,' I tell him, squeezing his hand. 'I think she's a bit overexcited.'

He just smiles and squeezes my hand back, saying nothing.

I want to ask him how he does that. How he is always able to make me feel better without saying anything at all. But it's not really the time or the place, so I just wait and soak up the occasion.

Jamie Richards and his perfect buttocks are standing in front of the altar, as they wait for the future Mrs Richards. Jamie's buttocks twitch nervously, and he looks around to the open church door where some late guests are just arriving.

Perhaps he thinks she won't show. His nervy arse certainly seems to be in doubt.

And then I think, perhaps she really *won't* show. I remember Paris. Her crying in the toilets. Her insecurities.

I look around at my mum's face, shadowed by her hat brim (with a circumference vast enough to circle Jupiter), but still generating radioactive contentment. It would absolutely crush her, and this is a woman who has been crushed one time too many. She would probably just fall apart.

I turn around and look at my brother. He seems to be thinking the same as me because he makes a worried face and then glances at mum. We both know that it could happen. After all, she's run away from things before. Perhaps she's decided to go back to Australia.

But just as a shadow of doubt passes across my mother's face, a communal hush fills the church and the organ starts to play *The Wedding March*.

I look around and there she is. More beautiful than she has ever looked, wearing a simple white dress.

She is being walked down the aisle by someone I assume is Jamie's father. There is something terribly sad about this sight and then I realise why.

I think of dad. I think of how much today would have meant for him. How much he would have wanted to be walking next to his youngest daughter on her big day. To be giving her away.

Hope catches my eye and smiles. I feel closer to her than I ever have. She is happy we are here and sharing in her joy. But the funny thing is, that is really how I am feeling. I really am happy for her. Her joy is really being shared. For once in my life there is no jealousy or anger or resentment that she has upstaged me.

I must be coming down with something.

The service starts. The vicar begins to talk. There are a lot of words like 'union', 'matrimony' and 'in the presence of God'.

There are more words and then they say their vows and their 'I dos' and Jamie turns to his best man, his brother I think, and takes the ring and places it on Hope's finger. My mum whimpers. Frank gently squeezes my hand.

They kiss. Eyes closed, like they mean it.

It's a perfect moment, and the whole congregation is ready to break out into spontaneous applause.

But as we walk out of the church into the bright golden sunlight, I am already thinking about the reception. And my promise to Frank.

Chapter Ninety

The reception is being held in a posh hotel two miles outside of the village. That poshness is evident in the slow gravelly crunch as we make our way down the driveway. It is also indicated by the string quartet who are playing outside the entrance and by the waiters, carrying silver trays over their heads, on the tips of their fingers. Oh, and by the hats. There are more hats than Royal Ascot.

When we arrive the place is already full and the canapé munching is well underway. While the men swig back drinks, female voices can be heard everywhere.

'Didn't she look lovely?'

'Wasn't she beautiful?'

'What a lovely vicar!'

'Oh, the *dress*!'

My mum is talking to Jamie's dad, Tom. He is handsome in a Sean Connery type way and he's got a broad warm smile. I remember Hope telling me he is divorced and I wonder, for a moment, if mum would ever settle down again with another man. She certainly seems back to her old self. There is a lot of nodding going on, and my mum still appears to be in heaven, working her proud-smile muscles to near fatigue.

My brother is talking to his flatmate in serious, hushed tones, as they nibble neatly on their anchovy-stuffed olives.

I wonder what they are saying.

They stand out, I realise, from the crowd.

They are the only ones in the whole room not wearing a smile, false or otherwise.

Well, apart from Frank. Maybe it's because he's confined himself to San Pellegrino while the rest of the room slurps on something a bit stronger.

'Are you OK?' I ask him, before sipping on my glass of champagne.

'Yes,' he says, looking slightly worried. 'Are *you* OK?' asks Frank, clearly wondering when I am going to tell my mum the truth.

'Yes,' I say. 'I'm fine. Fine. It's just ...' I spot Hope and Jamie taking a present from a small old lady '... is it OK, if we wait a couple of hours? Just until Hope goes to St Lucia. I can always tell Hope when she comes back, can't I?'

Frank looks at me, a slight look of doubt passing across his face. 'OK,' he says. 'Sure.'

'You do look smart,' I say, trying to make him feel better. And anyway, he does. His suit looks like it cost a bomb, and I start to wonder about the state of his bank balance.

Hope catches my eye and makes her way over, dragging Jamie behind her. The insecure woman I consoled a week ago in Paris no longer seems to be evident.

'Hi, Faithy,' she says.

'Hi,' I say. 'You look wonderful.'

'This is Jamie,' she says.

'Hi, Jamie,' I say.

288

He leans over and kisses me on the cheek. 'Hi,' he says quietly. 'Pleased to meet you.' Then he shakes Frank's hand. I realise, seeing him close-up, that he is just a normal person. OK, so he's a normal person who has patented his own style of butt-press and who will happily get sucked off at a restaurant, but still, he seems to genuinely love my sister. And that's good enough for me.

'And this is,' I look at Frank. 'Adam.'

'Oh hi, Adam, I've heard so much about you. I can't believe it! My sister! With a lawyer!'

'Yes,' I say, feeling embarrassed for Frank.

We exchange some more happy niceties and then Hope says she has to say hi to a few people before they fly off to St Lucia.

'OK,' I say. 'Happy honeymoon.'

After they disappear amid the crowd, I turn to Frank and say 'Sorry.'

He looks at me, then looks at the clock, wondering how long he has to keep up the Adam lie. 'It's OK.'

Chapter Ninety-One

Two hours later Hope and Jamie have gone off to Gatwick. And I have been trying to drink up the courage to tell my mum.

The room is starting to spin.

Everywhere are mad smiles and even madder hats.

'I think you should probably slow down,' Frank advises.

There is a door. A brown wooden door with the word 'Cloaks' inscribed on it. I grab hold of Frank's hand and lead him towards it.

'Faith, may I ask what you are doing?'

'Shush,' I tell him, loudly, as I open the door and then shut it behind us.

'Faith, why are we in the cloak—' He is unable to complete his sentence owing to the fact that my lips are on top of his mouth.

'Faith—' he says, coming up for air. But again my lips force him into submission.

I start to grapple with his shirt, loosening his tie, undoing buttons, in a restless frenzy of lust. He joins in too, for a moment, hoisting up my skirt, but then he stops.

'No, Faith, we can't.'

'What do you mean, we can't?'

'It's wrong,' he says, pulling away. He does up his buttons.

'But—'

He kisses my cheek. 'I'm not Adam,' he says. 'There's only one thing I want you to do for me. And that's to tell your mum the truth.'

'OK,' I say, sobering at the thought. 'I'll tell her now.'

Chapter Ninety-Two

We make our way out of the cloakroom and across the crowd until we get to my mum, who is over at the buffet table. She is looking at someone. I turn and follow her gaze to the smart suited figure of Tom Richards.

'Mum, I need to tell you something.'

She smiles. 'Oh don't tell me,' she says. 'You're tying the knot as well.'

'No,' I say, closing my eyes. 'It's not that.'

'Go on, then. What is it?' And then, popping a little flaky pastry thing in her mouth, she adds: 'Aren't these nibbles gorgeous?'

'Yes, mum. They are.'

'Go on, then,' she says. 'Tell me your big secret.'

'Well, you see, the thing is . . .' I look at Frank, who is clearly anxious for his true identity to be revealed. 'The thing is . . .' And then I look at my mother. I have never seen her this happy. Well, not since dad died anyway. Am I really wanting to puncture that happiness? Isn't it actually more selfish to tell her than to keep quiet? 'The thing is . . . Frank . . . we're . . . I'm . . . I'm getting promoted.'

'Promoted? Oh Faith, that's wonderful.'

Frank, however, looks less than happy with this made-up newsflash. In fact, he turns and walks out of the room.

My mum has me by my arm. She seems completely oblivious to Frank's sudden disappearance. 'Wow, so you'll be getting more money,' she says.

'Yes,' I say, already kicking myself.

'Congratulations, Faith,' she says. 'I'm so proud of you. And somewhere up there,' she points to the ceiling, 'your dad is smiling down on you.'

No. He is saying, 'Bloody hell, Faith. Just tell her the truth for once.'

'Mum, I'd just better go upstairs to our room. Check on Fr . . . Adam.'

'OK, dear. You run along.'

Chapter Ninety-Three

When I get back to the hotel room Frank is packing his suitcase. 'What are you doing?' I ask him.

'I'm going.'

'Going?'

'Yes.'

'But we're meant to be staying tonight.'

Frank doesn't look up, just carries on packing. 'I'm sorry.'

'But what will I tell mum?'

'Oh,' he says. 'I'm sure you'll be able to think of something.'

I don't like his tone. 'What's that supposed to mean?'

'Well, couldn't I have some important legal case to sort out. Something like that.'

Now I get it. 'Is this because I didn't say anything to mum?'

The silence tells me that it is.

'I'm sorry, Frank, I couldn't. I just couldn't. You saw her face. If I'd have told her it would have completely crushed her. Today was about my sister, not about me.'

But even as I am defending myself I know I am making things worse. Because I know what he is thinking. He is wondering which part would have crushed her. The fact that I lied, or the fact that my real boyfriend couldn't match up to my fictional one.

'It's all right,' he says, his lips sternly holding back any emotion. 'I understand. I really do. It's just that I'll never be able to live up to the man you've made up in your head so it's probably best if we just stop it before it starts. Because I would only end up letting you down. I'm not a career-minded lawyer. I'm a thirty-year-old student.'

I hesitate. I want to tell him that he is wrong. That I don't care what he is.

But I don't.

Something stops me. Because perhaps, deep down inside, I'm not just worried about my mother's approval, I'm worried about my own approval. Maybe he's right. Maybe he won't ever be able to live up to the man in my head. I mean, I certainly wouldn't have *invented* a recovering alcoholic whose main interest in life is exploring the possibility of alternative universes.

So my mouth opens and closes but there are no words to come out.

Frank zips up his suitcase and looks at me as if I have managed to disappoint him yet again. 'We are opposites,' he tells me. 'Total opposites. I couldn't care less about the things you care about. Looking good. I couldn't give a toss how I looked. I don't care about fashion or beauty or make-up and, last time I checked, you weren't that enthralled by the topic of universal sub-atomic matter.'

'But—'

'And don't give me that stuff about opposites attracting. Opposites don't attract. My mum and dad were opposites.

Opposites fall out and get divorced and then argue about who owns what. That's what happens to opposites.' He picks up the suitcase by the handle and moves around the bed, stopping right in front of me. 'I'm sorry, Faith. About your mum. But at least she'll think Adam really existed.'

I want to stop him. I want to pin him down to the bed and make him wait, but too much is going on in my brain right now.

'So, you're going back to Leeds?' I ask him.

'Tonight,' he says. 'Yes. But tomorrow I'm going to go to my mum's. And I'm going to stay there quite a while. I just need to be out of Leeds at the moment, it's just not healthy.'

'Your mum's?'

'In Edinburgh.'

'But where is she? I mean, what's the address?'

'You don't want the address. Faith, it's over. We've repaid our favours and it's over.' His face still stubbornly refusing to show any emotion.

'But I . . .'

He waits, expectantly. Looking, just for a moment like he wants me to finish my sentence. And I know there are words that could stop him, there are three words, to be accurate, but I don't know if they're the right ones. I don't know if I would just be telling yet another lie.

'I . . .' The words still don't come.

Frank sighs, as if the inability to say what I need to say is the final confirmation that he needs. I know I want him to stay. I *know* that. But what I don't know is *why*. Is it for mum? Or is it for me? And if it's for me is it only because I want to keep up appearances?

I don't know. And because I don't know I stand there motionless as Frank and his tartan suitcase leave the hotel room.

296

'Goodbye, Faith,' he says, turning at the door. 'I'll see you.'

He bites his top lip, and offers a sad farewell smile.

'I'll see you,' I say, blankly, not knowing what I have just allowed to happen.

Chapter Ninety-Four

I sit on the bed for about ten minutes. Part of me wants to follow Frank. A big part of me, but not big enough.

The thing is, today is about Hope. It is about mum. It's not about me, and I have no intention of turning it into the Frank and Faith mini-drama.

But as every Frank-less second goes by, I feel worse. I know that I've got to come up with some legitimate reason why Frank has suddenly decided to pack up and go, but for some reason I can't think of one.

This is weird.

I mean, this is what I'm good at. Making things up. But suddenly my capacity for bullshit seems to have abandoned me.

And I know why.

It's Frank.

I love him. Madly. And when I am with him he makes me feel happy to be me. That's the *me* me, rather than the me I make up to my mum. Because that's the thing, the reason I used to lie to mum wasn't just because she wouldn't like the truth. It was because *I* didn't like it.

But now I don't care. Frank has made me feel that there's more to being me than my job, or lack of it. That I am no less or more of a person, wherever I work. Or however much I earn.

I have realised that love has nothing to do with career prospects. Frank is thirty years old. He is in the middle of a PhD course looking into alternative universes. He couldn't be more unemployable if he tried.

But I still love him.

I am a part of him. I brought him back to life. I have helped him overcome his grief. No promotion could ever match that.

No raise in salary could match the sound of his voice. Or the way he looks at me. The way he seems to understand my every thought.

He has helped me see things more clearly. And even now, even by walking out he has made me see.

I have made a mistake.

But there could still be time to catch him. I run out of the room, through the corridor and downstairs out of the entrance, out onto the gravel drive.

He's either managed to find a taxi or he's gone and bloody run for the last train. Either way, I've left it too late.

'Frank!' I shout, pointlessly. 'Frank!'

I go back inside.

There are people everywhere. Drunk laughter. Tacky music. Dancing uncles.

I spot my mum, brother and Lee, over by the food. I head straight over.

'I need your car,' I tell my brother.

'My darling sister,' he says.

'I need your car. I've got to drive somewhere.'

'You can't drive,' he reminds me.

299

Good point. 'OK, but I need you to drive me some-where.'

'I'm over the limit,' he says. And, as if to prove it, he throws a stuffed olive into the air and attempts to catch it with his mouth. It lands on his cheek.

'Oh Mark, behave yourself,' says my mother.

I look at mum but can see from her eyes that she too is about ten glasses of champagne away from being a legal motorist.

'Faith, is everything OK?' I notice her tone is closer to cross than concerned.

'Yes, I'm—' No, Faith. No, you're not fine. I look out across the room to see if there is anyone sober enough to drive who I could bribe into spending the rest of the evening on the M1. But no one over the age of seventeen looks capable of tying their own shoelaces.

'No mum,' I say. 'No, actually I'm not very fine right now. You see, I really have to tell you something.'

'Is is about you and Adam?' she asks.

'Yes, mum. Yes it is.'

'You're not ... you're not ... you're not *swingers,* are you?'

Oh this is hopeless.

'No, mum, we're not.'

'Only I saw a programme about it the other week.'

'We're definitely not swingers.'

'Good,' she says, reassured. 'Because it all looks very unhygienic.'

'Mum, please, would you just listen. Just for a second.'

I look at Mark and his Lee, and realise it's not just my mum who I am telling this earth-shattering piece of infor-mation to.

I swallow. 'Mum, Adam is not who you think he is.'

'Oh really,' she says, slurring slightly. 'You know, I knew it. Right from the very first time I saw him, I knew it.'

'You did?'

'Why, of course I did. You can't fool me.'

'I can't?'

'Why no,' she says, taking a sip from her already empty glass of champagne. 'Of course you can't. You can see it a mile off.'

'You can?'

'Yes, you can see it in his face. You can tell from his hair line. So what was he before?'

'Before?'

'Let me take a guess,' she says thoughtfully, her finger on her chin. 'Adriana? Adele? Adrienne? Am I warm? Am I getting closer?'

'Mum, what are you going on about?' And then I get it. 'Mum, he hasn't had a sex change.'

'Oh,' she says, taken aback. 'Well what has he had done then?'

'He hasn't had anything done.'

'So what is it?'

'It's just that he's not who you think he is. He's Frank.'

I look at my brother, who seems to be getting there a little bit faster.

'Well, it's good that he speaks his mind,' mum says.

Oh God. 'No. Not *frank*, Frank. His name is Frank, not Adam.' My mum is starting to understand so I keep going. 'There never was an Adam. Well, there was, but not at first. It was an invention. I made him up.'

Sobriety has returned to my mother's face. Even her sense of balance seems to have been restored. 'I don't—'

'I know, I'm sorry. It was a terrible thing to do, but you have to understand I only did it because I ... because I

301

wanted you to be happy. Because I wanted you to be proud of me.' Right, that's where I should leave it, call it a day. That's enough confessions for one wedding. But I can't help it, it's like I've released some unstoppable force from deep inside me. Like a fountain of truth or something. As though all that matters right now is Frank, and how I've managed to let him down, along with myself. 'And I lied about my job as well. I never worked in PR. I was a make-up girl. I worked on the Keats Cosmetics counter. But now I'm unemployed because ... because ...' OK, some secrets should always stay locked away '... because I am. And Frank isn't a lawyer. He's about to start a PhD looking into the possibility of alternative universes. Which basically means he's as skint as I am.'

My mother is shocked, to say the least. You know those photos you get at theme parks which are taken just as you are about to go down the log flume or the steepest bit of a roller coaster and your mouth is wide open and your hair is all standing up and it looks as though you are going to be sick? Well, that's my mother's face right now. And I am responsible. Jesus, what an idiot. At my sister's wedding.

But just as I am on the point of collapsing from guilt, my brother stands forward, against the protests of Lee. There is a look of quiet resolution on Mark's face as he starts to speak.

'Lee isn't just my flatmate,' he says, looking my mum square in the eye. 'He's my partner. I'm gay.'

She looks confused.

'Mum, I'm gay.'

God is a very big fan of cheesy sit-coms. That moment, the moment my brother comes out of the closet after three decades of hiding his sexuality, is also the same moment that the wedding DJ plays 'In the Navy' by The Village People.

The irony is lost on my mother, who appears to have gone into some kind of vertical coma.

'Mum,' Mark is asking her. 'Are you OK?'

But she is not responding.

'Mum?' I say, waving my hand in front of her face. 'Mum? Can you still hear us?'

Still no response.

We wait, while the DJ slows the pace down with something soft and, in my current state of mind, heart-breaking. Dido, I think.

Then, from somewhere behind me, there is a man's voice. It's Tom. Jamie's dad.

'Doreen,' he is saying to my mother. 'I wonder if you would care to join me on the dance floor.'

Mum looks at him, her face still in shock. A different kind of shock though now. A happy shock.

'Oh,' she says. 'Oh yes. Yes. Why not?'

She trots off for her smooch as if nothing has happened. I look at my brother, whose raised eyebrows tell me he's as surprised as I am.

'What do you make of that?' I ask him.

'I don't know. Maybe we got her wrong. Maybe we should have been honest with her all along. Perhaps we just *assumed* she'd have a problem.'

'Oh well,' I say looking over at my mum on the dance floor with a handsome man. 'Tom Richards seems to have softened the blow.'

But now my mum seems well on the way to getting over her double shock my mind shifts back to Frank. I try and think of a way to contact him.

But he doesn't even have a mobile phone. Well, not one that works. It was cut off when he stopped his payments when his brother died.

I could call a taxi. But Sussex to Yorkshire would be quite an expensive fare, and I don't think mum's in exactly the right mood to lend me some money.

'Are you OK?' I ask Mark.

'Yeah,' he sighs. And then: 'I didn't mean to do that, you know, I didn't mean to say it like that. I didn't want to hurt her.'

'No. I know. Neither did I.' Before I know it I am crying. For Frank. For mum. For Mark. For the universe. For everything.

My brother hugs me. 'Hey, come on, sis, it's OK. It's OK.' I worry that I am getting tears on his neatly ironed shirt.

'I love you,' I tell him, for the first time since I can remember.

'I love you too,' he says. Then he laughs. 'Just go easy on the shirt, OK?'

Chapter Ninety-Five

My brother knocks on my door first thing the next morning. He is dressed. He is shaven. He is immaculate.

'Morning,' I croak, weary from the hour and a half's worth of sleep I've had.

'Come on then,' he says. 'Let's go.'

'Go?'

'To Leeds. I'm going to drive you back. Let's try and see if we can get you there in time. Before lover boy leaves.'

'I don't understand.'

'There's nothing to understand. Grab your clothes, and let's go.'

'But what about mum? What about Lee?'

'They're both still asleep. They probably won't be up for hours. I could be there and back by that time. And anyway, I've left mum a note. And we can phone her mobile from the car. Now come on, let's go.'

Mark is a maniac. Or at least, drives like one.

Seriously, he hardly drops below seventy the whole

journey. We make it to Leeds in under three hours, but we are still too late.

Frank has gone.

I thank Mark and apologise for his big waste of time and petrol. He hugs me and tells me if I need anything else to just call him. While we are hugging I wonder why I ever used to get jealous or annoyed about him, and his career in futures. I also wonder why he never told me he was gay and whether it was because he didn't trust me to keep quiet or because he didn't know how I would react.

'Drive carefully,' I tell him, as he starts the engine.

'I will. Take care, sis.'

'Yes. You too.'

Chapter Ninety-Six

The flat has never looked so depressing.

The orange carpet, the swirly wallpaper, the barred up kitchen window have lost what little characterful charm they once had.

How big is Edinburgh? Not that big, surely. I could find him, if I tried hard enough. I could get a train and walk the streets and scour the phone book and ask people in bars and coffee shops, the way they do in movies.

I lie on the sofa and stare out of the window, watching the pattern of rain forming on the glass. Already I am losing him, in my mind. His face. His whole physical presence. Perhaps I am trying too hard to remember, to picture him, to hear his voice. All I want to hear is him talking about alternative universes or Al Greene. I just want *him*.

The cushion is a poor substitute but it doesn't stop me hugging it, and I stay here, curled up on the sofa, thinking of a man who exists, but might as well not, until my eyes grow heavy and I drift off into sleep.

A while after – how long I have no idea – I jolt awake.

There is a sound.

A music sound.

This could still be a dream. This *must* still be a dream. A dream about Frank.

Because it's Al Greene. It's 'I'm So Tired of Being Alone'. And it's being played at full volume.

I sit up and pinch myself. Then pinch myself again.

This is not a dream.

I weigh up in my head the chances of there being a new basement tenant. And then the chances of that new basement tenant being a fan of Al Greene. While I am weighing up, a new song comes on. It's 'I'm Still in Love With You'.

Five seconds.

That's how long it takes me to get to my front door. I run down the stone steps and knock frantically on his window. 'Frank! Frank!'

I can hear, above Al Greene's soulful singing, the sound of a latch. The door opens.

It's him.

'Frank!' I say. 'Frank!'

'Hello, Faith,' he says.

'It's you!'

He looks down. 'It is.'

'But I thought you would be in Edinburgh.'

'I thought I would be too,' he says. 'But something seemed to hold me back,' he waits, prolonging my agony, before he adds: 'Some*one*.'

It is raining heavy but I can hardly feel it. I must look a total mess in this soaking baggy top, but somehow it doesn't seem to matter.

'I told my mum,' I say. 'I told my mum everything. All my lies. When you left the hotel I told her.'

He nods, but seems to be waiting for me to say something else.

'I love you,' I tell him. 'I really love you.'

He looks at me, confused. I don't think I have ever felt this vulnerable in my entire life. But I had to tell him because it is the truth. And because it is the truth I could stand here all day in the freezing wet rain saying the same thing.

He steps forward, out into the Leeds weather. He looks down at me, gorgeous and ungroomed, and holds my face in his hands. And that is when I know.

But it's still good to hear him say it. 'I love you too.'

He looks at me and as he looks I feel a million different things inside. I realise that there is nowhere more romantic right now. No Eiffel Tower, no Venetian gondola can compare with this wet doorstep in West Yorkshire.

I realise also that if we don't move inside pretty soon, one of us will die of pneumonia.

'This is where you kiss me,' I tell him, hurrying things along.

'Oh yes,' he says. 'Of course.'

Chapter Ninety-Seven

'But what about your mum,' I ask him, towelling dry my rain-soaked hair.

'I spoke to her,' he says. 'I told her about you and she completely understood. She said it was about time I found myself "a bonny wee lass." '

I nod, acknowledging the universal concerns of mothers. And then I remember something. 'But you weren't there. Your car was gone.'

'I did drive off,' he tells me, taking off his T-shirt. He then says something else but I am not concentrating on anything but his naked chest. But it's not a sexual thing. Well, it's not *just* a sexual thing. It's just that I had been so worried I would never see him again, and here he is, standing right in front of me. Half naked.

'Sorry?' I say.

'I said: I did drive off, but I kept on, you know, thinking.'

'No,' I say. 'I don't know.'

'OK,' he says, reluctantly. 'I kept on thinking that it was time to stop – I don't know, it sounds a bit crap – but I just felt it was time to stop running away from things. You see, ever since my brother died that is what I've been doing. I've been running away from having to deal with things. With life. And I just realised, halfway along the motorway, that you were one thing I couldn't run away from. Because you meant too much. So I turned around and drove back.' He pauses, remembering how it happened. 'Mind you, the bloody radio didn't exactly help. Every single station I managed to get was playing some soppy love song. I was OK during Elton John, but then it was that U2 one. You know, "With or Without You". And that just proved too much. I was in the slow lane by the end of the first verse, and I'd turned off by the time it got to the chorus. So if you want to blame anyone over why I came back and waited for you, you can blame Bono.'

'OK,' I say, smiling. 'I will.'

Later on, when we are both lying in his bed, he asks if I'd like to meet his father. Tomorrow. He says his dad wants to take us out for a meal, at Othello's.

Now obviously, this raises a number of questions.

Like, when had his dad invited us. If it was before all the kissing in the rain, which it must have been, then it was somewhat presumptuous. And also, Othello's is the priciest restaurant in the whole of Yorkshire.

Provoked by this thought, I ask Frank, 'What does your dad do again?'

'Oh,' he shrugs, awkwardly. 'I'm sure he'll tell you all about it.'

311

Chapter Ninety-Eight

This is nerve-racking.

I feel like Ben Stiller going to see Robert de Niro in *Meet the Parents*. Although I don't think Ben Stiller was wearing his best dress from Zara. And I don't think he'd spent an hour plucking his eyebrows and applying his make-up and straightening his hair.

But I couldn't exactly have said no, could I? Not after all Frank had done for me regarding mum.

So here we are, in the back seat of a black cab, travelling through Leeds on a mild Monday evening.

'Do I look all right?' I ask Frank.

'You look perfect.' He smiles. It's a nice smile, but a slightly distant one. The sort of smile someone would wear if they were arranging a surprise birthday party. Only, it's not my birthday.

Oh God, we're here.

I can see the sign, in sideways letters. Frank holds my hand and squeezes it.

'All right?' he asks, gently.

'Yes,' I say, copying my sister's yoga breathing technique. 'Absolutely fine.'

Frank pays the taxi driver, kisses my cheek, and then we get out. The crazy bongo player I haven't seen since the interview with John Sampson has returned to my rib cage, as we head up the steps to the restaurant.

This doesn't feel like Leeds. It feels like somewhere different. The little fairy lights, the gleaming glass, the illuminated sign and all the gorgeous pot plants. It could be somewhere on the French Riviera. And Frank, now I come to think of it, would fit in perfectly. He looks, well, quite stylish actually, what with the black shirt and nice jeans. But not *too* stylish. I mean, he's still Frank.

We get to the woman on the front desk and Frank says, 'We've got a table booked. It's under Blake. Three people.'

An alarm bell sounds in my head. I turn to Frank. 'Blake? But you're Black. Frank Black.'

He is shaking his head. '*Blake*. I'm Frank Blake. I thought you always knew my name. I thought the hospital told you.'

I remember the woman at the hospital, munching on her cheese sandwich as she told me his name. Why didn't I check? Idiot!

Is it possible to fall in love with someone without even realising their surname?

Apparently so, folks.

The woman smiles. 'Oh yes,' she says. 'Of course.' And then she grabs a couple of menus and starts to lead us through.

We turn the corner, and make our way through the sea of romantic couples and family outings, then I see someone I recognise.

313

A large bald man, sitting on his own, smoking a giant cigar. My heart thumps.

'Oh God.'

Frank turns. 'What is it?'

'That man. I know him. I used to work for him. Well, for his shop. He runs Bla—' I stop, waiting for the last piece of the jigsaw to be slotted into my brain.

Once it is, Frank smiles. 'You've got there.'

'He's your father?'

'Yes. It's OK,' he says, sensing my terror. 'Trust me.' I look into his eyes, and feel that comforting hand on mine. 'Trust me. It's OK.'

Oh my God. This is bad. This is a very bad situation which no lie will get me out of. He will surely know about me by now. Mr Blake. *The* Mr Blake. Frank's *dad*. He will know about the stock room. He will know about the male nudity. Of course he will. It must be the biggest piece of Blake's gossip *ever*.

Blake.

Frank *Blake*.

Mr *Blake*.

Chapter Ninety-Nine

How could I have been so stupid?

But how could I have known?

Mr Blake has spotted us. He is smiling. He can't have recognised me. Yet.

He places his cigar in the ashtray and stands to greet us. 'Faith, hello.'

'Hello,' I say, my voice a-wobble. 'Pleased to meet you.'

Frank's-dad-Mr-Blake smiles. 'Again,' he says. 'Pleased to meet you *again*.' His tone is jovial, but it does nothing to calm my nerves.

'Yes,' I say, wondering whether I am going to faint.

Frank pulls out a seat for me. We all sit down. Why hasn't Frank told me? And if his dad runs Blake's then why does Frank have to live in that grotty basement flat?

'Quite a surprise, eh?' says Mr Blake.

'Yes,' I say.

The waiter comes over for the wine order. Mr Blake orders some Château or other, a fizzy mineral water for his son, and then sucks on his cigar. 'You were sacked from my store,' he says.

'Yes,' I say.

'You were wrongly sacked,' he says, the words not yet sinking in. 'I had my security people look at the tape. There are hidden cameras in the stock room. Anyway Faith, you did nothing wrong. It was a terrible mistake to fire you.'

'It was?'

'You were a fine member of staff.'

I was a fine member of staff? How on earth does he know? He only met me once.

'Anyway,' he continues. 'We got rid of Lorraine Baxter. Not because she fired you, well, not just because of that. But while my security guys were looking at the tape they caught her pinching stock. Anti-ageing products. As much as she thought she could get away with.

Oh my God. So that is why Lorraine used to spend so long checking stock.

The wine arrives, not a moment too soon. As the waiter pours the wine, and as Frank remains in happy silence beside me, Mr Blake continues from behind a veil of cigar smoke. 'You saved my son's life. In more ways than one, as well. After his brother . . . my son . . . died . . .' For a moment he stares blankly in front of him, at the grief which has yet to diminish.

'OK, dad,' Frank says, tenderly. 'It's OK.'

'No,' he says. 'I just want to explain.' He turns back to me. 'I tried to stop him drinking. I told him I didn't want to lose another son. But he wasn't listening. In fact, he got so fed up with me he moved out. He could have moved anywhere. Got himself a nice city centre apartment or something. But no. He thought that would be disrespectful. So he rented himself a shit hole in Hyde Park instead.'

'Dad—' Frank interjects.

'Oh,' says Mr Blake, remembering I live immediately above said shit hole. 'I didn't mean any offence. But honestly, he's one of the major shareholders in Blake's and future heir to the company, so he could live anywhere he wants.'

I look at Frank. He shrugs.

'Oh, he hasn't told you that, has he,' Mr Blake says, smiling. 'Of course he hasn't. He's always reckoned that it was always better to not tell people, until they got to know him properly. His brother was exactly the same. They were two peas in a pod. Never wanted to attract gold-diggers.'

'I'm ... not ... a gold-digger,' I tell Mr Blake, not knowing what else to say.

'No, Faith my dear. I know you're not. You're just slightly insane.' He is laughing.

'Dad—'

'It takes a very brave or foolish girl to take on a challenge like that!'

Mr Blake laughs. I laugh too. Frank, suddenly wondering whether this is such a good idea, is not laughing.

'Thanks,' he says.

'And speaking of challenges,' Mr Blake continues. 'I've got another one for you.'

'You have?'

Frank squeezes my hand, under the table, apparently aware of what is coming.

'We're making a few changes, at the store. Big changes.' He stubs out his cigar. 'Department stores are entering a new era. Customers are expecting more, and if we don't give it to them, we'll lose it all to boutiques and the Internet. They don't just want to buy products anymore, they want to interact with them. It's all about offering the highest degree of personalisation possible. And that's where you come in.'

317

'It is?'

'Yes, Faith, it is. We're transforming the entire ground floor. Instead of just separate cosmetics counters, we're taking a more – what's that word they like to use nowadays – a more *holistic* approach.'

'Right,' I say, not having a clue what he is going on about.

'Beauty Heaven, that's the name we've come up with for it. The whole floor will be devoted to beauty and make-up. There'll be special makeover bars, a nail clinic – whatever that is – make-up consultants, a spa treatment area, skin-care sections. And none of it divided up by brands. Because although it's still about selling products, we're ultimately selling a beauty *service*. We're selling, in short, beauty heaven.'

'Right.'

'And it's the boldest move we've ever made. So bold, we haven't even done any market research. Because you know what market research is, don't you?'

'Um, yes,' I say, thinking of how important Adam used to make it sound.

'It's crap, that's what it is,' he says, lighting up another cigar and evidently on what must be one of his favourite topics. 'It's like what Henry Ford said about the first car ever built. He said, "if we'd have asked the customer, he'd have asked for a faster horse". You've got to take a risk.'

'Right,' I say.

'Dad,' Frank says before taking a sip of his mineral water. 'Perhaps you should just tell her.'

'Yes,' Mr Blake says. 'Yes. Quite right.' He leans back in his chair. The waiter arrives, ready to take our order but Mr Blake flaps him away. Then he turns back to me and says, 'Faith, I'd like you to come back and work for us.'

'That would be great,' I say. 'Thank you.'

'But I've got a new role in mind.'

'You have?' Oh my God. He's going to ask me to be a make-up consultant.

'Yes,' he says. 'I want you to be the manager of Beauty Heaven. The entire first floor.'

I must have developed a hearing problem. I could swear he just asked me to be the manager of the entire first floor.

'But . . . I . . . I'm just a make-up girl.'

'No, Faith. No, you're not *just* a make-up girl. You're the best make-up girl we've ever had.'

This feels great, for a second. But then it starts to feel wrong. I mean, it's a lovely gesture. And it's a great thank you for saving Frank's life. But there can be no denying that that's what this is about. It's not based on my own merits. It can't be. I mean, Lorraine was hardly likely to provide him with positive feedback.

These worries must be evident on my face because Mr Blake raises a calming hand.

'I know what you're thinking,' he says. 'You're thinking this is about Frank. A reward for pulling him out of a black hole. And I'd be lying to you if I said that it hasn't had some impact on my judgement. Frank told me all about it. How you found him, how you thought on your feet, how you waited at the hospital all night to make sure he was OK. Now, never mind all those outward bound management courses in the Peak District, that shows me a girl who is able to see a task through to completion.'

'Thank you,' I say, still a little uneasy.

'But do you really think I would employ you for this position on that basis alone?'

I sip my wine and glance at Frank. 'I don't know.'

'I'm a businessman, Faith,' Mr Blake says, as a cloud of smoke billows from his mouth. 'I only make decisions which are in the best interests of my business.'

'Believe me,' Frank tells me, perhaps remembering some childhood memory of his father. 'That's true.'

'The fact is,' Mr Blake continues, 'we've been watching you for quite a while. And in a way your suspicions are correct. I do want to employ you because of my family. And because a very close member of my family thinks very highly of you.'

I look at Frank. 'Yes, I know, but—'

'Oh, it's not Frank,' Mr Blake says. 'One day I am sure he could make a very good businessman, but right now he's a bit too busy stargazing and looking into other planets or whatever it is he wants to study.'

'Alternative universes,' says Frank, scanning the menu.

'I don't think I understand,' I say.

Mr Blake offers a warm smile. 'It's my mum,' he says.

'Your mum?'

'Frank's grandmother.'

I frantically search my brain for a Mrs Blake. 'I still don't—'

'You'll know her as Josephine.'

'I—'

'Or Josie.'

Josie.

The sweet old lady I do makeovers for. The one who uses rosewater on her face. The one Lorraine never bothered to talk to. The one who used to tell me everything would be all right.

'She always said you were the best on the floor,' Mr Blake continues. 'More attentive than any of the managers. You see, she's always helped me out in the store. For over thirty years she's come in every Saturday, never revealing her surname to anyone. She's my secret undercover agent.'

I am speechless.

Little old Josie is his secret undercover agent, working the shop floor for thirty years.

I look at Frank, who is enjoying my dumbfounded reaction. He pours me some more wine.

'I don't know what to say.'

'You don't have to say anything,' Mr Blake says.

But inside my mind the angels are already singing. This is real. This is really happening. The truth is suddenly proving more spectacular than any lie I have ever told my mum.

Mr Blake stands up. 'I'll just go to the men's room,' he says.

Left alone with me, Frank turns and says, 'So what do you think?'

'I think ... I think I'm not the only one who's been keeping a few secrets.'

'Hey,' he says, deflecting my words with his palm. 'I never lied about anything. You just assumed things. And anyway, what am I meant to say. "Hi, my dad's a millionaire." '

I smile. 'I can't believe it.'

'I know, it's probably all a bit much to take in right now, but he means it, you know. The job's yours if you want it. And you'd be brilliant at it, you really would. It's just about loving what you do and bringing the best out in people. And that's what you're made for.'

'Oh stop it,' I say. 'Now you're getting cheesy.'

'I don't care,' he says. 'I love you, Faith Wishart.'

I bite my lip. 'I love you too.'

Mr Blake arrives back at the table. 'Right,' he says. 'Obviously, your salary will match the responsibility, and

I'll have to run through what it exactly entails, but I want to make sure you have as much time on the shop floor, doing what you do best.' He pauses, for effect, then stares straight at me. 'You have a think about it.'

Is he mad?

'I've thought about it,' I say, without wasting a further second. 'And I'd absolutely love to do it.'

Mr Blake props his cigar in the ashtray and claps his hand. 'Great,' he says flamboyantly. 'Now let's order some food!'

Chapter One Hundred

When we get back to my flat, I'm still buzzing. 'I still can't believe it,' I tell Frank in my bedroom. 'I really can't.'

'Perhaps I should have warned you.'

'Yes,' I say, placing some make-up remover on a cotton wool pad. 'Perhaps you should.'

'Here,' Frank says, 'let me do that.' He takes the cotton wool pad out of my hand and gently starts to rub the make-up from my face.

'Hey,' I say. 'You missed your vocation.'

After he's wiped the foundation from my forehead he places a delicate kiss on my brow. He then adds more remover and starts on my cheeks, remaining silently absorbed in the task.

I should probably call my mum. Tell her the news. But it can wait till morning. Everything can wait till morning.

'Close your eyes,' Frank says, before starting to wipe off my eye make-up. 'There you go. More beautiful than ever.'

'You charmer,' I say.

'I mean it.'

He hugs me, and I feel his heart beating against my chest. A heart which could have stopped forever. I squeeze him closer and know I will never let anything bad happen to him again. And I know he will look after me the same way, whatever happens.

Over his shoulder I can see outside the window. A clear night reveals a sky full of stars. Somewhere beyond, there are all those alternative universes Frank told me about, with all those different possibilities.

And for the first time since he told me, I realise I don't want any other possibility. I don't want to belong to an alternative universe.

I'm perfectly happy with this one.

Turn the page to read more from
the painfully funny and
deliciously sexy Andrea Semple . . .

THE EX-FACTOR
Meet Martha Seymore:
relationship doctor

She's the girl who gets paid to sympathise with the cheated and jilted, the under-sexed and over-attached at *Gloss* magazine, but when she finds out about her boyfriend's one-night-stand, she starts to doubt whether she really has any of the answers.

Not only does she have to admit a failed relationship to her colleagues, but also to her old frenemy, Desdemona, blond, perfectly evil and newly engaged to Martha's very first boyfriend. Realising she's just as clueless as her hapless readers and tired of always doing the right thing, Martha decides it's time to ignore her own advice. She's going to go for what – and who – she wants, even if it's wrong . . .

THE MAN FROM PERFECT

In life – and men – be careful what you wish for . . .

After her experiences with ex-boyfriend Rob the Slob, Ella Holt has abandoned hope of ever finding the right man. So when she answers 50 questions on her perfect man in a glossy magazine, she has no idea that her responses will be used by a new state-of-the-art dating agency to find her perfect match.

Naturally, Ella scoffs at the very notion of a 'perfect man', until the man from the Perfect Agency, James Master, arrives on her doorstep. Not only is he gorgeous, but spontaneous trips to Paris, declarations of love and gourmet sex all become part of her daily routine. However, as 'romance fatigue' sets in, Ella's suspicions about the consequences of her answers begin to mount. And when Rob starts to change his slobbish ways to win her back, she remembers that she asked for a man who will do anything to keep her . . . and let no one stand in his way.